Sweet Mercies

ALSO BY ANNE BOOTH

Small Miracles

Sweet Mercies

ANNE BOOTH

Harvill
Secker

1 3 5 7 9 10 8 6 4 2

Harvill Secker, an imprint of Vintage, is part of the Penguin Random House group
of companies whose addresses can be found at global.penguinrandomhouse.com

Penguin
Random House
UK

First published in Great Britain by Harvill Secker in 2023

penguin.co.uk/vintage

Typeset in 12/15pt Garamond MT Std by Jouve (UK), Milton Keynes
Printed and bound in Great Britain by Clays Ltd, Elcograf S.p.A.

The authorised representative in the EEA is Penguin Random House Ireland,
Morrison Chambers, 32 Nassau Street, Dublin D02 YH68

A CIP catalogue record for this book is available from the British Library

HB ISBN 9781787302990
TPB ISBN 9781787303003

Penguin Random House is committed to a sustainable future
for our business, our readers and our planet. This book is made
from Forest Stewardship Council® certified paper.

Dedicated to the memory of my mum and dad,
Patrick Simms (1927–2017) and
Anne Simms (née Lennane, 1930–2014).

And with love and thanks to my wonderful
husband Graeme, for all his support.

Prologue

The others had gone, and he was alone. He boiled the kettle and made himself some tea, then took a chair and his drink outside so he could peacefully sit and look at the mountains and the sea, and take in the silence . . .

And then he heard it. Not so much in his head but in his heart, yet somehow part of the beauty that was everywhere around him.

'All shall be well,' it said.

And in spite of the unholy mess, the waste, the pain, the lies, the shame, the deliberate cruelty and the genuine mistakes, in spite of everything, he suddenly believed again, that it could be true.

Saturday 16th December 1995

One

It was Saturday 16th December 1995, and in the English town of Fairbridge, Christmas preparations were well underway. The skies were grey and cloudy, but the band of the Salvation Army was playing carols in the medieval market place, brightly decorated shops were playing cheery jingly Christmas songs, and crowds of Christian and non-Christian, religious and non-religious Fairbridge residents and students alike were milling around, enjoying roasted chestnuts and mulled wine and hot chocolate, chatting and busily buying festive jumpers and hats, jewellery and bags and Russian dolls and handmade chocolates and all sorts of different goodies, from the tinselled, Father Christmas-hatted stallholders at the Christmas market.

It was not snowing, but it was cold, and in Fairbridge's only travel agents on the corner, George Sanders had made the wise decision to put up fairy lights in the windows to advertise warm-weather holidays as presents – he had already sold an Italian Easter break, a Greek cruise and a summer weekend in Paris. In Pet Paradise, Fairbridge's only pet shop, the new assistant Jackie was muddling through whilst her uncle, the manager, was off sick – her enthusiasm was only just outweighing her chaotic wrapping and trouble with the till, but she was working as hard as she could, selling treats and Christmas presents for the pets of Fairbridge.

In the centre of town, next to but not part of the hustle and bustle, in the relative peace and quiet of the Victorian Roman Catholic Church of St Philomena, fifty-eight-year-old Sister Margaret and twenty-three-year-old Katy were in the empty church, putting the last touches to the stable for the crib. Father Hugh, the parish priest, wanted to have it put up for the Sunday before Christmas, just in front of the altar, with a cow and a manger already installed. He was going to preach a sermon about Mary and Joseph preparing to travel to Bethlehem. Then, on Christmas Eve, before the early family Mass, Mary and Joseph and the donkey would arrive, and Father Hugh would ask one of the children to place a baby Jesus in the manger, and the others, proudly wearing tea towels as head dresses, to bring sheep and shepherds.

'This is a lovely backdrop,' said Katy to Sister Margaret, slotting a beautifully painted scene of Bethlehem into the window of the wooden stable.

'Sister Bridget's sister Mary painted it for us, and sent it over from Ireland,' said Margaret. 'Thomas Amis made the stable itself, with the little window, and I remembered that Mary had been going to painting classes, and I asked her if she could paint a Bethlehem scene. I gave her the dimensions for the window and the painting arrived at the convent in a week.'

'She's really talented,' said Katy.

'I know. She hides her light under a bushel really. She is one of those people who needs a bit of encouragement to shine, and I think she doesn't really get it from her family,' said Margaret.

Setting up the church crib reminded Katy of Nonna Ellen, an important new friend of the Sisters of St Philomena who had visited them from Italy recently. Sisters Margaret, Bridget and Cecilia had met her earlier that year when they stayed at the hotel she ran with her grandson and his wife, during their summer of small miracles.

'Shall I take some photos and send them to Nonna?' said Katy. 'She loves cribs so much. The little one she gave the convent last week as a parting gift is so gorgeous.'

'That's a lovely idea, Katy,' said Margaret, smiling at her kind ex-pupil.

'It's a shame she had to go back to Italy before Christmas,' said Katy. 'I miss her.'

'We all miss her,' said Margaret, 'but we were so lucky to have her staying with us all these months, especially while we were setting up the Guest House. Her advice has been invaluable. I suspect she didn't want to be away from her beloved Cardellino for Christmas, now that Francesco and Maria are back from their travels.'

'It sounds so beautiful there. I'm definitely going to visit them when I finish my MA.'

And *maybe after that you will be starting your novitiate with us,* thought Margaret. Katy was the first young woman to be interested in joining the Sisters of St Philomena for some years. She had asked to live in the community for this year, as she studied for an MA at Fairbridge University, and they were getting to know her in a new way, not as the student the Sisters had taught when they ran the school, but as a candidate for religious life, and an impressively mature, resourceful and caring young woman. When she wasn't busy at the university,

Katy took the trouble to help out in the convent as much as she could, both in the B&B and in helping Cecilia set up a little museum of religious life, as well as joining the Sisters for prayers. As far as Margaret was concerned, Katy would make a wonderful religious Sister, should she take the next step and join the novitiate. Margaret often found herself thinking, with a pang, how much Sister Helen would have loved to see Katy joining the community. It was over a year now since her dear friend had died.

I miss you so much, and wish you were here, Helen. But I know you and the other Sisters are up in Heaven, praying for us, and our new adventure with the B&B, Margaret thought.

'I'll just go and light a candle, Katy, before we go back,' Margaret said.

'I'll light one for Mum. I know it's five years now since she died, but I still miss her, especially at Christmas,' said Katy. Her voice wobbled a little. Margaret put an arm around her shoulders and gave her a quick hug. Katy was such a cheerful, calm, private person, it was very moving to be reminded of how she had lost her mother when still studying for her 'A' Levels, a suffering that maybe accounted for her maturity and compassion now as a young woman.

'We never forget the ones we love,' said Margaret, and Katy, understanding Margaret's own loss, hugged her back.

They went and stood beside each other in the Lady Chapel. A few tea lights were already burning there, in the empty but open church, their flickering flames symbolising recent prayers said by people who had 'popped into' church to ask for help or give thanks for blessings: an unseen community. Margaret took the taper and lit it from a tea light, adding her prayer to that of whoever who had lit it originally, then she lit a new candle for Helen, and all the other Sisters who had died in the past years, and handed the taper to Katy, who lit her own one for her mother, then blew the taper out.

Margaret prayed silently, as the two new little tea lights' flames took hold, joining the others on the candle stand in front of the Madonna and Child. *Lord, please bless our community, in Heaven and Earth, all the Sisters who have gone before us, and Bridget, Cecilia and me. And bless Katy, and may her mother rest in peace, and bless her father and all their family. Thank you so much for sending her to St Philomena's. Last Christmas was so sad, with you taking Basil, Helen and Frances. I thought, with just the three of us left, we were going to have to close the convent. Thanks to you, and Nonna Ellen and her family, our debts are paid, and we have a new B&B to run, and Katy is living in the community. Thank you for giving us hope. Please bless us all this Christmas and New Year, and bless all those who will come to visit us.*

Over in Ireland, Mary Lynch opened the door of her large, detached modern house, built by her husband's firm in an exclusive development in a very smart part of Galway city. As Declan had explained, if he was to be known for his modern luxury homes, it made sense if he lived in one himself.

'Some post for Declan and a special parcel for you! I think it's from England,' said Martin O'Dowd, the postman. He had saved the parcel until last, as he always liked to have a chat with Mary, and he wanted to know if he was right in his guess about what it was. It didn't occur to Mary to be offended by this nosiness. Martin had been their postman for years, and she had seen him and his wife Nola and their family at Mass every Sunday for decades. Their four children, all younger than Mary and Declan's two, were very cheerful and sweet when they were little, and she had enjoyed preparing them for Holy Communion and Confirmation. They were all over in

America and England now. Mary never minded having a chat with Martin about whatever he delivered. When her own children left home, and before she had started volunteering at the charity shop, Martin had sometimes been the only person she chatted to all day. They never found themselves discussing postal rates or the problems of life at Mass on Sundays – outside church, on Mary's doorstep, it was a different matter.

Martin had learnt a lot about the family over the years.

'The only things she ever orders for herself are paints and art things,' he had said to his wife Nola only the week before.

'I've never seen her paintings though,' said Nola. 'I'd like to see what Mary paints. I've always liked her. She's very kind and gentle. There are no airs and graces with her, with all the money she has. Declan's very charming, but I never feel he thinks we're quite as good as him.'

'Maybe she's no good at painting, God help her,' said Martin. 'Poor Mary. She's no good at cooking, that's for sure – she doesn't even cook for Declan – I often see those big catering vans outside – it must have cost them a fortune over the years. They are always entertaining.'

'But Martin,' said his wife, wisely, 'that will be for the business. That's why Declan Lynch is so successful – he came back from England and he wined and dined the finest in Ireland to get all those deals. You don't want home cooking when that amount of money is at stake. All that entertaining. And inside, it's like a palace, I believe . . . Bernie O'Donoghue was working for the cleaning firm and she said it's all white, everywhere. She said you could eat your dinner off the floors.'

'I'd rather your home cooking than food in a palace,' said Martin, giving his wife a big kiss. 'But maybe I should take you out more?'

'I wouldn't say no, but I don't envy Mary,' said Nola. 'She might be married to a handsome millionaire . . .'

'Hey, hold on there, Nola!' protested Martin. 'Are you after Declan then?'

'I am not,' said Nola. 'I'm saying I don't envy her one bit being married to him. Too smooth.' She tutted at the thought. 'He was at Mass every Sunday when all those stories were going around, with the pictures in the papers with the models and the actresses, and not a bother on him! Smiling away he was, like a film star or a politician. Passing round the collection plate like nothing was happening. And poor Mary looked shook, even with the good clothes she had on. She carried on helping with the children's liturgy and the choir, and never said a word against him all those years, but it must have broken her heart. It's donkey's years ago now, but I'd say she never really looked happy after that, and I blame it on him. She's never been too grand, too big for her boots, even with all their money, but I think there's something wrong in a marriage when the wife and mother wouldn't say "boo" to a goose.'

'Well, we're all right so,' said Martin, laughing. 'You'd "boo" at any goose – you'd tell the Pope off if you met him.'

'Sure, after reading that book about our Bishop Casey, I've plenty to say to the Pope,' sighed Nola. 'I don't like secrets in families or churches – they are never good news.'

Mary looked at the post in her hands – two Christmas cards from friends across the country, a few letters from charities she subscribed to, a catalogue for comfortable shoes, and a handwritten envelope addressed to Declan as CEO of Declan Lynch Buildings, but addressed to their home. Maybe a business associate sending a family card? A nice thought. The handwriting was vaguely familiar. Maybe it was Colum from golf. But then why was it just to Declan? Mary put the post on the side table to sort out later and turned back to Martin, who was waiting expectantly. She weighed the parcel in her hands and smiled wryly. A quick glance at the address label confirmed what she knew already. It was from her sister Bridget in Fairbridge. Bridget had baked her a brack again. Even though Mary could have easily bought one from a local shop, Bridget had never got out of the habit of baking this Irish fruit tea cake for her and sending it all the way from England. Declan would be pleased. He said he could tell Bridget's cakes from any shop bought one.

'It's from my sister Bridget. She has baked us a brack for Christmas.'

'I thought so!' said Martin, unguardedly pleased he had guessed correctly. 'Isn't that grand?' he said, saving up the conversation to tell Nola. 'You have a blessed brack, all right, baked by a nun! She does that every year, doesn't she? But doesn't she know you can buy them here?'

'She does, but I think she likes to keep up with the Irish ways,' said Mary. 'The Irish ways she remembers, anyway. She always baked the brack for the family when we were young.'

'Will you be going away for Christmas?' said Martin.

'No, no. Declan always likes a family one at home. Deirdre and her family will come for dinner, and Noel will join them. He is coming back from Switzerland for a few days, staying with us and visiting friends too. And you?'

'Ah yes, we've got the gang home, thank God. Though they eat us out of house and home, and Nola is pulling her hair out getting the house ready and the food in,' said Martin. 'Sure, you know yourself,' he added, and immediately regretted it. Mary just smiled. She and Martin both knew that with cleaners, and caterers, and food delivered, she had nothing to do apart from buy the presents, get her hair done, and wait for her big house to be filled again.

'I'll look out for you all at Midnight Mass, and say hello. I've always been very fond of your four.'

'I'm afraid it will be just Nola and me,' said Martin. 'The young ones don't want anything to do with the Church any more, and that's the truth.' He looked at Mary's kind, sympathetic face and blurted out what was on his mind. 'It was Nola's birthday last week, and Geraldine sent her mother that book, you know, the *Forbidden Fruit* one, by Annie Murphy, the one your man Bishop Casey had a baby with and wouldn't acknowledge. She's been staying up at night reading it out to me. It's terrible all together, Mary. It would make you think, all the lectures we got growing up, and the fear of God they put into us, and all that carrying on. And it's been going on for years, of course. *The Gay Byrne Show* opened my eyes. And the industrial schools. The stories coming out there about the Brothers in Connemara. There were some fierce cruel nuns too. It's all coming out now, in dribs and drabs, and it's shocking. No offence to your sister though, Mary.'

'No, I agree,' sighed Mary. 'I don't know if Noel will come to Midnight Mass either, to be honest. But you know yourself, Martin, the Church has been a great comfort to me. There are still great nuns and priests and Brothers. With the cancer and everything, I don't know what I would have done without my faith. Lourdes – Lourdes was beautiful. There was real peace there.'

'I know. I try and tell the young ones that. That they mustn't throw the baby out with the bath water, and they're not all rotten apples. But they're angry, and I don't blame them. Ireland's not like when we were growing up, Mary. Ireland's changed.

And the young ones aren't putting up with any more nonsense. No more hiding things away.'

Mary sighed. 'Well, you know about Noel . . .'

'Is he all right?' said Martin.

'Yes. He's away working in Switzerland. Declan's made his peace with him, but there was a time when they weren't speaking, and Noel took it very hard.' He had a breakdown really, thought Mary. He was so close to his father, but Declan just couldn't accept he was gay, and Noel couldn't keep it hidden any more. It was killing him, to be honest, but when his father wouldn't talk to him, it nearly destroyed him. 'I ended up thanking God for my cancer, and that's the truth,' said Mary, 'as it made them talk, and my sister Bridget was a great peacemaker, God bless her.'

'Well, thank God for the good nuns,' said Martin, 'and she's one, and that's the truth, God bless her.' He looked at his watch. 'Anyway, I'd better be going back or they will send a search party out for me. Best to keep on the boss's right side before Christmas!'

'I was wondering,' said Mary, ducking behind the door to pick something up. 'Declan keeps getting given hampers by his clients, and we will never get through them. Would you have any use for this, do you think?' and she held out a wicker hamper and offered it to Martin.

'That's very kind,' said Martin, taking it. 'If you're sure?'

'You'd be doing me a favour,' said Mary. 'We're drowning in them.'

'Thanks a million, Mary!' said Martin, beaming.

'Oh, you're very welcome,' smiled Mary. 'Give my best regards to Nola.'

'I will indeed, Mary,' said Martin, carrying the luxury hamper back to his van. Nola would be delighted.

Mary took the post and Bridget's parcel into the kitchen. She put the letters on the kitchen windowsill to deal with later. She wanted to send some more money in response to the charities, though it always made her sad to read the case-studies, and have a look through that catalogue. She knew already Declan would hate those shoes but she really wanted something comfortable to wear. She would see if there were any that might pass the Declan test before she threw it away.

She sat at the table to open the parcel, certain it at least would pass the Declan test. Sure enough it was a brack and a card. Declan would be glad.

Half an hour later, back in Fairbridge, England, in the rambling Victorian house just a short walk from town, which was Saint Philomena's convent and, for the past six months, also Saint Philomena's Guest and Retreat House, Sister Cecilia was doing her morning chores. At ninety-one, the oldest in the community of four, she was passing a brightly decorated reception on her way to the laundry, with the convent kitten Pangur trotting behind her, as he always did, when he suddenly decided to practise the joyful art of living in the present moment, and legged it up the Christmas tree. Sister Cecilia, instead of praying for patience with the kitten, shifted her irritation onto Emily, or Em as she liked to be called, the irrepressibly friendly young receptionist, married earlier in the year to Chris, the convent gardener, and due to move in, with him, to one of the two new staff flats in the convent.

'For goodness' sake, Emily, how did he get up there AGAIN?' said Sister Cecilia, her light Edinburgh accent carrying an unreasonably accusatory tone, as if Em was responsible for Pangur's inability to resist a Christmas tree; a Christmas tree, moreover, that Cecilia considered had been put up far too early. Sister Bridget's insistence that it was really for the December B&B guests had not changed her mind.

'Sure, Em can't be stopping Pangur all the time, Cecilia,' interjected Sister, Bridget 'She has the guests to look after.' At seventy, the small, energetic Superior of the community had come to collect the post, and caught Sister Cecilia's tone and Em's flushed face.

'And Em is doing a great job,' added Sister Margaret, the youngest Sister, who had just come back from church with Katy. 'We've had a lot of compliments from the professors staying here. Dr Woodburn's art history conference is a great success and he says everyone wishes they had booked into our B&B. We'll have to build more rooms at this rate!'

Em beamed. She loved working for the Sisters. It was only Sister Cecilia who was the difficult one.

'I honestly don't mind getting Pangur off the tree,' said Em, 'I love him. The trouble is I know he's going to go straight back up as soon as I do, and I've got bookings and guests to deal with.'

Sister Cecilia grudgingly nodded her head. Each time he got stuck in the Christmas tree Pangur mewed loudly and urgently for help out of his precarious position, but he never learned. Unless he was physically removed from the scene of silvan temptation, he was liable to just shoot up the tree again as soon as his four paws were back on the ground, and Em was very busy and couldn't keep dropping everything to deal with his piteous cries.

'Well, I can see I'm just going to have to remember to carry him whenever we pass reception,' said Sister Cecilia, picking up Pangur and holding him firmly in her arms. 'I had hoped he would learn to ignore it, if it has to be there, but it seems I was wrong.' It wasn't the most gracious of apologies – she still sounded somehow affronted – but it was better than nothing.

Pangur purred as they left the scene of the crime. This was a very satisfactory outcome for the kitten – the indoor tree these past weeks had provided him with the fun of climbing up, batting shiny ornaments and peeping down from a swaying branch onto a rapt audience, or, if things didn't quite work out and got a bit scary, he could be, and was, often, rescued and firmly carried around in the arms of his favourite person in the world. Sister Cecilia wasn't someone who generally gave cuddles, so the carry was a particular novelty. Christmas, for Pangur, was win-win all the way.

'Ah, isn't that a lovely Christmas card from Mary?' said Sister Bridget, exclaiming with pleasure as she opened an envelope with Irish stamps on it, and showed it to Em and Margaret and Katy. 'Now isn't that painting of an Irish cottage absolutely gorgeous?'

'A Paul Henry, I believe, Sister!' said an enthusiastic professor, catching sight of it as he passed by on his way up the rather splendid wooden staircase to the bed and breakfast rooms above. As Fairbridge University had now broken up for the holidays, the remaining guests were no longer the term-time, shy, would-be students and their families, or parents visiting home-sick students, or even student-missing parents visiting perfectly happy scholars. Instead, the convent B&B was full of visiting academics. Dr Matthew Woodburn, art history academic and close friend of the Sisters, had bowed to eager interest and unashamed pressure from colleagues and organised an exclusive art history conference celebrating the work of Edwardian Fairbridge-born artist Jack Mortimer, many of whose works had been recently donated to a special gallery at the university. He had made sure that the leading speakers were all booked into Saint Philomena's B&B, to everyone's mutual satisfaction.

Bridget beamed.

'Thank you, Professor Jones!' she called up after him, before turning back to Em, Margaret and Katy.

'Mary wishes us all a Happy Christmas and says she has read great reviews of the B&B and hopes to come and visit next year. Of course, Fairbridge has always been important for them, it's where they fell in love,' said Bridget.

'I didn't know that!' said Katy. 'I thought they were both from the island you grew up on?'

'They were, and Mary was always mad about Declan, but he just saw her as a little girl. When she came over to join me in England, aged sixteen, Declan saw her in a different light, and the rest, as they say, is history. It was a whirlwind romance. They got married, with my parents' blessing, on Declan's twenty-first birthday, just before she was seventeen!'

'That's so young!' said Katy, shocked.

'Ah yes, but sure, the families had known each other forever, so no one was worried. It wasn't as if she was marrying a stranger. He absolutely adores her. She wants for nothing, and he couldn't have been a better son-in-law for our parents. They lived in comfort in their old age – he made sure of that. They have a son, and a daughter, whose husband works with Declan. He's very clever. He and my niece have a daughter, so I am a great-aunt, would you believe it?' she smiled proudly. 'Yes, my little sister married very well, thanks be to God! It will be fifty years this coming May since Declan and Mary's wedding, but in many ways, it feels like only yesterday.'

CHRISTMAS DAY

Monday 25th December 1995

Two

It was two o'clock in the afternoon on Christmas Day. The last cracker had been pulled, the last cracker joke groaned at, and the Christmas lunch plates had all been cleared away at the annual celebration hosted at St Philomena's Church Hall.

'Thanks be to God, it's gone very well this year,' said Bridget, ever grateful for her Sisters and this year's helpers. She stood with Sister Margaret and waved the last people off. Kind volunteers were linking arms with those who needed assistance out of the hall, drivers were giving lifts to those who needed transport back to their homes, and in the kitchen, a team of helpers were finishing the washing up. Outside it was cold, with soft heavy grey skies indicating snow might soon be on the way, but inside it was warm and surprisingly cosy for a church hall, festooned with bright paper chains made by Sister Margaret and Katy, and pictures painted by children of St Philomena's Infants School and the Cheeky Monkeys playgroup. As Doctor Matthew Woodburn, off-duty lecturer in art history and volunteer chair-stacker, noted – looking at the colourful Nativity paintings – reindeer and

Fireman Sam and Father Christmas were evidently frequent visitors to Jesus, Mary and Joseph, very much as the fabulously rich De Medicis turned up, unquestioned, at the lowly stables of the Italian Renaissance. There really was room for everyone at the inn.

'It didn't just go well – it went brilliantly!' said Sister Margaret. She smiled at Bridget, putting her arm around her shoulders and giving her a quick hug. 'Doesn't it always?'

'The money from the bingo covered everything, and with all the food donations we even have left-overs. We can use some of the food and the extra Christmas crackers tonight, and George and Matthew said they would drop some things over to the shelter later.

'People were very generous,' agreed Sister Margaret. 'The dinner was organised and cooked to perfection, your mince pies were gorgeous, and Father Hugh's Christmas cakes were a huge hit. His cooking has become so good these past months.'

'It has,' agreed Sister Bridget.

They turned back to the empty hall. Sister Cecilia was energetically and determinedly sweeping the floor – scraps of tinsel and party hats had no chance against her broom – and Katy and Matthew were helping Father Hugh and his curate Father Stephen stack chairs and tables. Bridget and Margaret went back to the kitchen, to finish clearing up.

George Sanders, Fairbridge travel agent, who had been on washing-up duty with Thomas Amis, the convent's volunteer handyman, a long-term friend of the sisters, and the widower of Sister Bridget's best friend, Rose, was draping a by-now very wet tea towel on the radiator. Decorated with a prayer celebrating the 'Lord of Pots and Pans and Things', it joined an equally wet collection: an 'Irish blessing' one about roads rising up to meet people, a somewhat alarming prospect if you weren't used to an Irish turn of phrase, one with a picture of St Peter's in Rome, and an old calendar one for the year 1983. Sister Bridget swiftly assessed the situation, opened a drawer, extracted a new dry one, and gave it to George.

'Thanks Thomas, you go and join the family now. You've been a great help, as always. Now, how is your hip today? When is the op?' Sister Bridget said, guiding their great friend out of the kitchen as Sister Margaret took over washing up.

Unfolding the dry tea towel, George was faced with a smiling picture of Sister Bridget's favourite Irish singer. 'Daniel O'Donnell! I am honoured!' said George, raising his eyebrows as he held out the new tea towel to properly appreciate its charms. 'That's heroic of Sister Bridget to let him out of the convent.'

'Oh, it's not the convent one,' said Margaret. 'Bridget has a spare one kept here for the washing up after bingo.'

'I suppose he is like God, always with her,' mused George, as he started to dry the last of the teacups. 'Sorry, Sister Margaret. I don't mean to be disrespectful. You accept my absence of faith, and I should respect the presence of yours.'

'Don't worry, George. I know it sometimes seems as if Daniel O'Donnell's image is everywhere Bridget is, but not even Bridget worships him, so no blasphemy is involved from either of you,' Margaret laughed. 'There are certainly no apologies needed when you have spent all day volunteering with us.'

'It was a pleasure! It helped me avoid Christmas lunch alone with Mother,' said George, making a face.

'She looked like she was enjoying herself,' said Margaret, sympathetically. Everyone knew George's mother was not the easiest of people to please, to put it mildly. Mrs Annabel

Sanders, widow, or 'George's mother', as she introduced herself to everyone, was not a relaxing person to know. Not a church goer, or a member of St Philomena's parish, and rather solitary, she had somehow consented to meeting Margaret and Katy who, out of kindness and because of their friendship with her son, now visited her regularly. George's mother had even been persuaded to attend the weekly bingo, which she clearly adored, though she always complained about it.

'She was sitting with her bingo crowd, queening it over them as usual,' said George. He checked his watch. 'Sorry, I'd better get Mother back in time for the Queen's Speech, or she will never forgive me. Not that she's such a big royalist, she just believes in things being done right.'

'Thanks so much for all your help, George. Will we see you tonight?'

'Yes, please – it will be nice not to be on our own with Mother all evening. It will be a pleasure! We have a little present for you all, anyway.'

It was seven o'clock in the evening. Across sea and land, in his smart suburb of Galway city in the West of Ireland, Declan Lynch watched his wife doze in the armchair opposite him. The house was quiet at last. He stretched out his legs and, cupping his hands around the bowl of his son's present of a new brandy glass engraved with 'Dad', sipped appreciatively from the fine French cognac his daughter Deirdre had given him to go with it that morning. Deirdre and Tom and Fran had gone home, Noel off to stay with a friend – Declan hadn't asked who, and Noel hadn't offered, so that had avoided any unpleasantness. It was better that way. Noel certainly looked well-dressed and happy – Switzerland was suiting him – and he had been especially thoughtful. Mary had been so touched with the paintbrushes Noel had given her – you'd think they were diamonds. Yes. Christmas Day had been everything he would have expected it to be. Mass in Galway Cathedral, back home to an excellent meal and presents and games. Mary was a good home cook for just the family, but she had always got in such a state about cooking for company, or big feasts like the type of Christmas dinner he expected, that he had long ago arranged to get it all done and brought in professionally, that way nobody was shamed. All she had to do was keep the house and garden looking nice and welcome people, though he knew even that had put a terrible strain on her. He had made sure that she had money for regular hairdressing appointments and good clothes, and there was a regular cleaning firm in to keep the house up to standard. There were a couple of times, after the babies had arrived at last, in the early years of marriage, when he had come home to a mess, and children's toys everywhere, and he could see she just wasn't able to look after the children as well as the home, so he didn't listen to her protests and got in help. Then they could both relax. Give her her due, when there was family, she was particularly good at welcoming. When she played charades or set out the board games with the children and Fran he saw her laugh in a way she never showed in company. When she was with people she loved she shone, but she was a lost cause when it came to impressing strangers.

Her charming sister would have been better as the society hostess, that was for sure, a perfect match for an aspiring businessman, he had always known that, but what could he have done? She had chosen another, and even Declan, who was famous for never letting a competitor best him, knew when he was beaten. So he had made his sacrifice to God, and settled for pretty, adoring, shy Mary. He had made the best of it, give or take a few lapses when he was younger – all confessed to a priest now, never discussed with Mary – and God had rewarded him. He was well satisfied. She was a good Catholic woman, a wife to enter old age with, and after a while trying, when he had wondered if he had made the right choice after all, God had given them a healthy boy and girl. Maybe Noel had not turned out exactly the way he would have hoped, but he had brains and was doing well working for a pharmaceutical company. Deirdre had married a dynamic young man, and the business was in good hands with his son-in-law. Yes, he was proud of his fine family, and Declan Lynch Buildings was known throughout Ireland. They might have started with next to nothing, just some savings and his experience working with his mother's brother in England, until he inherited the business and re-named it for himself, but his Mary was a rich woman now. He had managed to not let Mary's shyness, or lack of her sister's natural gifts, hold him back, and once he had shown clients their home, the perfect show house at the first meeting, he was in the habit of taking business contacts out to dinner or away for weekends, alluding to Mary being an 'artist' as an excuse for her reticence. So everyone was happy.

Not that you could tell she was an artist from the house, thank God. She kept all that side of her in Connemara, in the family home he had bought back for her. He had updated it with a new kitchen and bathroom, and a loft conversion for extra bedrooms, but she had wanted little changed. Other women would have wanted diamonds, cruises, even a yacht. He had had a few relationships when he was a young man where women had expected good jewellery in exchange for discretion. All his Mary had ever asked him for was an old cottage by the sea, the house she and Bridget had grown up in. This had actually proved an excellent investment, bless her. Connemara houses were reaching sky-high prices in sales, and holiday rentals brought in a fortune. Though they hadn't needed the money, Mary had surprised him this last year, renting out the house to tourists rather than using it herself. She had their daughter Deirdre involved, organising the lettings, fixing up the house, popping down to check. Good thing really, as Mary was no good with money. She had always been a soft touch for the latest sob story. That's why it was always best if he was in charge of the finances. Now Deirdre was a chip off the old block – she was a business woman. She would be all right. Keep an eye on Mary if . . .

But why would the worst come to the worst? There was no point worrying her. He had the best of doctors on the case. His heart needed fixing, but money was no object for treatment. Look at Mary herself – she had that cancer scare, but he had got her the best of treatment and sent her off to Lourdes, and she was back as fit as a fiddle. She looked very good for sixty-six, kept herself trim. She had always been pretty, like her sister, even if she had never had Bridget's energy. Yes, Declan and Mary Lynch were a fine-looking couple. People had always said that. Still did. He knew he was a handsome man. Cary Grant, someone had said he was like, and he wasn't going to argue. He wore well-cut suits, he looked after himself. At seventy he was still relatively young – his father had lived until ninety and he had not had half the advantages Declan had had. He had always kept himself fit. True, there hadn't been much Health and Safety when he started off back in the 1950s, on the buildings over in England, but it was a long time since he'd got his hands dirty. There was no need to worry. It could be fixed. He could always work things out. And in May, on his birthday, he and Mary would have the biggest Golden Wedding anniversary party Galway would have ever seen! No one could say that Declan Lynch didn't know how to party!

He finished the brandy and instead of just leaving his glass on the side as he would normally do, in a burst of Christmassy good will, he opened the dishwasher Mary had already emptied and put it in. Why not – it was Christmas, and he had time. He looked around the clean kitchen with pleasure, but frowned a little at a pile of papers on the kitchen windowsill. Mary must have absentmindedly put them there – she was a great one for carrying little piles of things around to deal with later, and then forgetting them. That's why she would never have made a good PA for the family business, and why they needed a cleaner.

He smiled indulgently as he went through the pile. Letters from charities, thanking her for her donations. He gave her an allowance, and she seemed to spend most of it on helping others. Bless her. They could just go in the bin. A catalogue for comfortable shoes – now, there he would put his foot down. They were hideous. Mary couldn't wear those. The catalogue joined the charity letters in the bin. A couple of Christmas cards she had forgotten to open. He took them out of the envelopes and put them on the windowsill. They were from families they knew. He was sure they would be in response to cards she had already sent. She was very worried about upsetting people and always started sending Christmas cards way in advance. Declan disposed of the envelopes, but, warmed by the brandy, he remembered to tear the stamps off and put them in the tin Mary had marked 'used stamps for guide dogs'. He might ask his secretary if she could start saving work stamps too, and then he would bring them back for Mary. He knew she would be pleased. What was this, though?

Buried at the bottom of the pile was a letter to him as CEO. He tutted. Now that was a bit irritating of Mary. It didn't do to offend business contacts. He'd have to deal with that.

He opened the letter and read it. And then wished he hadn't. He folded it up and put it in his pocket, grateful that Mary hadn't seen.

He went to the dishwasher, took out the 'Dad' brandy glass, and topped it up again. He was sitting opposite Mary, drinking brandy, when she woke, just as he had been when she fell asleep.

'Is everything all right, Declan?' Mary said, seeing him lost in thought, his face serious.

'What?' said Declan, and quickly turned on a brilliant smile. 'Sure, everything's grand, Mary.'

Three

It was eight o'clock in the evening on Christmas Day, and Sister Bridget was sitting at the head of the long convent dining table, beaming at their friends all gathered in the dining room, a yellow paper cracker crown perched a little wonkily on her veil. If truth be told, Bridget was slightly affected by the unaccustomed glass of Prosecco from a bottle brought by George, but, '*in vino veritas*', as they say, and Bridget's 'truth spoken in wine' was only making her more cheerful and delighted with the day and the company.

Thank you, Lord, Bridget prayed. *I can't believe the miracles you've performed this last year for us. The new B&B is doing so well, and I am looking forward to getting things ready so we can give retreats. Thank you for all these lovely friends you've given us, and bless them!*

Outside by now it was cold and dark, but inside it was cosy, the gas fire on, the room filled with relaxed chatter and laughter. The dinner plates had been cleared away after their evening Christmas meal, and a Christmas pudding had been set alight and shared out. They sat, full and happy, their empty bowls in front of them, and lingered to chat some more. It was Heaven.

To Sister Bridget's right was Sister Cecilia who, as the oldest member of the community, had had the honour that morning, before first Mass, of placing the newborn baby Jesus in his place in the manger in the beautiful Italian crib or Presepe on the mantelpiece, the one given to them by their dear friend Nonna before she went back to Italy for Christmas. Margaret, sitting next to Cecilia, helped Katy explain Cecilia's Christmas cracker joke to her.

'Why are pirates great? They just aaaar!' repeated Katy, throwing herself into the part with gusto. Sister Cecilia just shook her head, puzzled. 'I don't understand what pirates have to do with Christmas? And they really aren't great, Katy,' she said. 'They are actually very unpleasant criminals.'

Katy and Margaret exchanged glances.

'You'll probably like the one I got best,' said Katy. 'Who delivers presents to cats?'

'I don't know – who DOES deliver presents to cats?' said Margaret, in support as Sister Cecilia watched.

'Santa Paws!' finished Katy

'I think I can see the point of that,' Cecilia conceded. 'Though we normally say Father Christmas here, of course. I imagine that joke is American.'

'It probably is,' said Margaret, trying not to smile. Cecilia was trying her best.

'Who said "presents"?' said George, who had been chatting to Father Hugh and Matthew, seated further down the long table 'We have one for you all, don't we, Matthew?'

'We do,' said Matthew, rather shyly, and reaching behind his chair, he brought out a thin, flat Christmas parcel, which he gave to George, who took it up and handed it to Sister Bridget to open.

'Ooh, exciting! Thank you both so much!' said Sister Bridget, unwrapping the package with gusto. The paper tore off to reveal a newspaper cutting, beautifully mounted and framed.

'We thought you could put it on the wall in the entrance hall of the B&B – it's a copy of your first review from that Sunday supplement!' said George.

'That's so kind!' said Margaret, as Bridget passed it to her to admire. 'I wish Nonna was still here to see it. She was such a help with setting everything up.'

'Ah, God love her, sure she's having a great time back in Italy with Maria and Francesco,' said Bridget. 'There's no place like home.'

'We actually also sent a framed copy over to Cardellino for them,' said George. 'After all,' he continued, 'quite apart from Nonna's expert hotelier advice, our favourite B&B would not exist now without their gift of the Jack Mortimer paintings, which helped pay off the convent's debts, and more.'

'It was extraordinarily generous,' agreed Matthew. 'Fairbridge University wouldn't have the Jack Mortimer Gallery without the newly discovered paintings now in the collection.'

'And St Philomena's Church would be falling down without their kindness,' said Father Hugh. 'Let's raise a glass to our dear Italian friends!'

He got up and went around the table, topping up everyone's glasses. First he served Sisters Bridget, Cecilia and Margaret, then Katy, then Father Stephen, who was seated at the bottom of the table with him. Next to him was Mrs Sanders – George's mother, as she preferred to be known

('Those churchy people are not my chosen personal friends, George,' she had said when her son protested. 'They can address or refer to me as George's mother, or Mrs Sanders, but we are not on first name terms') – George, Matthew and, next to Bridget, Sarah, Matthew's twin sister and local district nurse.

'Maybe you could propose the toast, Sister Bridget?' said Father Hugh.

'Well, all right,' said Sister Bridget, getting to her feet and raising her glass. 'To all our friends, here and in Italy and Ireland, God bless them, and with thanks to God for the launch of St Philomena's Guest House, and asking for God's help in the New Year. Amen!' said Sister Bridget, excitedly mixing a toast with a prayer.

'Amen,' said everyone, church-going or not, laughing, and clinking glasses.

'Now, let's hear this wonderful review again!' requested Father Hugh from the bottom of the table.

'Yes, please read it out, Katy dear,' said Sister Bridget, clasping her hands in excitement, even though she had read it many times since it had first appeared.

'Well, the title is "St Philomena's – a Heaven-Sent new B&B",' said Katy. There were delighted and appreciative noises from the others, even though they had all read the review already, and she continued. 'This old Victorian house in the university town of Fairbridge, still a working convent for three nuns, is a charming getaway offering very reasonably priced bed and breakfast and, for no extra cost, peace.'

'Peace,' said Sister Bridget, happily. 'That's a sign we're doing it right.'

'The beds are comfortable and the bedding of the highest possible quality.'

'As Nonna advised us,' said Margaret.

'The guest rooms are simply decorated and spotlessly clean,' continued Katy. 'The breakfasts themselves in the formal dining room, at tables covered with crisp white table-cloths are superb.'

'I am glad they noticed that,' said Sister Cecilia.

'Thanks to you, Cecilia,' interjected Sister Bridget. Cecilia inclined her head. She had taken over the laundry duties, something she had never done before in all her life as a religious Sister, and, helped by the two brand-new washing machines installed for the purpose, was finding the job, which as a younger sister she had slightly looked down on, suited her very well.

'We are offered a wide choice, a truly continental breakfast, or the standard full English, with vegetarian options. Delicious home-made bread and jam add the finishing touches.'

'I must say, I am proud of our breakfasts,' said Sister Bridget, happily. 'Nonna was spot on about having freshly made bread, wasn't she?'

'The garden, open to guests, is tranquil, with places to sit and meditate, and although still beautiful in November, I can imagine that in spring and summer it will come into its own.'

'Thomas and young Chris are doing a great job,' said Sister Bridget, 'and Em is wonderful as receptionist. I can't wait until they see their finished staff flat. They are with their families today but they are excited to be moving in in the New Year.'

'This new B&B appears to be Heaven-sent. The cheerful young receptionist and all the staff are very friendly, there is a delightful convent kitten . . .' As if on cue, scratching on the door was heard. George got up and opened it and little Pangur appeared, ignored everyone else and made a beeline for Cecilia.

He jumped on to her lap, and was firmly removed by her and placed on the floor. Katy leant over and picked him up and gave him a cuddle, but very soon he wriggled free and curled up by the desired person, a small adoring white furry ball by Sister Cecilia's sensible black-shoed feet. '. . . and if you are lucky enough, as I was,' Katy read out, 'to actually have a chat with the Superior, the welcoming and wise Irish Sister Bridget, I guarantee you will go home refreshed in body and soul.'

Everyone burst into a spontaneous round of applause.

Sister Bridget blushed and beamed, then had a fit of coughing.

She's worn out, thought Margaret. *I have to talk to her about slowing down in the New Year. She needs a break.*

Katy went to get Bridget a glass of water, but in the meantime Sister Bridget accidentally downed all of her newly filled glass of Prosecco.

'I can do magic tricks!' Sister Bridget suddenly proclaimed, enthusiastically, her crown wonkier than ever. 'Can't I, Katy?'

Katy shyly agreed. 'Yes, well, Sister Bridget did show me some.'

'Would you like to see them?' said Bridget, getting to her feet.

'Go on then, Sister,' said Father Hugh, who had been expertly fielding some rather uninhibited and searching questions from George's mother, who had no qualms about asking a Catholic priest everything she had always wanted to know about his life.

He found it startling but quite refreshing, but he could tell his serious young assistant Father Stephen was getting increasingly alarmed at the intrusions. Sister Bridget's magic tricks were a welcome distraction.

'Go on, Sister Bridget!' said George, sitting next to Matthew and Sarah, his heart full of love for the little Irish Sister who had walked into his travel agents that year and transformed his life by her acceptance and kindness.

'Go and get the bingo bag, Katy dear,' said Sister Bridget.

Katy looked over at Sister Margaret, who smiled and nodded. This was a new one.

Sister Cecilia looked a little concerned, but she was more than occupied trying to stop the kitten, who was himself occupied in swinging on the tablecloth. She picked him up firmly and put him on her lap, and he immediately sighed and fell asleep.

'Isn't he a dote?' said Sister Bridget, fondly. 'He is very at home with you, that's for sure. Pangur Bán, the little white cat.'

'Hmm,' said Cecilia, resolutely trying to ignore him, though aware of his warmth and weight. She kept her hands awkwardly by her sides, but Margaret noticed she had raised her knees slightly to make sure he was safe on her lap. For someone who did not care about the kitten, she was making herself rather uncomfortable on his behalf.

Katy came back with a blue drawstring cloth bag, embroidered in gold-coloured chain stitch with the words 'bingo balls'. The balls themselves were a random collection of old tennis and ping pong balls with numbers in permanent marker written on them.

'Listen, everyone,' said Sister Bridget. 'Believe it or not, I can tell the numbers of the bingo balls without looking at them. I discovered my gift by accident.'

'I didn't know this,' said Sister Cecilia, looking at Margaret.

'It's all right, Cecilia. It's a joke,' said Margaret quietly. 'It's a magic trick. Wait and see.'

'Never! I don't believe it!' cried George loudly and

obligingly, getting into pantomime mood. Matthew smiled fondly at him.

'No word of a lie, young George,' said Sister Bridget. 'Now, Katy love, get me a blindfold. A clean tea towel from the kitchen drawer – that would be good.'

'TWO tea towels!' yelled George. 'I want to be sure there is no cheating.'

'Two tea towels it is,' agreed Sister Bridget. 'You put them on me, George, so you can't complain later.'

Duly blindfolded, Sister Bridget dramatically instructed Katy to pull a ball out of the bag.

The first ball Katy brought out was a ping pong ball with the number eight on it. She showed it in silence to the assembled group, and then handed it to Sister Bridget, who carefully felt it all over.

'Number eight, St Francis is great!' announced Sister Bridget, decisively. Father Hugh clapped, and Sister Bridget beamed as she pulled down the tea towels and was proved to be right. Admiring oohs and aahs followed.

'It's a fluke!' heckled George, enjoying himself. 'Or you peeked!'

'It is not!' replied Sister Bridget indignantly. 'And you can't say I peeked, George, as you put the blindfold on. I'll do another one now to prove it. No, another three. Go on Katy. I won't rest until this unbeliever accepts I am right.'

'I'll choose then,' said George, and picked out a tennis ball with the number ten on it. He paraded it around the group before handing it to the blindfolded Sister Bridget, who examined it carefully.

'The Ten Commandments – number ten,' she proclaimed, to the room's applause.

'Well done, Sister Bridget,' said Sarah.

'Go again now – you choose, Sarah.'

Sarah pulled out a tennis ball with twelve on it.

'Now, that's either the twelve apostles, or Daniel O'Donnell's birthday – the twelfth of December, God love him. We'll do one more now – Margaret – you choose.'

Margaret chose a ping pong ball with seven on it.

'Number seven, may we all go to Heaven, even you, George, doubting my word,' said Sister Bridget, confident in her answer even before she had pulled the tea towels down.

'I give up! I should never have doubted you, blessed Sister, please forgive me, have mercy,' said George, dramatically falling on his knees before her, his hand on his heart.

'Ah, get up you silly boy,' laughed a delighted Sister Bridget, throwing her arms around him and giving him a big kiss on his cheek.

'You should be on television – a celebrity magician nun!' said Father Hugh.

'I think it might be something to do with the size and surface of the bingo balls themselves,' said Father Stephen, genuinely intrigued, if a little tactless.

'Ah no, it's magic, I'm telling you,' said Sister Bridget.

'No, but Father Stephen is right. I think some of the bingo balls might be more dented than others,' said George's mother, who had been watching Sister Bridget and George rather disapprovingly. 'And of course, if all the double numbers are tennis balls and single numbers are ping pong balls and if you are using them every week, it would make sense that you would get to know their size and the feel of their surface, rather like Braille. Let me see the balls.' She got up and went to the top of the table. Katy passed her the bag of balls. George's mother started taking them out and looking at them carefully.

'Mother – don't spoil things,' said George, quietly.

Father Stephen came over to examine the bingo balls too, and George, who was now seriously annoyed, joined them to stand next to Sister Bridget and make sure his mother and Cecilia hadn't deflated her excitement.

Pangur Bán, woken up from his nap decided that looking at the balls was not as much fun as patting and chasing them, and climbed into the bag to find some more. The flash of his little white tail and the ensuing wiggling bump under the cloth alerted Sister Cecilia, who extracted the little cat and put him back on her lap, from whence he climbed up on to her shoulder and promptly fell asleep again. Cecilia, who over the last months had come to see tiny Pangur Bán and his obsessive devotion as a spiritual trial sent to test her, once more gave in to the inevitable and let him stay there. He was very soft and warm, after all, and Sister Cecilia suffered from the cold.

'Yes – here it is. Number two is a ping pong ball with a definite dent for example,' said George's mother, holding it up triumphantly. 'Although I must say that would still take some memorising to recognise all of the balls separately.'

'Well, Sister Bridget IS very clever,' said Katy, smiling.

Sarah got up and started to collect the pudding plates. As the others gathered around the top of the table discussing the bingo balls, she took the opportunity to speak quietly to Father Hugh. 'Sister Bridget has done a great job, but she is not as young as she thinks she is, and she looks very tired. She can't keep going at this pace, running the guesthouse and the parish bingo and goodness knows what else. I can't believe she cooked most of the Christmas lunch for the parish, and then more dishes for tonight!'

Father Hugh grimaced. 'Well, it would take a stronger man

than me to persuade her to slow down. I think it would need divine intervention!'

George and Matthew joined Sarah in clearing away the pudding plates and leaving them on the side in the clean and orderly kitchen. Katy and Margaret had already loaded up the other plates in the new dishwasher, which was dutifully quietly whirring away.

Sister Cecilia started to fall asleep in her chair, but was gently woken up by Katy, who lifted Pangur off Cecilia's shoulder and helped her up the stairs to bed.

'Happy Christmas, and thank you, Sisters!' their guests all said, realising it was time to go, hugging each other and setting out home into the cold winter's night.

Once Sister Cecilia had undressed and knelt by her bed to say her last prayers of the night, as she had done every night since she was a child, she heard a scratching at her door. She opened it, and Pangur ran past her and jumped up and curled up in his usual place at the bottom of her bed. In the five months since they had got him as convent kitten, Sister Cecilia had learnt that nothing she could do or say to Pangur Bán could stop him from being near her when he wanted to be. He was not intimidated by her glares or upset by her indifference. She never petted him or played with him, as the others did, but he was constantly trying to sit on her lap, pushing his head against her, following her around, purring. In all her years she had never met such persistent love from a living being. He loved everyone, and everyone loved him, but the person he had decided was especially his, was Sister Cecilia, and nothing would persuade him to leave her alone. The room, in spite of Sister Bridget getting new radiators put in, was not warm. Sister Cecilia got into bed and little Pangur shifted obligingly to lie on and warm her cold feet. She didn't move him.

ST STEPHEN'S DAY

Tuesday 26th December 1995

Four

'The wren, the wren, the King of all birds. St Stephen's day he was caught in the furze,' quoted Sister Bridget, washing up the convent's breakfast things and looking out at the garden, lightly covered with snow. 'That's what we always said at home. I must check the cupboards and the bookings for when the B&B opens again tomorrow.'

'Bridget – why don't you have an end-of-year break? We can manage for a few days. You could go to Ireland and see your sister?' said Margaret, concerned at how pale Bridget looked.

'Ah, she'll be tired after Christmas,' said Bridget. 'And I have to be here for the B&B.'

'We can manage. Maybe you could ask her if you could stay at the cottage,' said Margaret. 'I'm sure George could help you get a cheap ticket. I think it would do you good to get away.'

'But it has snowed,' said Cecilia, unnecessarily. 'Why would you want to travel now?'

Margaret resisted the temptation to roll her eyes and tut

loudly. Cecilia could be exasperating. A little bit of moral support would have come in handy – it was hard to get Bridget to take time off, particularly when she most needed to take it.

'We've been there before when it snowed,' argued Margaret. 'Declan drove us. A few years ago. I remember it being very cosy. And the mountains looked beautiful. It was like the psalms. It could be a retreat.'

'I will ring her. Anyway,' said Bridget, 'I didn't manage to speak to her yesterday. I'll do it when we get back from Mass this morning.

'After the party for the altar servers today, I've nothing urgent scheduled for the rest of the week. I can help out at the B&B instead.

'I just want to get the preparation for the New Year's bingo party over with. I'm so glad we're doing it. In this cold weather the hall will be a warm place to see in the New Year, and it brings together the Church and even those in the bingo crowd who never go to Mass. I promise – in the New Year things will change.'

Please God, make that happen, prayed Margaret. *She won't listen to me, that's for sure. For a good person she is very stubborn.*

'So Mum, I've had a quote back about the boiler. Could you write me a cheque?' Mary frowned at the receiver as her daughter launched into the financial details without stopping to enquire how her mother was. No 'Hello Mum, how are you?' or 'Thanks for a lovely Christmas.' Not that there was anything new to report about her day, or say, but shifting quietly at the back of her mind was the thought that once, just once, it would have been nice to be asked.

'Mum? Are you still there?' Deirdre's voice was irritable, impatient.

'Yes. Shall I post it to you?'

'No – I need it today. I'll send Fran round . . .'

There was a muffled protest, and a hissed 'Yes you bloody will, Fran . . .'

'Right, Fran will be over this morning.'

'That's fine,' said Mary.

'So you will?' The relief in Deirdre's voice melted her.

'Of course I will, Deirdre,' said Mary. 'If the boiler needs fixing, it needs fixing, that's all there is to it.' She paused, willing that Deirdre would say something, anything, about what was going on.

'We have to keep up standards if we are to rent the cottage out,' said Deirdre, bossy again.

'And we do still need to rent the cottage out?' asked Mary, tentatively.

'Yes. That's OK, isn't it?' said Deirdre, and again that insecurity in her voice twisted Mary's heart, pushing down the other thing, the unnamed thing that scrabbled at the back of her mind and kept her awake at night, the thing that howled, the thing she tried to quieten with prayer and trying that bit harder every day.

'Of course it is, love,' she said, and put down the phone. She would put the washing on. Declan was out playing golf with a friend, and he preferred not to hear machines running when he was at home.

In the presbytery over in Fairbridge, Father Hugh and Father Stephen were washing up the breakfast things before going over to the church to say Mass.

'I meant to say, Stephen – I noticed you talking to Maura at the Christmas lunch.'

'Yes – yes, poor woman. I was so shocked at the way her

45

family have been treating her. She has had to come back to Fairbridge for Christmas instead of spending it with her children and grandchildren. You would think they would honour their widowed mother. I am so glad we were able to give her a good Christmas dinner at least,' said Stephen. 'She has asked me to lead a morning rosary group she wants to start up now she is back in the parish. Of course, I said yes.'

'Oh dear. I should have said something. Maura . . . it's not always simple. I don't want to speak ill of her, but Maura has a history. Every summer since her husband died just over five years ago, she has gone to stay with one or another of her four children, with the idea that she might want to live with one of them, and it just has never worked. Each time she is back just before Christmas, after a big argument.'

'That's very sad,' said Father Stephen, concerned.

Father Hugh searched for a way to continue charitably. 'You are right, Stephen, it IS very sad, but it is not quite as straightforward as Maura might say. I think her children DO love her, but she is not easy. The other thing I would just warn you about is her rosary group. It's not the first time she has started one. There's a bit of a history there too.'

'What could be wrong with a rosary group?'

'Well, she started one a year ago, and people joined it after Mass, but she kept adding more and more prayers and petitions and novenas at the end, and it took longer and longer to say, and people were missing buses and appointments but she wouldn't listen. In the end people stopped going. In fact they started up another one, on Wednesdays, at Bridie's flat. They have tea and cake afterwards and it's a very jolly meeting. We should go one week. I would have taken you there before, but the school wanted us in on Wednesday afternoons. Maura was invited too but she was offended and refused. The only person left in Maura's group was Hortense Brown, who was too kind to leave. I think it was a relief to poor Hortense when Maura went off to stay with her son.'

'Oh dear,' said Father Stephen, rather worriedly.

'I used to be in Maura's group too, but in the end, I said I had to say my Divine Office as an absolute duty and I didn't have time. If it gets too much you can always blame it on me and say I have asked you to do things after Mass.'

'It seems very hard if nobody wants to pray with her,' said Father Stephen. 'After all, Jesus said he is there where two or three are gathered . . .'

'The problem is, Stephen, I am not sure if her image of God is quite as loving as yours,' said Father Hugh, touched by Father Stephen's attempts to look for the good in a woman Father Hugh found a real trial. 'I just want to counsel you to take care. She's . . . she's a troubled woman. I'm here to talk to you, should the need arise.'

'Thank you,' said Father Stephen, trying not to feel daunted.

'So, you're off after Mass? I hope you have a good time home with your family, Stephen. Thank you for all you have done. You're back on the thirty-first?'

'Yes, thank you. I'll be back in plenty time for evening Mass and the New Year vigil prayers and the parish New Year party.'

'Well, maybe you could pop over to Bridie's on New Year's Day when you're back? She would enjoy a visit, and I think that it would begin 1996 well for you,' said Father Hugh. 'I always find that seeing Bridie does me good.' *Especially after spending any time with Maura,* he thought, but did not say it out loud. Maura was a problem. He definitely needed to pray for her more.

*

George was making Boxing-Day breakfast, a Spanish omelette. He beamed over at Matthew, who was sitting at the table in his striped pyjamas, tall and thin, suitably academic with his glasses on, but his fair hair adorably tussled. He had a mug of tea in front of him, and was reading the newspaper whilst leaning down and stroking Sebastian, George's big rescue cat, who was purring and rubbing his head against him.

'Where shall we go on holiday in the spring, my love?' said George.

'Well,' said Matthew. 'I'd like to devise a student study trip to look at the landscape painting of an Irish artist called Paul Henry. I want to teach it next year, but I'd need to go over to Ireland myself first and plan the itinerary. The thing is, some of the places in the west are very remote, and badly served by public transport. I think I would need your help to drive . . . ?' he ended hesitantly.

'Give me a list of places you need to go, and I'll sort it,' said George. He put the plate down in front of Matthew with a flourish and gave him a swift kiss, then burst into song: 'I'd drive anywhere for you, dear, anywhere, for you mean everything to me . . .'

Matthew's eyes suddenly filled with tears.

'Darling, what's the matter?' George stopped and put his arm around him.

'I don't know, George. It's just so wonderful. I don't deserve you.'

'Rubbish, Matthew. I'm the one who doesn't deserve YOU. After Miguel died, I thought I would never find love again. I can't help thinking he's up there in Heaven, with his angels and saints, pulling strings for me. You're the kindest, gentlest, cleverest, most wonderful man. I can't believe my luck. I'm punching way above my weight here!'

Matthew smiled over at George, small and dark and cuddly, full of energy and ideas.

'This time last year I had no idea you would be in my life,' he said. 'I can't believe it. You're my miracle.'

'Well,' laughed George, going to collect his own plate and mug of tea, and coming back to sit opposite the shy, gentle man he loved so dearly. 'I don't like to boast . . .'

St Stephen's Day Mass on Boxing Day was always the time when the newest altar servers, drawn from the children of the parish, were rewarded for their first year or so of service with a special Guild of St Stephen medal on a red cord. Father Hugh would officially present each boy or girl with a medal during the Mass, and they were then allowed to wear them around their necks over their white servers' costumes or albs, like the older servers. Special prayers were said for all the servers, new and experienced, their commitment pledged or renewed, and then, after Mass, there would be a special party for them and their families in the church hall.

Sister Margaret, as parish Sister, had taken Katy with her before Mass to set up the hall with party food and lemonade. Now they were back in the pews and she was trying not to feel cross. *These are lovely little lads, and older lads too, Lord, and I am very happy to organise a party for them, but why are there so few girls?* she prayed quietly.

At least girls were allowed to be altar servers now, and since the reforms of Vatican 2 back in the 1960s, women could stand up on the sanctuary and do the scripture readings, if not the Gospel readings. When Cecilia was a girl, and even in Margaret's memory, they used to not even be allowed on the sanctuary – only men in the holiest part of the church. She was glad she had asked Katy to read today. It would inspire the girls. Though the first reading itself was rather daunting, it was supposed to inspire everyone – brave and gentle St Stephen, the first martyr of the church, stoned to death for being a Christian. Not the cheeriest of texts. Though being a saint, Stephen went straight to Heaven, so that could be seen as a happy ending. The point was, they were ALL supposed to be martyrs, or witnesses for the Faith – men AND women. Boys AND girls. So why not women deacons – why not women priests? Though the Pope had specifically written a letter last year ruling out discussion about that. Gosh, she was getting cross. *Sorry Lord. Help me concentrate and pray.*

The Gospel reading wasn't easy either, even though Father Hugh read it out in a very kind and gentle way. There was no avoiding the fact that Jesus warned that families would be divided because of Faith in him, and Margaret was distracted and irritated by Maura Ryan nodding vigorously as Father Hugh read it out.

Sorry, Lord. I really don't like Maura. What was it C. S. Lewis said in The Screwtape Letters? *Something like she's the kind of woman who lives for others, and you know the others by their hunted expression . . . Oh dear, 'Judge not and you will not be judged.' I know you love her. But she frightens me really – there is something very mean and bitter about her, dressed up in piety. I don't think it is easy for her family when she is with them but I wish she hadn't come back here, to be honest. She bullies everyone. I am a bit worried she will be moving in on Father Stephen too. Please bless her, but protect us from her. If that isn't too dramatic. It probably is. Sorry. Sorry I am being so horrible about someone you love so much. Please help me pray now.*

Margaret managed to focus on her prayers for the rest of the Mass and made sure she paid a visit to the church crib after the service to look at the baby Jesus lying in the manger, Mary and Joseph on either side, the donkey and the cow and the sheep kneeling before the sweet scene. The Holy Family always cheered her up. Life and people were complicated, but it was nice to remember that sometimes a family really could just simply be good, and loving, and full of peace. But right now there were altar servers and their families waiting in the hall. Father Hugh was going to tell them that all the altar servers were getting free tickets to the parish panto trip. There would be cake and lemonade and huge excitement. She had better get over there and help Katy serve them before it all went pear-shaped.

Five

Back in her kitchen in Galway, Mary was definitely lacking Christmas peace.

'It isn't broken, you know, Granny,' Fran blurted out, as she waited for her grandmother to write the cheque.

'What isn't broken?' said Mary.

'The boiler. There isn't anything wrong with it. We were there before Christmas and it was fine.'

The thing with no name sat up sharply inside Mary, alert. She didn't tell it to lie down, but she refused to let it dictate what she said to her granddaughter and how she said it. She deliberately made her gaze kindly and vague as she looked at Fran. Her granddaughter's eyes, which had been mutinous and angry, now had the panicked look of someone who has said a little too much and wants to take it back.

'I didn't know that you went to the cottage, Fran. When did you go?'

'Dad and Mum had another row and she said she needed to get away. So we went for a few days.'

'How was it?' said Mary, the thing scrabbling inside her.

'Boring,' Fran shrugged, but she must have noticed something in her grandmother's expression.

'Mum was just on the phone shouting at Dad all the time. The cottage was lovely though. I really liked your paintings.'

'How did you see my paintings?' said Mary surprised. 'They are all locked away.'

'Mum got the key to the studio. I think she was thinking she might put another bed in there, so that she could rent it out to bigger groups.'

Mary closed her eyes for a moment and counted to ten.

'I think they are really good. Why don't you do them any more, Gran?'

Mary opened her eyes and shrugged. 'I don't know, Fran. Life, I suppose. Let me get my cheque book.'

There was a silence.

Mary signed her name a bit more energetically than she normally did, and the energy with which she ripped the cheque out of the book contrasted with how mildly she spoke to Fran.

'Here you are, love. Tell your mum I would like to talk to her about the cottage, will you?'

'Are you all right, Gran? Forget what I said about the boiler. It probably *was* broken and I didn't notice. I'm just in a bad mood, I suppose.' She looked suddenly forlorn, and a bit scared. Mary wanted to give her a hug, but knew that Fran might not welcome it.

'Christmas can be difficult. Couples can row when they love each other.' Though she and Declan never did. She had never liked conflict, and Declan liked to be right. It had always been easier to give in.

A great tiredness overtook her. Keeping the thing with no name from rampaging was taking all her energy.

'Gran – are you all right?'

'I'm fine. I'm just a bit tired. I think I just need to lie down. I'll be fine.'

She was touched when, in the hall, her granddaughter suddenly turned and hugged her before going through the front door.

'Bye Gran,' she said. 'And . . . can you forget what I said about the boiler? Don't tell Mum.'

'Don't worry,' said Mary. 'I won't tell her.'

Mary closed the front door. The phone was ringing and she went to answer it. She could have let the answerphone take it, but somehow, she never did.

'Well, everything is absolutely fine in Ireland,' said Bridget, beaming as she got off the phone. The Sisters were back from Mass and the small celebration in the hall for the altar servers. 'They had a tremendous Christmas, apparently. To be fair, Mary sounded a bit tired all right, but she always needs a rest after company. It's the way she was made, God love her. Ever since she was little.'

'Did you ask about the cottage, Bridget?'

'I did, I did ask if it was free for a few days, but apparently there is work needed done on it. It was a good idea, Margaret, but I think it was a bit short notice. She rents it out now.'

'I wouldn't have thought that they needed the money,' said Margaret.

'She's very busy with the family, of course, and volunteering, and the church. And Declan still runs his business, of course.'

'He must be seventy now – doesn't he want to retire?' said Margaret.

'Sure, what would he do? It's like a vocation with him,' said Bridget.

What vocation? Making money? thought Margaret. She had never really warmed to Declan, Bridget's brother-in-law. He reminded her slightly of the Bishop. He was a bit too good looking and sure of himself. Margaret preferred Bridget's sister. She was a bit surprised and disappointed that Mary too seemed to be so focused on making money, when they really didn't need it.

'Well, if you won't go to Ireland, Bridget, let's have some trips out of the parish,' said Margaret, back in the convent. 'Fairbridge Gardens are open today – let me at least take you there this afternoon.'

'But they will be covered in snow,' said Sister Cecilia.

'It will look very pretty, and the tea rooms are open on Boxing Day,' said Margaret, wishing Cecilia wouldn't say, 'But you can have tea at home.'

'But you can . . .' started Cecilia, but Bridget, to Margaret's relief, had started talking at the same time.

'I would like to go to Fairbridge Gardens,' said Bridget. 'We could take Thomas – he used to court Rose there. It's good for him to get a chance to talk about her. He misses her so much. He always will. A love like that never dies, no matter how many years go by.'

'Why don't we go straight after lunch? Cecilia and Katy, would you like to come?'

'I will be working on my History of Catholic Fairbridge,' said Sister Cecilia.

'I won't, thanks. I'm going to pack to visit Dad tomorrow, and catch up on some reading,' said Katy. 'Then I'll make dinner for us tonight.'

'Lovely!' said Margaret, before Bridget could protest or get involved in menu planning.

'A change is as good as a rest,' said Bridget happily as they walked the paths around the gardens. She and Thomas got OAP rates to visit Fairbridge Gardens and House, which pleased them both, and Sister Margaret, who was too young to qualify and had to pay full rates, was also somewhat encouraged to be reminded that she might have retired from teaching, but she was still classed as of working age.

'Do you remember the fun we had back in the fifties, Thomas?' Bridget asked, as they went through the turnstile into the formal gardens, now pretty with powdered snow over bushes and fountains. 'Rose and I meeting you both at the bottom of the garden, behind the topiary, on our half days, and hoping nobody would catch us?'

She looked younger, her face lit up with memories.

'They never did catch us. I always said you had the luck of the Irish,' said Thomas. 'Then we would go to the dances. I don't know why we took the risk really. We could have met you both at the hall.'

'Ah no, there was a big, long dark path to go down before the road – you were gentlemen – you wouldn't leave us to walk there on our own. You and Rose were always great dancers, I remember,' said Bridget.

'Oh, you're one to talk! Didn't you and Dec win prizes for it?' said Thomas. 'Does he still dance?'

'I don't know. I have never asked him. I don't think they've had the time, with the family and the business. You should get back in touch with him. I'm sure he'd be pleased.'

'How old were you when you all met?' asked Margaret,

pleased to see Bridget's and Thomas's enjoyment, both smiling at happy memories.

'Well, Declan and I were in the same class at school. He went over to England first, to work with his mother's brother in his building firm. You were working there, weren't you, Thomas, before you joined the postal service?' Thomas nodded. 'Fairbridge College, the finishing college they were running at Fairbridge House at the time, were recruiting for girls to work there, live-in. Father Ryan told my mother about it. They thought it would be a good thing for me to join in but to be in a safe place. I had to see Declan, after all, everyone thought we were practically engaged, my parents and his were all for it – Father Ryan too, truth be told, but I knew deep down that wasn't where God was calling me. They shipped me over so I could see Declan and decide better about where my vocation lay, and I know they wanted it to be marriage with him. But I found the Sisters of St Philomena, and the rest is history.' She sighed happily.

'It must have been a shock for Declan,' said Margaret.

'It was,' said Thomas. 'They were the golden couple.'

'Yes, but it all worked out for the best, thanks be to God,' said Bridget, easily. 'He has a grand marriage with Mary. Now, isn't this beautiful? Even with the bare trees, there's beauty in every season, I always say. Thank you, Margaret, this was a great idea you had.'

The kitten Pangur Bán was in disgrace. He had climbed on Sister Cecilia's lap when she was writing and swiped at her fountain pen.

'Stop that now!' she had said firmly, but Pangur had persisted, knocked the pen out of her hand, and now a big ink blot had been added to her careful notes.

Sister Cecilia was irritated beyond words. She picked up the errant kitten, who inappropriately purred with delight at such attention, and strode furiously down to the kitchen to deposit him in the utility area. Katy was there, reading a cookery book, planning Boxing-Day tea.

'Please – take him. I cannot work. He is an utter nuisance. Someone else needs to have him. He appears to think my pen is a toy.'

'Maybe that's what he needs,' said Katy. 'More toys. He's so little still – he just wants to play, that's all. I'll entertain him for a bit, though I know I'm second best to you!'

'But why does he always want to play with me?' said Cecilia, exasperated.

'Maybe it's just because he loves you so much?' said Katy, unaware of how those words hit home.

Sister Cecilia turned to go back to the library, but, on impulse took a detour to the chapel. To her surprise, she found herself thinking about the Annunciation by the angel Gabriel to Mary. It calmed her, as she thought about the young girl chosen to be the mother of God. That had been a really big thing, and here she was, getting so frustrated about a kitten. Her anger ebbed away, and she felt sorry for her fury. She sat in front of the tabernacle, the candle inside the red votive light holder beside it flickering, and her guilt and irritation were gradually replaced by peace, as she allowed herself to sit in the presence of a God who loved her even more than that small white cat did. It was hard to get used to. It was good, but a bit unsettling, to be so loved.

'I am sorry, Lord,' she said. 'I shouldn't have been so impatient.' She had some money from her allowance. Maybe she would buy Pangur some new toys. A new high scratching post she could put in the library so she could write in peace whilst he entertained himself. Yes, that is what she would do. She would go to the pet shop the next day.

After lunch Father Hugh drove for a couple of hours to a run-down area in London. He parked up by a block of flats. Abandoned syringes and smashed bottles on the pavement, graffiti on the walls, a broken window on the ground floor and loud music blaring from upstairs. It was a world away from Fairbridge. From a flat on a middle floor came the raised voices of people arguing.

He scanned the car park for anyone loitering, and made sure nothing tempting was on show. Father Hugh's car was old and not a desirable make, but he knew the temptation a wallet on display could be.

The heavy great entrance door, with a square of grimy steel-mesh glass inset, opened to a dark stairwell which smelt of urine and spilt beer and, in the background, a pungent, sweeter smell Father Hugh recognised from earlier parish work. The lift worked, but was filthy.

A heavy smell of incense hit him as he walked down the corridor of the second floor, but there was no sound of accompanying hymns, and the windows were not beautiful stained glass, sending colours across the floor, but wired, cracked and grimy. Someone had been sick on the floor and the furious argument he had heard from outside was coming from the flat next door to the one he stopped at.

He rang the doorbell and when a tall, slim, bearded man about his own age opened it to him, stepped inside into a different world – a refreshingly clean, simple sitting room, so bare it was almost like a monk's cell. There was a frail figure holding rosary beads in a chair in the corner.

'Hello Peter,' Hugh said to the tall man. 'Hello Jimmy.'

'Hello Father Hugh! It's grand to see you,' said Jimmy. He tried to get up out of his armchair.

'Please don't get up,' said Hugh, noting how weak his old friend had got. He was only in his mid-sixties, but looked so much older. 'How are you?'

'Ah, can't complain,' said Jimmy.

'Well, I can,' said Peter, crossly. 'I rang the police at one point. I don't know how you have stood it so long, Jimmy. The neighbours say these last six months have been hell, but you never mentioned it to me at the day centre.'

'I didn't want to be a bother. They weren't as bad before,' said Jimmy. 'If it wasn't for the old chest giving me bother, I'd have managed.'

'Well, if it wasn't for your old chest, I wouldn't have come to stay, and then I wouldn't have heard what was going on,' said Peter. 'I took him to the doctors, as I told you,' he said to Hugh, 'and they sent him for an X-ray. He has a shadow on his lung, and they say that a lot of his problems come from working on the buildings all those years ago. No health and safety then, and asbestos everywhere. People should be in prison for this.'

'Sure, I always had a weak chest, even as a boy,' said Jimmy, peaceably. 'And they didn't know about that asbestos donkey's years ago.'

'Well they should have known,' retorted Peter. 'They knew enough about making money, and that's for sure. That's all they cared about. Anyway,' he said to Hugh, 'I've taken leave from the care centre and I'm going to look after Jimmy until we have sorted something better for him. He can't live like this. I've packed his suitcase. There was hardly anything to do, to be honest. He doesn't exactly have many possessions. The furniture is going to be picked up by the centre tomorrow.'

'How are you, Jimmy?' said Father Hugh, bending over and taking Jimmy's hand in his. Jimmy's voice was quiet, his Irish accent strong.

'Not too bad at all, Father, thanks be to God. Sure, haven't I got the best friend a man could want in Peter?'

Father Hugh looked back over at Peter, his eyes filled with tears. There was a tangible atmosphere of peace emanating from the frail, sick man, in spite of the raised voices and swearing next door.

A door slammed and the arguing voices stopped. Footsteps in the corridor were accompanied by tuneless, angry drunk ranting. A bang on the door and an anti-Irish oath rang out, and Father Hugh and Peter tensed, but the footsteps thankfully went on. Next door, the radio came on, loudly. In the flat above, another resident turned their music up, and the bass beats shook the ceiling. Somewhere else, a baby cried, and outside a car revved its engine loudly. Father Hugh was anxious to get back down to his.

'You were right to call me,' said Father Hugh to Peter. 'We'll think of what to do tomorrow, but you can come back to mine today. You can't stay here a minute longer.'

'Well, I don't want to be any trouble,' said Jimmy.

'What trouble?' said Father Hugh, affectionately. 'I'll enjoy the chat. Father Stephen is away for a few days, and it will be nice to have your company. It will be like the old days.'

'Come on, let's get you out of this hellhole, Jimmy,' said Peter. 'Things are going to get much better.'

Wednesday 27th December 1995

Six

It was the day after Boxing Day, back to work for many. Declan had to go into the office early to sort something out, and wouldn't be back until much later. Mary was glad she was on the rota for the charity shop. Lizzie the shop manager was there already and the shop had no customers as yet, so they had time to chat as Lizzie made a new window display and Mary tipped a donated jigsaw on the shop counter and started to assemble it. When she had first started volunteering, Mary had been surprised at how important this task was, but now she was familiar with the regular customers, she understood how the 'jigsaw complete' sticker was an essential component of a sale. This one, according to the box, was of two kittens indoors in a washing basket, so a piece of blue sky, for example, could be immediately set aside as belonging to another puzzle, maybe the Riviera scene next to be sorted. She already had customers in mind for each of them.

'How was Christmas then?' said Lizzie, who had climbed into the window and was arranging a silk scarf around the neck of a favourite shop dummy, Dolly.

'Fine.'

'What's up?' said Lizzie, recognising that tone. They were such different women, and Lizzie was only thirty, ten years younger than Mary's daughter, but they had formed a real friendship over the years. Lizzie was the only person Mary talked to about her art, as they had first met at evening art classes. And Lizzie, who at first had been intimidated by Mary's perfect clothes and hair had soon realised that Mary was actually very lonely, and very kind.

'It's Deirdre. Something Fran said. She said they had been down at the cottage before Christmas.'

'What's wrong with that?' said Lizzie, frowning as she tried different coats on Dolly, settling on a green Donegal tweed cloak, fastened by one button at the neck.

In the quiet, warm, colourful shop, so different from the muted taste of her home, with this younger woman she felt closer to than her own beloved daughter, Mary felt safe enough to talk. 'You know Deirdre has been renting it out. They have . . . money troubles. Declan doesn't know.'

'I know. You said.' Lizzie considered herself a heroine for not sharing with Mary exactly what she thought of her daughter.

'Deirdre rang me to tell me the cottage needs a new boiler. I gave her a cheque. But Fran says it doesn't – that it was warm.'

'Yes – but Fran isn't an engineer, is she?' said Lizzie, reasonably, stepping down and rummaging in the hat basket to find a suitable one for Dolly. An Aran beret in sparkly wool was retrieved. Dolly was going to a party.

'No. But . . .'

'What?'

'I just have this feeling. And . . .'

66

'And what?'

'I don't know.' Mary was surprised to feel tears coming to her eyes. 'Don't mind me. I'm just tired. How was yours?'

'Oh, you know. He was with his wife, but he popped round in the evening. I know you don't agree.'

'Oh Lizzie. I just think marriage is for life.'

'So does he. That's the trouble. Even though they don't love each other any more. And I, like a fool, love him so much. And he loves me. He says it, and I know it's true.'

Mary sighed. 'I'm not surprised at anyone loving you, Lizzie,' she said, not saying any more. Lizzie was so open and kind – too kind. Her married boyfriend had been a fellow student at their art evening class, and Mary understood why the shyer older man had fallen for her brightness. Maybe, as he said, he was in a loveless marriage. But having an affair with a married man was wrong. She knew by now they wouldn't get anywhere talking about it. Mary just had to keep praying for her.

The shop bell rang as the door opened, and a pair of regular customers came in, a woman Lizzie's age and a little boy of about three.

'Hello Sinead! Hello Rory!' Mary said. 'Did you have a lovely Christmas?'

'We did!' said Sinead. 'But we need to get something from you today.'

'Don't tell me – your grandmother has finished her jigsaw already?'

Sinead laughed. 'She has. She loved the last one, thank you, Mary. She said Connemara ponies were her favourite and brought back memories of growing up in Connemara. It's funny – she never talks about that normally.'

'I'd love to meet her one day and chat about her childhood!'

smiled Mary. 'That would be a treat for me! I think she's about the age of my husband, so seventy?'

'She is sixty-eight. That would be lovely, Mary. She broke her leg before Christmas and she is so bored.'

'Well, for a change, how about a scenery one? If she liked the ponies she might like another Connemara scene? I've got a five hundred piece one of Kylemore Abbey? I checked it before Christmas, and it was good fun to do.'

'That's perfect!' said Sinead, passing Mary the money.

'And how about you, Rory? Would you like a puzzle?' said Mary. 'I've got a great one of *Bananas in Pyjamas*! I've done it myself, so I know it's good!'

The little boy nodded solemnly and took the box and Mary popped a pound of her own into the till.

'Oh Mary, you're too good.'

'Not at all! I'm only training him up for the big ones! You're our best customers for jigsaw puzzles. I feel I know your grandmother through the puzzles, too!'

'It really would be great if you met her,' said Sinead. 'We do our best, but she's lonely since Pop died, and Rory is at nursery and Dad and Mum and Rory's dad and I have to work most days, so she needs more company.'

'That's my New Year's Resolution, then,' said Mary, and waved goodbye to them as they left the shop.

Lizzie, still arranging the window, gave the sparkly beret a more jaunty angle. She looked at Mary, carefully back to doing the jigsaw, and impulsively stepped down from the window and gave her a hug. Mary smelt her perfume and felt her curls tickle her cheek and turned round to respond. The two women hugged, feeling each other's mutual love.

'Have you been painting, Mary?'

Mary shook her head.

'Honestly, Mary, that's a crime. I know Deirdre has been renting out the cottage, but can't you paint at home?'

Mary shook her head. 'I don't know. The cleaners come in – I just feel like I'm in the way. I can't relax with the paints and there is nowhere I can put the paintings. They're not Declan's cup of tea.'

'Mary – it's your home!' said Lizzie, shocked.

'It's Declan's too, and he likes everything white and clean for when he shows off the house and entertains. He has to – that's his business.'

'Hmm,' Lizzie said, and put some more sparkly tinsel in the window for New Year. 'I thought the deal with Deirdre was that when the cottage wasn't booked, you'd have the studio for your painting? And that this whole arrangement was just temporary, to get them through a hard patch?'

'Yes.'

'And you've still got keys?'

'Yes – but she has probably got people in for the holidays.'

'Without a working boiler? Why don't you ask her?'

'I . . . She's in a funny mood, Lizzie. And Fran said she was opening up the studio and looking to see if she could put more beds there.'

'What? That's outrageous! Have you asked her about it?'

'No – I know I'm just a coward, Lizzie. I hate it when she gets angry.'

'You're gentle and easily bossed about, but you're not a coward,' said Lizzie, smiling at her friend. 'Why don't you ask Deirdre if anyone is booked there for these few days?'

'Why?'

'Because I have tomorrow off, and you aren't on the rota. We could drive down to the cottage and see what is happening. You are the owner – if there are people there you can just say you were told that the boiler wasn't working. And we can go to the studio and check the paintings, and maybe you can get your paints out. It will do you good.'

'I wouldn't want to intrude or spoil anyone's holiday.'

'It's your home, Mary! The studio is apart from the house. Look – if it makes you feel better I can ring. What's the booking number?'

Mary gave her the card. Deirdre answered quickly.

'Hello,' said Lizzie, putting on a posh Dublin accent that made Mary smile. 'I was thinking of a few days in Connemara. Can you tell me, does your cottage have any vacancies, starting from tomorrow?'

There were eager sounds from the other end of the phone. 'Oh, great. And tell me – what about the heating – I have heard horror stories of friends on holiday and the boilers breaking down. I presume there is a traditional turf fire – but is there central heating too? There is? All toasty? Good. And the cost? Thank you. Hold that for me, as I'm definitely interested. Goodbye.'

Lizzie beamed. 'Right – nobody is in there this week. The boiler is working, and the cottage is toasty warm – she has been there recently. So it sounds like Fran is right. You're going to have to tackle Deirdre, Mary. Something is up.'

Mary bit her lip.

'Look. We'll drive down and make a day of it,' said Lizzie. 'We'll pop over to the cottage and check it out. We can bring things for lunch. You can paint. I'd like to get back into it myself. Remember that time you invited the art class down? That hunky visiting tutor really fancied you. Not that he had a chance leading you away from Declan.'

Mary blushed. 'He was very nice about my painting.'

'He was. I do think he fancied you – but really liked your

work too. We all did. You light up when you're painting. This last year, since Deirdre's been letting the cottage out, it's been like someone put you on dimmer switch.'

'I do feel like that. I'm so tired. Coming here to the shop cheers me up, but at home I just keep falling asleep.'

'Well, my therapist would say it's because you are suppressing things. So that's settled then? I'll pick you up at eight, and we'll have tea and cake in Clifden and buy some treats for lunch, then pop over to the house, and on our way back we can have a slap-up dinner in Roundstone. That's settled then!'

'So you're off to the cottage?' said Declan that evening, surprised. He hadn't actually been at the office that day. In fact, he had decided, on impulse, to give his secretary and staff the rest of the week off. Doing the various blood tests and ECGs had taken all day, and, after that letter, he had been feeling curiously depressed. Whilst he didn't have the results yet, and had no plans to share the contents of that awful letter with Mary, he had taken it for granted he would have her company to take his mind off things. 'Shall I come?'

'No – no, Declan. Not today. I think Lizzie wants to talk with me in private about something,' said Mary. She hated lying, but if Deirdre was up to something at the cottage, she did not want Declan to find out. 'It's . . . women's issues.' She knew that would frighten Declan off any more awkward questions. 'We won't be late. I'll be back in time for dinner.'

'I'll book us a table to eat out,' said Declan. 'I'll book it for seven. That should give you plenty of time to get back.'

Not plenty of time, Mary thought, trying not to feel disappointed. She hoped that cancelling a delicious meal in Roundstone wouldn't be too disappointing for Lizzie. Why would Declan take time off, all of a sudden?

71

'Don't worry about me. I'll go over to Deirdre's for lunch,' said Declan. *Unnecessarily reassuring,* Mary thought, suddenly exasperated. Surely she could go away for the day without the world coming to an end?

Mary opened her mouth to warn him not to tell Deirdre where she was going, but realised that that would strike him as odd. Maybe it would be good for Deirdre to know her mother was going down to the cottage. After all, it was hers. As Lizzie said, it was supposed to be a temporary arrangement.

'I'll finalise the details for the New Year's party whilst I am over at Deirdre's. She said she would get caterers in.'

'How much did she say it will cost?' said Mary, unexpectedly. She never normally asked about bills.

'It doesn't matter. Whatever it is, we can afford it, Mary,' he reassured her. 'It's a long way from the island we are now. It'll never be like back there again, I promise.'

Thursday 28th December 1995

Seven

Sister Cecilia woke as she did every morning, to Pangur's purring right next to her, and his green eyes looking at her.

Little Pangur had become her constant companion, but she was still not entirely sure how this state of affairs had come about. It had certainly not been her decision. She knew nothing about cats and had no desire to be in charge of one. A day or so after he arrived in the summer, when he was very little, he had somehow managed to climb the stairs up to the landing and slip inside her bedroom's half-open door while she was paying her last visit to the bathroom before sleep.

'Oh no! How on earth did you get here? What are you doing?' she had said when she returned, but he had ignored her and curled up on the bottom of her bed. He seemed so tiny, fast asleep, and because she was tired, and the convent was dark and quiet, and she had never picked up a kitten before, she had decided to ignore him just that once, and get into bed without disturbing him. He slept well all night and in the morning he followed Sister Cecilia down and, without prompting, used his litter tray in the utility room, which was a bit of a miracle.

The second night she was aware of the little white shape on the landing again.

'No, you are not to come in with me,' Cecilia said firmly to the kitten, who sat still, only the tip of his tail twitching. She closed the bedroom door when she went to the bathroom, but somehow she mustn't have pulled it shut quite as firmly as she had intended to, because Pangur was there again, curled up, his eyes shut, when she came back to bed, and yet again, ignored by Cecilia, he slept all night without causing any bother.

He had slept in her room every night since.

Cecilia sat up in bed, and, as ever since she had first signed up for religious life, she resolved to make her first words a prayer. She began 'Our Father . . .' and Pangur immediately climbed over the bedclothes and sat on her lap, purring.

The first morning this happened, soon after he had first started sleeping in her room, she had tried to push Pangur from the bed before she prayed, but he so determinedly kept climbing back up each time he was pushed off, it had interrupted the prayerful beginning of her day. The next day she had compromised by sitting up rigidly in bed, arms at either side, ignoring his little warm furry presence, but as she had prayed the words out loud the tiny cat's body had thrummed with pleasure and approval, and now her first prayers of the morning, spoken out loud, were more and more often accompanied by the absentminded stroking of a rapidly growing Pangur, whose warm furry weight was utterly unignorable and whose loving purrs, getting louder by the day, were the choral background to her words.

So now, without anything being officially decided, Pangur

and Cecilia had an agreement. Pangur would be beside Sister Cecilia in the convent day and night, and Cecilia would neither encourage nor discourage him, just accept his presence. As everyone was very busy, Cecilia had taken out a book on kittens from the library. He had come litter trained and Bridget and Katy had gone out and bought a few toys and scratching posts which were put around the convent. Cecilia fed him and made sure he had fresh water to drink, but apart from those first prayers in the morning, she never spontaneously cuddled him. This made absolutely no difference to Pangur's attachment. He was a very friendly cat, and enjoyed playing with Katy and Sister Margaret and Sister Bridget and Em and Chris and any visiting B&B guests, but it seemed his true happiness lay in just being tolerated by Cecilia, and his vocation was to be wherever she went.

Sister Cecilia was now in charge of the laundry of both the convent and the B&B, and was finding it very rewarding. There had been an interesting documentary on washing machines on the BBC, and she had to admit to feeling a delayed admiration for the work of all those lay sisters she had lived with for years, who had done the convent laundry by hand. In the old days, as shown by a photograph of no less than St Thérèse and her community in the Carmelite convent in Lisieux, France, a whole day would have been dedicated to a convent's laundry. Now, thanks to the marvels of science, and two washing machines, Sister Cecilia could fit her laundry duty into the rhythm of her day without really interrupting her study. It was marvellous.

Pangur followed Sister Cecilia into the chapel for Morning Prayer, and then Sister Cecilia and Pangur put the table linen and tea towels collected the night before into the machine before Mass.

The First Liturgy of the Laundry, the same this day as every day, went like this:

Entrance of nun and cat to laundry room. Nun inspects basket full of tablecloths and tea towels and loads them into washing machine.

'No, Pangur, come out of the machine.'

Small white cat is lifted out of machine and put firmly on floor.

Response: Purr

'No, Pangur, come out of the machine.'

Small white cat is extracted from washing machine and put firmly on floor a second time.

Response: Purr

'Now, the powder is in and the machine is on. Come along Pangur.'

Response: Purr.

Ceremonial exit of nun and small white cat.

Sister Cecilia always found it very gratifying when she and Pangur left the laundry room, hearing the machines whirr and knowing that the laundry would be being done even as she ate toast and drank her tea.

After breakfast Pangur had a little nap in his basket in the utility room, or, to be honest, on the windowsill or on a chair in the kitchen, whilst the Sisters went off to Mass. But he was always there waiting for Sister Cecilia when she came back and went to take the laundry out.

It was a struggle to get Jimmy back down the stairs at the presbytery that morning. He and Peter were staying in Father Stephen's room whilst he was away visiting family so this was only going to be temporary and it was evident to Father Hugh that if Jimmy was to have any life at all, he needed to live on a ground floor.

Father Hugh left Peter and Jimmy watching breakfast television and went over to pray in the church before Mass.

'Lord, Jimmy has struggled for so long. Peter introduced me to him in the shelter over thirty years ago. Isn't it time for him to have a break? He has been so brave fighting his alcohol problem, and you know he is more sinned against than sinning. He had the worst start possible as a boy, and the Church has to take responsibility for that, and then there are the problems caused after all those years on the buildings. Please help us to help him. They can't stay here, but I am dreading finding him new accommodation. I felt we had no choice but to get him out of that hellhole, but now I am daunted by what we have done. I leave this with you, Lord.' He made the sign of the cross and went to get up, then remembering a postscript, crossed himself again. 'And, dear Lord, please bring peace to Peter. There is a sadness and a grief in him that only seems to get worse with the years, and I don't know how to help him.'

Lizzie and Mary had an early start. Once they had left Galway City, around Clonbur, the scenery began to get wilder. The road twisted and turned past the choppy slate-grey waters of Lough Mast, and along the side of the road the fuchsia and wild rose bushes were pushed by the breeze. Mary felt her spirits rise even as sheets of rain moved across and partially obscured the mountains in the distance.

'It's just beautiful, isn't it?' she said to Lizzie. 'It always looks gorgeous, in whatever weather. Thank you for taking me here today.'

'No problem,' smiled Lizzie, slowing down to a halt for a sheep which had wandered on to the road and just stood there, looking at them, the wind blowing its wool. It moved to eat grass from the verge and they drove on. High up on either side of them sheep and cows looked down from fields with stone walls. In front of them dark grey silhouettes of the mountains lay like shadows under soft grey clouds.

The yellow signs at every bend warned of twists and turns, and increasingly, as they wound their way towards their destination, gaps in hedges along the narrow, undulating road showed glimpses of wind-ruffled sea, grey, lichen-covered dry-stone walls, and whitewashed cottages.

The wind blew the clouds away and the winter sun shone pale golden on the blue mountains ahead of them. They drove through a dark forest of conifers, and the road took them out and into the light. The landscape opened up to fields and cottages and rocky shorelines. Mary opened the car window a little and breathed in the smell of peat fires and seaweed, and a donkey walked to the edge of a field and looked at them as they drove by. They passed a man in a flat cap cycling slowly along, and in front of them a smaller, local hill rose up green and brown against white and grey clouds.

Then another twist in the road, and they were driving over the bridge to the island. It was almost too beautiful to be true. The rain clouds had moved on, so now the blue range of mountains was clear to be seen, reflected in the sea. They passed tumbledown cottages in dry-stone-walled fields. There were some smart new bungalows, some with boat houses and large driveways, and renovated cottages.

'It's as gorgeous as I remember! Do many people live here all year round?' asked Lizzie.

'Not many now, if any,' said Mary, her heart aching with the loveliness. How could she have stayed away for so long? 'That house there – there were seven children and they all emigrated – some to England, some to the USA. None of them stayed. And the parents died ten years ago. It was sold to a German professor. He lives there all year round and writes, I believe. That cottage coming up – that was Mary John Jack's – that's been sold to a man in TV in Dublin. He has been coming every summer for the last twenty years. The next one is a holiday home, but the owner lives in Clifden and rents it out most of the year.'

'They must miss seeing you, Mary. You used to come so often. Which fork do I take now?' The single road had divided in two, and they were to take the right-hand way, which was on a slight incline. The road was bumpy, and Lizzie drove carefully to prevent the car's suspension being ruined, and from being scratched by fuchsia bushes reaching out over the walls of a ruined home. They came to the top of the little hill and the view opened up again. Directly beside the road the land was boggy, with little pools and wild grasses moving in the breeze, but down below them was a patchwork of fields, an old graveyard and a few cottages in the distance, one with smoke coming out of a chimney. The fields sloped down to the sea and a rocky shoreline with seaweed and birds. On their right, hidden in a hollow, only the slate roof and a chimney to be seen, was the cottage. The cottage she and Bridget had grown up in, the home she had never stopped loving.

They left the car at the top of the hill, at the end of the road, and walked down to the house.

'Mary John Jack's uncle came back from America and brought a gramophone player home with him. One spring night he brought it over here and we wound it up on that rock, and we all danced,' said Mary, as they walked past a flat rock. 'Those fields on the right used to be hay, and in those fields on the left we used to grow the finest potatoes. Cabbages too. And that tree – my father gave me an apple to eat and I grew the tree from one of the seeds.'

'Why did you ever leave, Mary?'

'Ah well, it's a long story. Bridget was over in England, and making a life for herself, and she came home and persuaded my parents to let me come over and work there for six months. She knew she wanted to be a nun and that growing up I had had a big crush on Declan, you see, and she wanted me to have a chance with him. So I went to join Bridget, and it turned out that when Declan saw me all grown up he was interested . . . and the rest is history, as they say.'

Lizzie wondered at the flatness in Mary's voice when recounting her romance. It sounded, the way Mary told it, as if the decision had just been made by Declan and Bridget. Surely Mary had something to do with it? But she didn't comment on it. Mary's marriage was off limits. Lizzie might have her own opinion as to whether Declan was the right husband for her sensitive artistic friend, but she knew Mary wouldn't want to hear it, and bit her tongue.

'Declan was from this island?'

'He was – if we had taken the left-hand fork back there, we would have passed his house. His parents died, the Lord have mercy on them, when he was a young man, when he was over in England with his uncle, his mother's brother. It was a hard time for him, and he the only child. He used to enjoy being part of the gang of island children.' Mary smiled at the memory. There had been a lovely group. Bridget and Declan had been the leaders, of course, but she had had her own friends too. One particular, gentle boy she would never forget, but nobody knew where he was now. She shook her head and brought herself back to the present. 'Declan sold the home long ago,' she continued, 'to some English people who rent it out. He used the money he got from it to build his business in Ireland.'

'But you bought your old home, the cottage?'

'We were left it, by my parents, when they died. They actually left it to both Bridget and me, but Declan paid the convent the money for Bridget's share, and he gave it to me. He had heating and water put in, and the kitchen extension, bedrooms and bathrooms built for me.'

It was the only thing she had ever asked him for. Her home, back with her.

They had got to the little wooden gate set in the dry-stone wall which ran around the house, enclosing the yard. The cottage had no windows in the side facing them, but a traditional red wooden door, split horizontally across the middle so, if wanted, the top could open and the bottom remain closed. The little area outside the door was clean and swept, with neatly trimmed fuchsia and rose bushes. Mary felt between the stones in the wall and drew out a key, before walking down the path and unlocking both the top and bottom of the door. They entered a bright, clean holiday home, simply furnished, with wooden chairs and a comfy sofa, a traditional dresser full of striped blue and white mugs, tin cups and willow-patterned plates. It was not cold, and some unobtrusive radiators indicated central heating had been installed, but there was still the original big open fireplace, with black hooks hanging down and a kettle hanging on one, with a basket full of turf waiting to be burned beside it. There was a small dining table and chairs by the window, and the window looked over a small garden with a washing line, and, beyond it, the sea. On the horizon, across the water, you could see a long line of colourful buildings – the houses and pubs and shops and restaurants of the nearest village.

'It's just how I remember it,' said Lizzie. 'I love how you have left it as it was when you were growing up.'

'Well, not really. It was the only room when we were growing up,' said Mary. 'The kitchen next door and the downstairs utility area are add-ons, and we had to have a roof conversion to put in the two upstairs ensuite bedrooms. We've converted one of the two downstairs bedrooms into a bathroom. But sometimes, when I sit here, I can remember what it was like when we were growing up, getting our water from the well, and using the oil lamps at night.'

They stepped down into the kitchen, modern, but not gratingly so. Declan had done his job well and kept the cosy cottage feel here too. The window looked across the farmyard to some stone buildings, which used to be stables, but now had a sign over the main wooden door proclaiming 'STUDIO'.

'Go over and check on your studio and I'll make us tea,' said Lizzie, producing some milk from a bag and finding tea-bags in the tin by the electric kettle. Mary took them both by surprise as she threw her arms around her.

'I'm so happy to be home!' she said, and taking a set of keys marked 'studio' from a drawer, rushed to see if anything had been changed.

Eight

On returning from Mass, Margaret and Katy found out from Em which guests had checked out. They cleaned rooms and stripped beds and brought the used towels and linens downstairs. It was time for Pangur and Sister Cecilia to pay another visit to the laundry together.

There was another mini-liturgy then too, enacted word for word every day.

Entrance of nun and small white cat to laundry room.

'Ah, all done. Good. No, Pangur, don't climb into the basket, that's for the clothes.'

Small white cat is lifted out of the basket.

Response: Purr

'No, Pangur, don't climb into the drum.'

Small white cat is extracted from washing machine.

Response: Purr

'No, Pangur, those clothes are wet, don't climb on top of them.'

Small white cat is lifted off basket.

'Come with me and we will hang them out.'

Response: Purr

Ceremonial exit of nun carrying basket of wet clothes, with small white cat following.

They would then go to hang it out on the washing line in the garden, or, on rainy or cold days, on the wooden racks and pulley system in the old boiler room. Pangur was equally enraptured whichever method was chosen. If they were in the garden he could run around, stalking invisible insects, pouncing on pebbles, climbing into buckets and empty watering cans, or wander off to see what Thomas Amis and Chris were doing. In the boiler room he could leap on the wooden slats and, as Cecilia hoisted them into the air, try to stay on them and get higher and higher before she noticed. Once, to Sister Cecilia's annoyance, he managed to walk across a slat and tumble a tablecloth to the floor, falling in a tangle with it. It had scared him a little. She got him out of the folds of cloth and once he was clearly OK, tutted very loudly about how she would have to wash the tablecloth again. But she had picked him up that day and even cuddled him, which Pangur had thoroughly enjoyed.

Today was a hanging-clothes-in-the-boiler-room day, as it was too cold for clothes to dry outside. Pangur was remarkably good, and there were no climbing accidents. Afterwards, Pangur and Sister Cecilia would normally have gone together to the library for a couple of hours, then off to Midday Prayer. Today, however, the routine was to be slightly different. Sister Cecilia remembered Katy's words. Instead of quiet time in the library, she had decided to go shopping. Pangur followed her to the front door, but, as if understanding Sister Cecilia was going out, and he could not go with her, he jumped up on to the reception counter and allowed himself to be petted by Em.

'I am going out for an hour,' said Sister Cecilia. 'Please look after Pangur,' and she left.

Em tried not to feel cross at her bossiness. Sister Cecilia was the only nun she found hard to work with. Ever since she had started the job, back in July, Sister Cecilia, unlike Sister Bridget, had never seemed to want to chat, or ask questions, and always seemed slightly irritated with her when she was friendly.

'I'm supposed to be friendly – that's my job,' she had complained to Chris, over breakfast at her mother's house, where they were staying. 'I don't know why I annoy her so much. I thought nuns should all be friendly too – surely that's her job?'

'Sorry, Em. She's a bit grumpy and stuck in her ways, I suppose,' said Chris. 'But you do like your job, don't you? Because we are going to move into the house if we take up one of the new staff flats, so if you aren't happy you need to say.'

'I'm REALLY happy, Chris,' Em had replied. 'It's brilliant working in the B&B, and meeting all the guests. I know I'm really good at my job. Sisters Bridget and Margaret and Katy are all great. And Pangur. And when we get the flat we can move out of Mum's and bring our own kitten. So I can't wait! Don't worry. I'm not going to let Sister Cecilia spoil it all.'

Em stroked Pangur. She loved it when he visited her on reception. For a cat who had so firmly attached himself to the most undemonstrative of the Sisters, he was very keen on fuss, and could always be relied upon to purr with pleasure when stroked.

'I've got your sister, Kylie, you know,' said Em. 'I'll be bringing her here with me next week. I wonder, will you remember each other?'

He pushed his head against her arm and purred deeply. Pangur was a very happy cat.

Sister Cecilia arrived at Pet Paradise at the same time as Matthew.

'After you, Sister,' he said, as they both entered the shop, and then, embarrassingly, they both found themselves standing next to each other in front of the cat toy stand, the two least social members of the social group centred around Sister Bridget.

'Well, I hope that you had a very happy Christmas, Sister,' said Matthew. 'Thank you all again for that delicious Christmas dinner.'

'I did, thank you for asking. And you?'

'Very good, thank you. I've actually been asked to occasionally appear again on *Antiques Roadshow* next year,' he found himself blurting out, just for something to say. 'Just as a general expert on early twentieth-century paintings.'

'Really? You were very good on that special programme when a Jack Mortimer painting turned up, so I am not surprised,' said Sister Cecilia. *Antiques Roadshow* was her favourite programme.

'I'll let you know when it's on,' said Matthew, grabbing a discounted cat's Christmas stocking to give to Sebastian as a surprise.

'Do you think Pangur Bán would enjoy that?' said Sister Cecilia. 'I need things to keep him occupied.'

'Um. I don't know really. George's cat Sebastian is not a lively kitten any more,' said Matthew. 'He is really rather a sedate cat.'

'Do you have a lively kitten, Sister?' said Jackie, the

enthusiastic shop assistant, who had been hovering in the background.

'Yes. Very lively. I would like something to occupy him.'

'That's very good. I wish more owners took that care,' said Jackie.

'We do have some toys already, but he appears to be bored with them,' said Sister Cecilia. 'I would be grateful for advice.'

Loaded up with another scratching post and more enrichment toys and catnip balls, and a discounted Christmas stocking for kittens, Sister Cecilia waited at the counter as Jackie, beaming, rang in the purchases. This was the best sale of the day. What a sweet old nun, buying kitten toys.

'I didn't know that nuns could have cats,' she said, chattily.

'Oh yes. Indeed many saints and holy women are seen depicted with cats,' said Sister Cecilia. 'As I am sure Dr Woodburn, who is an art history lecturer at the university, will attest to.'

'Yes, yes indeed,'

'That's fascinating. Of course ... witches have cats too, and they have special powers as well,' said Jackie, but tailed off, rather hurt, when Sister Cecilia did her best school librarian glare at her.

'Nuns and witches have absolutely NOTHING in common with each other,' retorted Sister Cecilia, in high dudgeon.

'Sorry. No offence meant Sister,' said Jackie, hoping that her uncle hadn't heard. She had been doing so well too. She had finally got the hang of the till, and her wrapping was really coming on. What a nasty nun. That wasn't very nice. She didn't need to be so huffy. Bit of a mean witch herself really. Poor little kitten.

Sister Cecilia went through the door Dr Matthew courteously

held open for her, inclining her head in graceful thanks as she did. She was well pleased with her purchases, and had no idea, as she went off to join the other Sisters back at the convent for Midday Prayer, that she had ruined the morning for the kind assistant who had helped her.

After Midday Prayer, Pangur and Cecilia put on a new wash for the sheets and towels from check-out, and then went to the boiler room to check on the things drying. After lunch Pangur joined Cecilia in a short nap, and then, before starting her reading in the library, Sister Cecilia got out the first of the new toys. A small wind-up mouse was a huge hit and kept Pangur very busy whilst Sister Cecilia made some more notes. That girl in the shop had done a very good job.

Mary opened the door of the studio and sighed with relief. Deirdre had touched nothing. Her finished paintings were stacked by the wall, and the one she was working on was still on the easel. She was surprised by a feeling of pride as she looked at it.

It was a simple painting of the cottage itself, and the field and trees beside it, but the love and feeling with which it was painted sang from the canvas. The apple tree beside the cottage was not yet finished, and Mary found her hands automatically reaching for a paintbrush.

'That's absolutely gorgeous,' said Lizzie from behind her. 'You've got to get back to this.' She set down a hot cup of tea on the side. 'Why don't I go for a walk, Mary, and then I'll curl up with one of those Maeve Binchys I've seen on your bookshelf. I'll leave you to do some painting for a couple of hours. I think that will do you good. Then maybe we'll go and have a late lunch back in town, and then set off home, if you're sure we can't make a longer day of it?'

'Declan is expecting me back for dinner. I don't think he thought I would be away today. I'd better get back,' said Mary.

'Hmm,' said Lizzie, with great restraint. 'Anyway, I'll go for a walk whilst the rain holds off, and then I'll check back with you in a couple of hours. Does that sound OK?'

'Thanks. That's great,' said Mary, already putting on her painting apron, her eyes on the easel.

Lizzie smiled as she closed the door behind her.

Friday 29th December 1995

Nine

'So, are you happy if I suggest you can help the Sisters?' said Father Hugh to Peter. Jimmy was asleep in the presbytery lounge, and Hugh was in the kitchen, telling Peter his big new idea. He had looked down at the congregation as he had prayed during morning Mass, and felt convinced that God had shown him the answer to their problems, confirmed immediately after Mass by Sister Bridget coming to ask him for advice about someone to cover for Thomas whilst he was in hospital. 'One of the new convent staff flats would suit you. They are at the level of the garden, adapted from rooms which were previously the old Edwardian below-stairs quarters, like the butler's pantry, and had been used for general storage for years. They will be peaceful for his last days. I know a good GP here we can register him with. I know you will be a God-send to them whilst Thomas is away.'

'I'm worried you-know-who will ask questions,' replied Peter, drinking his tea.

'I'll have a word,' promised Father Hugh. 'I'll tell her you are a very private person, that you have a good reason for not talking about your past and I'll ask her to respect it.'

Peter made a grimace.

Father Hugh looked at him. 'It seemed like such a Heaven-sent opportunity when she asked me after Mass if I knew anyone who could help out with gardening and odd jobs around the convent. I hadn't heard the full story then. Are you sure you want to go on with this?'

'Yes, I'll be all right. I'll just keep out of her way. It'll be grand. We need to focus on Jimmy.'

Peter got up and cleared the table and started washing up. His back was straight, and he washed up energetically, scrubbing away as if the sink was full of filthy dishes, not just mugs they had had their tea in. Father Hugh watched him with concern.

'Peter – you know what they say. Not forgiving someone is like buying poison for your enemy and then drinking it yourself.'

'Look – I've gone through enough in my life to know that, Hugh. When I left the seminary the drink and the anger nearly killed me. I had to forgive – or at least forget – or I would die. AA got that across to me, even if the Catholic Church didn't. But some things are easier to forgive than others, that's all.' He turned and smiled at Father Hugh. 'Don't worry, Hugh. My focus is on the present, and on Jimmy. This is too good an opportunity to turn down, and he needs all the help he can get. Thank you for sorting this out. The past can stay in the past, as far as I'm concerned.'

Father Hugh wasted no time, and arranged his visit to the convent to coincide with the Sisters' tea break.

'Sisters – you asked me after Mass this morning if I knew

anyone who could help out whilst Thomas is in hospital and recuperating, and I have to say I have the perfect man. He won't be coming on his own though, so I need to fill you in on that, and it will only work if they both get to live in one of the staff flats.'

'That sounds good,' said Sister Bridget. 'So has he a wife?'

'No. It's a little complicated. It's my friend Peter and the person he needs to bring is a mutual friend of ours, a good soul – a saint really – and an unfortunate man, who is very frail, with a shadow on his lung. His flat in London is a bit of a hellhole – it's not the place anyone should spend his last days. We had to get him out of there, and into somewhere peaceful, as soon as possible, so we brought him to the presbytery last night, as Father Stephen is away visiting his family, but we are looking for somewhere peaceful to transfer him to, and I thought of your empty staff flat.'

'None of us are nurses,' said Margaret, a little worried, taking the cups Cecilia was drying and putting them back in the cupboard.

'There is nothing that can be done. He needs rest and good food.' Sister Bridget looked interested immediately. 'And he needs somewhere quiet and safe. His neighbours are drug dealers and there is a lot of noise. The stress is terrible. Just going in there to pick him up was horrible. I can't imagine what it has been like living there.'

'There is only one bedroom in the flat,' said Margaret.

'We want Jimmy to have the bed, and Peter is happy on the sofa, or I am sure we can borrow a camp bed from somewhere.'

'We actually bought good sofa beds for the flats, thanks be to God,' said Bridget. 'That's settled then. It will be an honour to have him live out his last days with us, poor craitur,' she said warmly, pouring the dirty washing up water down the sink and rinsing the bowl.

'If Peter is out and about working for us, then won't Jimmy be left on his own too much?' asked Margaret.

'He's been on his own most of his life,' said Father Hugh. 'Confidentially, he has spent a large part of his life on the streets. He had a drink problem. Peter knew him when he was young, and then he found him again through his work with a charity. He got him some help a few years ago, but the accommodation has ended up being a nightmare.'

'I suppose Katy and I could pop in to check on him during the day,' said Margaret. 'She's away at the moment, visiting her father, and she has her MA work to do at the university, but in her free time she might be able to do some reading in his room. I know she asked me for texts about the Order so she could help Cecilia with her research, and to help with making her decision about joining us. She's a very kind girl, and always keen to join in with the community's pastoral work, but I don't want to ask her to do too much. She's still only a candidate after all, and is already helping out with the B&B during her holidays . . .'

'Honestly, he's really a saint. He sits in his chair saying his rosary most days, and he likes quiz shows on TV. You have a TV in the flat, don't you?'

'Yes. I thought it would be a nice thing for whoever lived there,' said Sister Bridget. 'We enjoy our one.'

'He doesn't smoke or drink. He's no trouble,' continued Father Hugh.

'I will come and say the rosary with him,' said Sister Cecilia solemnly.

'I'll be popping in every day I can,' said Father Hugh. 'He was a daily Mass goer, so I'd like him to have Communion as often as possible, Sister. And I'll get Father Stephen to visit too. The GPs have said they'll get the nurses to come and check on him.'

'I am sure we can all take turns sitting with Jimmy,' said Bridget. 'It sounds like he doesn't have long for the world, poor man.'

'I plan to spend some afternoons working on my book on St Philomena's parish. Dr Matthew has very kindly given me some information about the Stations of the Cross painted by Jack Mortimer which are in the church and I would like to include them and adapt the index and notes accordingly. I could sit and read in the flat if needed,' said Sister Cecilia.

'So when can your friends come?' said Sister Bridget.

'Today?' The Sisters looked at each other. 'I know it's short notice. They are actually in Fairbridge already, but Father Stephen is only away for a few more days. I'm sorry. I know it's a big favour to ask – but I couldn't think of anywhere else to go. I don't mean to force your hand. It's just we had to get him out of that hellhole, and you are the only people I know with a spare flat, and, as I say, Peter can genuinely be a help to you. It felt Heaven-sent. But I know I've sprung it on you.'

The Sisters looked at each other and nodded.

'They are very welcome today,' said Sister Bridget.

'I can make up the beds, and we'll put some tea and coffee and milk and breakfast things in the kitchen,' said Sister Margaret.

'They'll eat with us, won't they?' said Sister Bridget. 'There is a little kitchenette, but it might be nice for Jimmy, if he is up to it, to join us, and Peter will need company too. And of course, we have to pay Peter if he is going to work for us. I've been talking to Thomas about paying him too when he comes back, now the B&B is up and running so well.'

'Peter says he just wants board and lodging. He doesn't need payment. He has his pension and money of his own put aside and he has taken sabbatical leave from his job for six months. It was all arranged before Jimmy's problems. He was going to travel, but he has decided to use as much of it that is needed to help Jimmy.'

'That's settled then,' said Bridget. 'Tell your friends that they are very welcome. Bring them over this afternoon. The flat will be ready. We'll put the heating on now.'

Father Hugh and Peter moved Jimmy into St Philomena's that afternoon. Later, on her way to the chapel to say Evening Prayer, Sister Bridget popped over and knocked on the door of the flat.

Peter answered it quickly and was perfectly polite, but Sister Bridget was a little taken aback, seeing him close up, by how tall and handsome but unsmiling the bearded man was. She beamed and twinkled at him, but her fellow countryman was unbending.

'Hello Peter. Welcome. My name is Sister Bridget, and I am the Superior here. Just checking if we can do anything to help you settle in?'

'Thank you. Jimmy is sleeping still. I've rung the GPs and the district nurse is coming round to assess him tomorrow. Then I can work out when I can get away to do the work you need.'

'Oh, no hurry at all,' said Sister Bridget. 'I wasn't asking for that. I think we can wait to talk to Sarah – I expect she will be the nurse coming to assess any care plan – and then we are all at your disposal. The mornings are a little busy for us, with the B&B, but I am sure Sister Cecilia can sit with Jimmy for a while every morning, and Katy, who is living with us, is a very helpful girl, so I am sure will be glad to pitch in. We'll all take turns. Father Hugh says he is a very holy man, so being in his company will do us good.'

Peter's expression softened, and he nearly smiled. 'Yes, he is very holy,' he said. The coldness returned. 'Thank you, Sister. I will let you know what the nurse says. Father Hugh will be coming to visit too.'

'Would you like me to bring you both over some soup?' said Sister Bridget. 'We are having some for dinner.'

'No need, thank you Sister. I'll be making some myself,' Peter said, his face inscrutable.

'Oh,' said Bridget. 'What kind of soup?' She sniffed the air for cooking smells.

'I don't know yet,' said Peter, bluntly. 'I'll decide in a minute.'

'Well, if you want any herbs or stock cubes or anything, let me know,' said Sister Bridget, determinedly helpful and cheerful.

'I don't need your help,' said Peter, bluntly, unsmiling. Sister Bridget felt a little winded by his rudeness. He stood in the door, adding nothing to the conversation. She was normally good with people, good at winning awkward people around, but this man was impervious to her charm. There was something niggling her about his eyes, his voice. She was sure that he was a Connemara man. Peter Sims was not a Connemara name she recognised, but there was a familiarity about this stranger.

'So, if that's all, Sister?' said Peter.

'Yes, that's all,' said Sister Bridget.

But later at Night Prayer, she sat in the chapel, ruffled. How could Peter say he didn't need help when that was exactly what they were giving him and Jimmy? There was no call for such rudeness. But she knew she had to forgive. She prayed blessings on Peter and Jimmy, but she had an unfamiliar feeling of annoyance, which, when she went to bed spread into a troubled dream. She was calling the bingo and getting the numbers wrong, and everyone was very angry and Daniel O'Donnell burst into the hall and told her he didn't like the songs she was playing. She had never ever seen him cross like that. It wasn't like him at all.

Saturday 30th January

Ten

When Sister Bridget woke the next day, the feeling of upset from her troubled dreams remained. It subsided during Morning Prayers but resurfaced at Mass after Communion. Why was Peter so standoffish? That morning after breakfast Peter had barely passed the time of day with her when she had called round to see if they were all right.

Sister Bridget never minded people reacting strangely to her because she was a nun – she knew from long experience that once they got to know her as a person, they would inevitably come to like her. She knew God had given her charm, but she really tried not to abuse it – charm had to be linked with sincerity and true love, and should never manipulate. But it wasn't manipulation to be genuinely kind to people, to help them out, to cheer them up. It was what she did – God's gift – but one that wasn't working with Peter. Surely Peter didn't have a problem with nuns? He had agreed to come and live and work in the convent, after all.

'Please Lord, bless Peter and Jimmy, and may they settle in well,' she prayed.

After Mass she went into the sacristy, where Father Hugh was hanging up his robes. 'Would Peter like to come to Mass?' said Sister Bridget. 'We could take it in turns to look after Jimmy so he could. I didn't think to ask.' She hesitated, and continued, not quite managing to sound as casual as she obviously hoped to. 'I thought from his accent he might be a Connemara man. Is he not a Catholic?'

Father Hugh looked at her with affection.

'Now, Bridget, I want to talk to you about Peter. He has his own reasons for not talking about himself. I know them – well, most of them – and I respect them. I have known him for decades, and I have the highest possible regard for him and his work with the homeless, and so I need to tell you he is a Catholic, but I also know he has his reasons for not attending Mass any more. I pray for him to come back to the Church, and I hope you will pray for him too, but I never bring up the subject. So, I know you love to know everything about people, Sister Bridget, but can I ask you just to give him a bit of space and not analyse his accent.'

'He is a Connemara man though, I'm right?' said Bridget.

'I won't say, Bridget. Please, leave it.'

'It might help him to talk to another person from Connemara. Sure, I might know his family,' said Bridget.

'He doesn't need our help, Bridget, apart from prayers for him. He certainly isn't asking for it, and if you ask too much it will be a problem. He needs to be here with Jimmy. Jimmy is the priority here. Please, Bridget.' Father Hugh sounded unusually tense, and Sister Bridget backed down immediately.

'Sorry. Of course, I will respect his decision. I'll pray for him. And we'll all welcome Jimmy.' There was a slight pause, then Bridget could not help herself. 'Does Jimmy mind talking about himself?'

'You'll have to ask Jimmy,' said Father Hugh, half laughing, half sighing. 'Jimmy is a very different case than Peter. You'll see. There's a great peace about him. But most of all, Bridget, Jimmy needs to be loved in the present. "The Sacrament of the Present Moment", as we say. And we all know how good you are at that.'

Back at the B&B a little while later, Sister Cecilia had hung out the washing. There were no new loads to put in, so she attempted to help Sister Bridget with the sweeping of the dining room floor, but little Pangur Bán spent all his time jumping on the broom. Then he followed Sister Cecilia to the kitchen, where he was making a tremendous nuisance of himself trying to climb into the dishwasher whilst she loaded it. Sister Cecilia prayed for patience, as each time she turned to put a cup or plate in, a little white kitten made another attempt to get in with them. She picked him up for the hundredth time and was surprised to hear a loud purr. It seemed impossible to destroy Pangur Bán's good humour.

'Be good,' she said sternly, and put him gently down. She looked for something to distract him. The bag of new toys was still up in the library, so she picked up an empty yogurt pot, just rinsed to pass on to the primary school for their arts and crafts club, and put it on the floor whilst she put the tablet in the dishwasher and switched it on. Pangur Bán loved the yogurt pot. He stalked it, pounced on it, rolled it with delicate paws, chased it across the kitchen floor where it rolled under the dresser. Then he lay, full stretched out, eyes glittering with interest, stretching out paws to hook it back. Out it came, and the pouncing, rolling, chasing game began again. Sister Cecilia, at first irritated by the noisy rattle of plastic on the floor, became fascinated by the kitten's total abandonment to play, and found herself uncharacteristically standing still, a tray in one hand, dishcloth in the other, watching him.

'Thank you, Cecilia!' said Sister Bridget, coming in to put the broom away. Bridget took over cleaning the kitchen surfaces, whilst Sister Cecilia immediately busied herself finishing wiping down the trays the dirty dishes had been on and stacking them neatly away.

'You are working so hard, Cecilia. I'll put the kettle on and we'll have our tea,' said Sister Bridget. 'Aah, look at Pangur Bán, the little angel.' The kitten, finally tired out, had fallen asleep in a patch of sunlight on the floor.

Katy and Margaret joined them for mid-morning teas and coffees. The rooms were cleared, beds changed. The floors and windows and windowsills of the dining room were sparkling clean, new white tablecloths, ironed by Sister Cecilia the night before, were on each of the tables, just as the review had commented approvingly.

'Well done, everyone,' said Sister Bridget. 'Just to say, I rang the hospital and Thomas is doing well. I will pop in this afternoon. Katy – we'll check after Evening Prayer how many are booked in for breakfast tomorrow, and can lay the tables tonight accordingly. Now, rooms Faith, Hope and Charity checked out today, and they are all ready for tonight's guests.'

'Has anyone seen how our new guests in the staff flat are getting on?' said Margaret.

'Well, I checked in with Peter, and apparently Jimmy had a good night,' said Sister Bridget.

Margaret noticed a funny tone in her voice.

'Is everything all right, Bridget?' she said.

'Oh, yes. Everything is fine. Peter is an old friend of Father Hugh's, and he vouches for him absolutely. Nothing to worry about there at all. Father Hugh says that we aren't to ask Peter any questions about his past. Where he is from, and things like that. That he is a very private person. So, I think that's important to remember.'

Poor Bridget, thought Margaret. *She's the one who has to remember. She obviously got a warning off from Father Hugh. It's not really something the rest of us are likely to do.*

'Thank you very much, Sister,' said Katy. 'It's good to know. I won't say anything.'

'Thank you, Katy. In the religious life we have to learn to be discreet, to be able to receive confidences and not betray them. We may not be priests, bound by the Sacrament of Confession, but people trust us, nevertheless.'

Yes, but it's obvious that the problem is that Peter Sims is not telling you any confidences in the first place, and it's driving you mad, thought Margaret, simultaneously amused and sympathetic. How interesting. Margaret had never seen anyone not open up to Bridget before. Bridget was irresistible. Normally.

'I will call in and introduce myself to our visitors too,' said Sister Cecilia. 'I will make my availability to sit with Jimmy clear, but I will be mindful not to ask any intrusive questions of either man.'

'Thank you, Sister,' said Sister Bridget, solemnly, in what looked like a state of extremely low self-awareness. Sister Margaret wanted to laugh. The idea of Sister Cecilia, famously uninterested in others (at least, others who weren't long dead), promising to Bridget, by far and away the nosiest member of the community, that she wouldn't pry, struck her as very funny. She bit her lip and quickly collected up the used cups, so she could leave the table before her amusement with her fellow Sisters was noticed.

*

Declan had not gone golfing that morning, like he'd told Mary, but was sat at the desk in his office. It was unusually quiet, even for the weekend, because the staff were not back to work until after New Year's. All around him on the walls and on the shelves were signs of his success. Photographs of him on building sites, handsome as ever, smiling, with a clean spade, doing the symbolic first cut into the ground, or dressed in a dinner suit, shaking hands with mayors, or politicians. There he was at a dinner with the great and good, receiving an award for contributions to Irish industry. There he was at a party, with that actor whose house they had built. He was proud of how Lynch's Buildings had been praised for their design collaborations. He had always worked with the best architects, and it had paid off. He couldn't have come home to Mary in the evenings knowing he had produced bad quality housing. He took the letter from Christmas Day out of his pocket and read it for the umpteenth time. What was he going to do about it? What would Mary make of it? Over the years her quiet judgement had become more and more important to him – she was his conscience, though he had never really said that to her. He realised, for the first time, that there was no recent photograph of her up in the office. He would have to get that sorted – book her a nice spa day and get a good photographer – she was a bit camera-shy – but when she was relaxed, she was so pretty.

He checked his watch. Any minute now his golfing buddy would ring. The golfing buddy who was a heart specialist.

The phone rang and he picked it up.

'Declan—' came the voice.

'Colum, good to hear from you. Happy Christmas!'

'I'll cut to the chase, Declan. I'm afraid there is no easy way to say this. You are living on borrowed time and you need an operation on your heart.'

There was a tiny pause, and then Declan responded with his normal energy.

'OK. Fine. What do I need to do? Money is no problem.'

'Come in to see me tomorrow afternoon and we'll discuss options.'

'But that's New Year's Eve!' Declan said, the urgency just hitting him.

'I know,' said Colum, calmly. 'But you are an old friend, and we should act soon. I'll start ringing about. I'm happy to do the operation. Let's hope we can find a bed in the next few days.'

Sister Bridget popped in to see Thomas in hospital, waiting for his operation at the end of the day. He was concerned by her unaccustomed quietness.

'Are you all right, Sister Bridget?'

'I'm fine. Just a bit of a headache. It's been a busy few weeks and I am tired, I suppose,' said Sister Bridget brightly. 'How are you feeling?'

'I'm glad it has come at last, but I'm sorry to be out of action these next months. There isn't too much to do in the garden that young Chris can't do, but I had hoped to fix a few things for you around the convent,' said Thomas.

'Don't worry about that. Father Hugh asked us to give accommodation to a couple of his friends. One man is ill, but the other can do some work for us,' said Sister Bridget. 'Father Hugh says he is a bit of a handyman. Now that we have the two staff flats set up and decorated, we gave the spare one next to Chris and Em's straight to them. With the kitchenette and sitting room and a big bedroom, they're sorted and private.'

'The flat is so nice, he might not want to leave after the few months are up!' said Thomas, trying to sound positive but struggling with an unaccustomed twinge of jealousy. His connections with the convent were important to him. His daughter Linda and her family were all very important to him, but as a retired widower he had come to rely on the little community of St Philomena's for support and friendship too, and he loved his role as odd-job man. He didn't need the staff flat – he never intended to leave the little house he and his wife Rose had been so happy together in, but it would be hard to give up the work.

'Ah, no. I don't think poor Jimmy has long to go in this life, and Peter doesn't strike me as a man who wants to settle here,' said Bridget. 'We'll be only too glad to have your friendly face back in the convent, Thomas. I miss our morning chats and cups of tea. I'll be popping round as soon as you can have visitors, you can be sure of it!'

'Well, that sounds good,' said Thomas. 'Say a prayer for my operation, Sister.'

'We will, Thomas. Thanks for everything you do and don't worry. We'll check with Linda and the family about visits. We will be praying for you every day. We'll be fine while you're away, and you must concentrate on getting better, but we'll count the days until you're back!'

NEW YEAR'S EVE

Sunday 31st December

Eleven

Because of the snowy weather forecast, and the number of elderly parishioners, Father Hugh had decided that he would celebrate an early New Year's Eve Mass at five o'clock, and afterwards everyone could choose to go home early or go over to the hall and see the New Year in playing bingo with Sister Bridget and her regulars with a good conscience.

After Mass Father Hugh and Father Stephen arrived to help set up for the New Year's bingo party. Father Hugh had baked a chocolate cake, and Father Stephen, who had spent three years studying in Rome before being assigned to Fairbridge last summer, had found a traditional Italian panettone cake to bring. To everyone's surprise, Peter and Jimmy turned up, Jimmy in a wheelchair. Jimmy had already been to Mass with the Sisters.

'I thought Peter was picking you up to take you home?' said Father Hugh to the smiling Jimmy, who was delighted by everyone's surprise.

'I was!' said Peter, rolling his eyes. 'But he insisted he wanted to come and play bingo, and wouldn't take no for an answer. First time I heard he was a bingo fan!'

'Sure it will be a craic. I couldn't let him stay in on New Year's Eve,' said Jimmy to Father Hugh. 'That's no way to start the New Year. I thought I'd play some bingo and maybe win a cake! I can sleep all tomorrow!'

'You're more than welcome. You and Peter can sit with me and Father Stephen and see if you bring us luck!' smiled Father Hugh. Jimmy did look very positive and determined – maybe simply getting out of that terrible accommodation was giving him a new lease of life. Peter allowed himself a wry smile as he sat down – a more reluctant bingo player would be hard to find.

Matthew, Sarah and George and his mother arrived next. Together they had brought a very generous cheese platter with crackers and various pickles from the Fairbridge Christmas market, and some bottles of Prosecco. They put it all on the table in the hall. Matthew found Bridget and gave her a little wrapped parcel.

'But you have already given us a lovely Christmas present, Matthew!' she said, delightedly opening it up. 'Oh – what lovely paintings! Look at the mountains and cottages and lakes! Beautiful! Just like the Christmas card Mary sent.'

'I saw this book on sale of Paul Henry's paintings of the West of Ireland, in Connemara, and I thought of you,' said Matthew. 'I already have a copy because I'm preparing to teach a course on him, and other images of Ireland, after Easter.'

'Well, it was very kind of you to think of us. Thank you. Katy dear – will you look after it, and when we get home, we can leave it on the coffee table in the sitting room, and we can look at it when we need inspiration.'

More and more people arrived, many leaving snacks and drinks on the table. There was definitely going to be a New

Year's feast! Margaret and Katy and a number of helpers were putting out the chairs, six to a table, and laying three bingo cards and a pen at each place. Margaret did not recognise all of the helpers as being from the parish. One of the strangers, a young man with a shaved head and tattoos and piercings, was particularly helpful. Bridget was right – many of the regular attendees of St Philomena's bingo were parishioners, but many others went nowhere near the church, that she had seen.

Apart from the New Year snacks and refreshments, on a trestle table to the side of the hall Sister Bridget had placed the bingo prizes: a freshly baked chocolate cake, covered in chocolate buttons, and a plate each of six butterfly cakes and flapjacks she had also made. Each plate was labelled 'Full House', 'Line' and 'Line'. At the top of the hall, facing the table, was Sister Bridget's seat and table, with the simple blue drawstring cloth bag, embroidered in gold-coloured chain stitch. Also on the table was a little olive-wood crib from Bethlehem, and some tinsel 'To remind them of the real meaning of Christmas – because it's not over until the sixth of January,' said Sister Bridget, who had jazzed up her veil with some silver tinsel, reminding Margaret of a school nativity shepherd or angel.

Sister Bridget put on one of her trusty Daniel O'Donnell albums – *Christmas with Daniel*, the one that was a present from her sister the previous year – as parishioners and bingo regulars entered and took their seats, and Margaret and Katy went behind the hatch and made tea and coffee and served mince pies to the delighted people.

The music was very cheery, and people carrying their cups and saucers back to their tables had to resist moving in time with the music and spilling their tea as they found their seats.

They all greeted each other as if it had been much longer than ten days since they had last seen each other at bingo.

The parish of Saint Philomena's in Fairbridge had attracted lots of young Irish immigrants in the 1950s, and so there were many Irish pensioners in the parish, with Sister Bridget's bingo especially appealing to the older Irish women. Not all of them would be staying on until the clock struck midnight, but there were other people too, including a couple of younger, obviously homeless individuals, and a very smartly dressed older couple.

A few brave souls took the floor, dancing to the Country and Western music and the crooning voice of Sister Bridget's favourite singer. Women danced with women, as well as men dancing with women, and a few couples did fancy twirls. The very smartly dressed couple were semi-professional in their skill, and took it all very seriously, whereas most people were laughing or smiling, but it was clear all were having a good time. Sister Bridget was beaming, going from table to table, chatting to people, and laughing uproariously at people's jokes.

'Sister Bridget really knows how to throw a party!' said Katy, admiringly. 'This is amazing!'

'*She* is amazing!' said Margaret, fondly. 'God bless her.'

As Daniel O'Donnell started to sing about rocking around the Christmas tree, Sister Bridget looked at her watch and started to make her way back to her table, as the dancers waltzed and twirled around the room and other people, seeing Sister Bridget move, began to gather up teacups and saucers and bring them back to the hatch to Margaret and Katy, who were washing up. The tattooed young man got a dishcloth and quickly wiped any tables that needed it, so that all was cleared and ready for the main business of the evening.

Like a well-rehearsed piece of theatre, everyone was back in their seats, waiting expectantly with pens in hand by the time Daniel O'Donnell finished the next song. Sister Bridget tapped the microphone three times, beaming.

'Can everyone hear me?' she asked.

'Yes,' numerous people cried.

'What's that? I can't hear you?' said Sister Bridget, putting her hand to her ear.

'Yes, yes we can,' everyone shouted.

'Grand! Well now, happy New Year's Eve to you all! Pens ready? Right, we're off. Eyes down for the first line – we're playing for a plate of butterfly cakes for everyone on your table.' She rummaged in the bag, and brought out a ping pong ball.

'On its own, number one – but of course, we're never alone when God is with us,' beamed Sister Bridget, shamelessly exploiting the captive audience, who didn't seem to mind. She put it in its hole in a big wooden bingo card on a stand that Thomas Amis had made especially.

'Two little ducks, twenty-two,' she added, and flapping her arms made quacking noises, which the bingo players, full of mince pies and tea, found hilarious.

'Number seven, may we all go to Heaven,' was followed by 'Number six – the sixth of January is the Epiphany, when the Three Kings visit Jesus, and, here's something to remember St Nicholas – the original Santa Claus – did you know his Feast Day was the sixth of December?'

'That's my birthday, Sister!' shouted a cheery man from the back.

'Remind me next year, Sid,' replied Sister Bridget. 'What would you like as a present?'

'To marry you!' he cheekily replied, and everyone laughed.

'Ah, well I'm taken, Sid,' said Bridget, her eyes twinkling. 'But I'm sure there are many ladies here who would love to oblige! And – now, how lovely. It's number twelve . . .'

'That's got to be the twelve apostles, surely?' said Katy to Margaret.

'Number twelve – and of course that's our dear Daniel O'Donnell's birthday – the twelfth of December!' said Sister Bridget, excitedly.

'Are you sure you're not married to HIM, Sister?' shouted her admirer from the back, but he was busy checking his card for the number too.

'Line!' shouted George's mother triumphantly, and came up, to clapping, for a plate of butterfly cakes, which she brought back to share with her table, where Margaret noticed Hortense Taylor and Bridie Kenny and Cuthbert Brown sitting too. They were kind people – they had invited Maura Ryan to join them, and she was looking marginally less miserable when with them, and they had welcomed difficult Mrs Sanders as a regular member. Normally Thomas Amis would be on their table, but he was absent because of his hip replacement operation.

'I have to say my mother looks more cheerful than usual,' said George, looking over at his mum, who had abandoned him and Matthew and Sarah to sit on her regular table. 'She has really nice friends there, even though she will never admit it,' he said. 'God bless Sister Bridget, that's all I can say.'

'Twenty-one, key of the door. Sweet sixteen, never been kissed,' continued Sister Bridget, to friendly but not jeering laughter. 'We don't believe it!' shouted Sid again. 'Ah, here's a nice one, legs eleven,' said Sister Bridget, and did a little impromptu jig, which was a crowd pleaser. And on she went, pulling out balls from her little bag, until the flapjacks had been won by the table the smartly dressed dancers were at, and the Full House, and the gorgeous chocolate cake, by the young, tattooed man who had put out so many chairs.

Sister Margaret had helped at bingo a few times, and each time she never failed to be amazed at the kind attention of the bingo crew. Sister Bridget seemed to be totally free of any sense that there were recognised terms – she announced bingo in the free form way a jazz musician improvises, mixing in local and national news, people's birthdays, saints and little moral asides and sermons and facts about Daniel O'Donnell. And everyone loved it. And her.

When the cake was won, the game was over, and a jolly compilation of New Year's songs was put on. The used bingo cards were collected for recycling, and the pens gathered up. Those who felt unable to stay until midnight made their way home, after thanking Sister Bridget.

Peter had a go at persuading Jimmy to head back, but Jimmy was having none of it.

'Sure it's just getting going,' he said.

Bridget had an especially animated chat with the young tattooed man who had won the cake, and who left with a number of older bingo players.

'Who was he, Bridget?' said Margaret. 'I haven't seen him about.'

'He's lovely. He's Ben, the new curate at St Mary's, the Anglican church – he has a wife and children. He brought a couple of people from his parish here as they said they were keen to play bingo. He says they won't stay for New Year, as it's a bit late for them and he wants to spend it with his family, but he will bring them again on Thursday.'

'I would never have guessed!' said Margaret. 'Honestly, you're great Bridget. You know everyone!'

Bridget made her way back to the microphone.

'Now, please, everyone, we have dancing and entertainment laid on until Big Ben strikes – I have a radio ready for us to listen together. Come and help yourselves to food! People have been so kind and brought lots of delicious plates to share, I've made a cheese and onion quiche, a big bowl of salad, and there's home-made bread which Sister Cecilia is cutting up into slices.'

The guests had a wonderful meal, and then Father Hugh and Father Stephen insisted on clearing up, taking the glasses and plates and cutlery into the kitchen.

'Who would like some music? Peter here has a great voice,' said Jimmy to Katy, who had come to join them at their table.

'That's true – Peter has a great voice,' said Father Hugh. 'He could be a professional.'

Peter shook his head.

'I didn't bring my guitar with me,' he said.

'But you have, haven't you, Katy?' said Jimmy, mischievously. 'Weren't you playing it at Mass? Ah, come on now Peter. Give us a song. Could he borrow it, Katy?'

'Of course!' said Katy, and with everyone's enthusiastic approval, she fetched her guitar for him to play on. Peter, resigned to performing, started tuning it up, and was obviously at home with the instrument and playing to a crowd.

'What would you like me to play?' he said, in a soft Irish accent, coming up to the microphone.

'Is that a Galway accent I recognise?' said Sister Bridget, excitedly, forgetting her promise to Father Hugh, who coughed a warning.

Peter did not answer Sister Bridget, and started strumming.

'A folk song, perhaps?' said Sarah. 'Do you know any?'

'How about this one?' Peter said, 'It's not exactly a traditional song, but it is definitely folk.' He finished tuning the guitar, listening intently as he plucked the strings and turned the pegs, then began to play and sing, in a beautiful voice full of emotion, the Ralph McTell song 'It's a Long Way from Clare to Here'. The room fell silent as he sang about a lonely Irish immigrant feeling far from home, and then everyone clapped, some wiping tears away from their eyes.

'That was beautiful,' said Matthew to George. 'Very moving.'

'A little bit sad though Peter – let's have a few jolly ones to round off the night,' said Father Hugh, coming up to the microphone and loosening his dog collar. 'How about "The Irish Rover"?' and, in his English accent, he enthusiastically led the song, claiming loudly and somewhat unbelievably to have been a wild rover for many a year, who had spent all his money on whisky and beer. Peter, who had much more of the ex-wild rover vibes about him, good humouredly strummed along, and then accompanied Katy as she sang Fairground Attraction's song 'Perfect'.

Sister Margaret noticed Sister Bridget frowning at Peter as he played.

'I feel I know you from somewhere?' she said as he made his way back to the table, but Peter made as if he hadn't heard, and started talking to Katy, congratulating her on her voice. Sister Bridget said again, 'You have a Galway accent, that's for sure. Connemara even. And Sims is not a Connemara name. Of course, I'm Bridget O'Sullivan, and that's a Kerry surname – my father's father was from Kerry. Is it something like that with you?'

Sister Margaret could clearly see that Peter was deliberately not engaging with Sister Bridget. She glanced at the clock.

'Oh look – it's nearly midnight!'

Katy switched on the radio and positioned it next to the microphone so everyone could hear Big Ben chime in 1996.

'I'll fill up any empty glasses!' said George, and he and Matthew quickly made their rounds of the hall.

Everyone counted down to midnight and clinked glasses, then linked arms for 'Auld Lang Syne', and gave each other hugs. Margaret noticed Peter actively avoiding one from Sister Bridget, going over to pick up the guitar and put it in its case when he saw her coming towards him.

'Happy New Year everyone. Thank you so much for a lovely night,' he said.

'Thanks a million, everyone!' said Jimmy, coughing a little, but beaming with happiness. 'That was great craic. I'll sleep well now, that's for sure!'

And they left.

Sister Bridget suddenly looked shattered, and sat down.

'Are you all right, Bridget?' said Margaret, concerned.

'I'm fine. Just a bit tired. Not used to Prosecco, I suppose,' Bridget smiled.

'We'll help clear up,' said Father Hugh. 'Many hands make light work.'

In no time at all many helpers had cleared up, collecting rubbish, stacking tables and putting dirty glasses and plates in the hall sink.

'I'll come tomorrow and wash them,' said Father Stephen. 'Thank you for a lovely evening, Sisters, Katy.'

'Yes, leave it all now. God bless you. Thank you and Happy New Year!' said Father Hugh.

The two priests collected their coats and went on their way home.

Matthew, George and Sarah, aware of how pale Sister Bridget was looking, all suddenly realised at the same time that they needed to go.

'That was a bit odd,' said George in an undertone to

Matthew, once they were safely outside on the street. 'Did you notice Peter not answering Sister Bridget's questions? He clearly didn't want to tell Sister Bridget what part of Ireland he was from.'

'Well, he doesn't have to,' said Matthew, reasonably. 'He may have his own reasons for privacy. He told me he had been working with the homeless for a long time. I got the impression he is a man who may have had some hard life experiences himself.'

'Funny he wasn't very friendly to Sister Bridget though,' said George, defensive of his friend.

'I liked him,' said Sarah. 'I liked his air of mystery. He has a lovely voice, and he's gorgeous looking, in a silver fox kind of way.'

'If you like those sort of rugged Irish good looks,' said George. 'Personally, I prefer them tall and English and thin and shy.' Matthew blushed a little and could not stop a bashful smile.

'My mother is getting a lift home with one of her bingo pals. Apparently he has a very nice car!' said George. 'We'll walk you home, Sarah, and then Matthew is coming for a nightcap over to mine,' said George.

Sarah laughed. 'Honestly George, since my brother met you he has turned into such a party animal!'

'I won't be too late,' said Matthew.

'Don't worry,' laughed Sarah. 'You can party all night as far as I am concerned. You've got years of catching up to do!'

George's mother, once dropped off in style at home by handsome Cuthbert Brown in his immaculate Morris Oxford, spent the first hour of the New Year at home, a glass of sherry at her side, replying to Christmas cards from women she had been at school with. They were not exactly friends, but they had been in her life as long as she could remember, and she had things to tell them at last. She hadn't seen them since her husband's funeral, but they had sent Christmas cards. She knew Julia would be happy to visit, and had offered to come, but up until now there hadn't seemed to be any point. She'd had nothing to say. When George's father had been alive she had at least been able to boast about their cruise holidays, but she had fallen behind in the boasting stakes in recent years. Now she had two interesting conversation topics she was 100 per cent sure they could not compete with. She knew a real-life TV celebrity – Dr Matthew Woodburn – and she had become practically best friends with a convent of nuns – surely that counted for novelty value. And one of the nuns baked the most exquisite cakes she had ever tasted – and she and her husband had always eaten at the best restaurants, so she knew what she was talking about. A nice donation to the convent or some charity, and she was sure that she could get hold of a chocolate cake from Sister Bridget. It would be a major talking point at the tea party she planned to throw for the girls. Yes, 1996 would be the year she got back into circulation.

Just after one she finished writing her first letter and put it in the already stamped and addressed envelope: Julia Wellington, 'The Briars', St Anselm's Street, St Albans, Herts. If Sister Margaret and that new girl Katy who sang really very well and, bizarrely, wanted to be a nun, were insisting on calling round every week, as if she was some kind of charity case, they could at least make themselves useful and go and post it. Sister Margaret should be pleased to do it – she was the one who, all those months ago, had suggested she should get back in contact with her old school friends, and nuns were supposed to do good things, after all. She had gone through her address book and with much grumbling, had written and sent off the cards – well, George had posted them – and she had to admit there had been a gratifying number of Christmas cards and letters back this year. It turns out that water IS just as thick as blood, after all. Maybe the Girls of Caberley Manor did stick together *per omnia*, as the school song had said. And Julia had always been – well, she had been a friend. Her husband was dead now too, according to her Christmas card. She had written Julia a very upbeat letter about Fairbridge and the nuns and the bingo, and had employed all her old skills as editor of the *Caberley Chronicle*. She had even made herself laugh. Her description of Sister Bridget doing Irish dancing at the weekly bingo had been particularly witty, if she said so herself. Julia had always laughed at her jokes. It might be nice to have her to stay.

Annabel Sanders, née Brewer, found herself humming the old school song as she licked the envelope and put it on the side, and made her way to bed. Yes, she would like to see Julia this coming year.

The Sisters and Katy had finished Night Prayer when there was a prolonged ringing on the doorbell. They looked at each other as they left the chapel.

'It's very late,' said Cecilia.

The doorbell rang again.

'Do you want me to come with you to answer that?' said Peter, opening the door of his flat down the corridor from the chapel as the bell kept ringing, more like a fire alarm than a door bell.

'I think I'd be grateful,' said Sister Bridget. 'It might be someone worse the wear for drink.'

At first, on opening the door, their suspicions were confirmed. A strong smell of alcohol and cigarettes hit them, and the man leaning in with one hand on the door frame was very drunk.

'I need to see Sister Bridget,' he said to Peter.

'Declan?' said Sister Bridget, coming forward.

'I have to speak to you,' said the man, swaying.

Peter put an arm around him to steady him.

'Come in, Declan, come in,' said Bridget, concerned.

'It's Sister Bridget's brother-in-law,' said Margaret to Katy and Cecilia.

'But he should be in Ireland!' said Cecilia.

'Thank you, Peter,' said Bridget as they walked Declan into the hall. 'Declan – does Mary know you are here? It's New Year. Aren't you having a party?'

'I have to talk to you, Bridget,' Declan repeated, loudly.

'Could you help him through to the kitchen, Peter, then I can take it from there?' said Bridget, alert, and all signs of tired tipsiness gone.

'I think he needs to go wherever he can sleep it off,' said Peter. 'If I leave him here in the kitchen you'll never shift him.'

'I'll get the key for the other staff flat,' said Margaret. 'It's all set up for Em and Chris moving in.'

They brought him to the vacant flat and Peter helped him into a chair.

'I'll put the kettle on for some coffee or tea,' said Katy. 'And bring some water. It will help him if he isn't dehydrated.'

'Have you eaten, Declan?' said Bridget, gently, leaning forward and taking both of his hands in hers.

He shook his head and started to cry. Bridget crouched down.

'Aah, Declan, what's the matter?' she said, but he just leant forward and sobbed in her arms.

'He needs watching,' said Peter. Sister Bridget was a bit shocked at the slight tone of contempt she thought she heard in Peter's voice. She shook her head – surely she was mistaken? 'If he falls asleep lying down and is sick, he is in danger of choking,' continued Peter. 'I'll sit with him if you like. Jimmy is asleep.'

'No, you go to bed now, Peter. I'll sit up here for a while and pray. I'll call you if I need you,' said Bridget.

'You can't stay up all night.'

'Have you never done Lough Derg?' twinkled Sister Bridget, but Peter did not smile back. 'Sure, I have a nice comfortable armchair here and a quiet flat. It'll be like a retreat. It will do me good. Go – we don't know if you will be woken up for Jimmy. And I will call you if I need you.'

'I could sleep in your flat, Peter, if you need someone to be on call for Jimmy,' said Katy. 'I have a sleeping bag. I could put it on the sofa bed.'

Peter looked at Declan, who was still weeping. He was a similar age to Jimmy, but definitely not the frail pensioner Jimmy was. This was a tall, strong, fit, well-dressed man, and Sister Bridget was not physically up to dealing with him on her own.

'If Jimmy wakes and needs you, I will come and tell you,' said Katy. 'I used to listen out for Mum in the night when she was ill – I won't sleep through.'

'I think that makes sense,' said Sister Margaret. 'Let me help you sort out the bedding, Katy.'

'Thank you, Katy,' said Peter. 'The sofa bed is out already. Jimmy is asleep in his room and the bedroom door is open.'

'I'll just settle in quietly,' promised Katy.

'I should really phone Mary, in case she doesn't know where Declan is,' said Sister Bridget, worried. 'It's very late, but surely she would have told me if she knew Declan was coming here.'

'I will go to bed and pray,' said Cecilia.

'Thank you, Sister. We need it,' said Bridget, as Cecilia and Pangur disappeared up the stairs.

Twelve

Bridget dialled the number, and the phone was picked up immediately.

'Declan – is that you?' her sister's worried voice answered.

'No, Mary, it's me, Bridget.'

'Oh Bridget – sorry it's just that Declan . . .'

'I know, Declan is here with us.'

'What? Oh thank God! But why?' Mary spoke to someone else, 'He's found – he's over at Aunty Bridget's. Yes – in England. I know! No, I don't know why. But he's OK. Bridget – he rushed off to go golfing *again* this morning and just never came home. His phone was off. No contact at all. The family are round for New Year and he isn't back. I've been out of my mind with worry. I was going to ring you to pray I would hear, but I never imagined he would be over with you. Can I speak to him?'

'He's . . . he's a little worse the wear for drink, I'm afraid,' said Sister Bridget.

'Declan? But he is never the worse for wear for drink,' said Mary. 'I don't understand.'

'I don't understand either, Mary, but you mustn't worry. He's safe. I can't get any sense out of him and he is in no state to speak on the phone. We're putting him to bed and will sit with him tonight.'

'I want to speak to him, Bridget.'

'Honestly, Mary, he can't stand up. I can't bring him to the phone. We have a man staying here who helped bring him to the chair and that's where he will stay until he sobers up. Try not to worry. I'll try to find out what is the matter, and send him back to you tomorrow. Everything will be all right,' said Bridget to her little sister. 'I'll get him back to you. Now, who is with you?'

'The children are with me. They didn't want to go home – they were concerned about their father. What a way to see in the New Year!'

'Well, that's good you are not alone. The best thing you can all do now is go to bed and rest. Whatever has happened, he is safe here and there has been no accident. He is fine. We'll get to the bottom of this in the morning. But for now, try to relax and sleep.'

'Thanks Bridget,' her tearful sister said. 'I just don't understand.'

'We'll speak in the morning. Don't worry,' said Bridget. 'God bless.'

Bridget walked back into the flat, troubled. Peter and Margaret were still there, and Declan was drinking the tea Katy had made.

'I've told Mary you are safe. She was out of her mind with worry,' said Bridget. 'It's New Year's Eve – you should be home with her.'

'I'm a bad man,' said Declan. 'What can I do, Bridget? I'm going to Hell.'

'Now, now Declan, whatever it is, I am sure we can sort it.'

'Can you sort out the lives I've ruined? God sent me this, Bridget, and today I learnt I may only have months – weeks – days to live. It's a punishment.' He took out a crumpled letter from his inside suit pocket and held it in a shaking hand.

'Declan – what are you talking about – days to live? And how have you ruined anyone's life? Sure, you're a model husband and father, and you've given work to hundreds! All those lovely homes you've built too . . .'

'I've built my house on sand, Bridget, I've built my house on sand. This letter makes it clear. I want to put it right. But how can I?' Declan said.

'We'll sort this all out in the morning, Declan. Put your legs up and lean against these pillows. I'll be here. Go to sleep now and don't worry.'

They helped him to take off his shoes and then helped him off the chair and put him to lie on the sofa bed, propped up with pillows. He fell fast asleep immediately.

'Go and rest, Peter,' Bridget ordered. Peter hesitated, glancing over at the sleeping man. Sister Bridget was shocked to see a definite look of distaste, even disgust in his eyes as he looked at her sleeping brother-in-law. So she hadn't imagined it. She was disappointed at Peter, in the job he did, judging Declan for drinking to excess. Declan was a good man, a model husband and father and grandfather. Something must be terribly wrong to have led him to do this.

'I'll give you some privacy,' said Peter.

'You go and use the bed in there, Peter. It's all made up. I'll stay here and watch Declan, and if I need you, I will call you. Katy is fine next door, and she will let us know if Jimmy needs any help in the night too.'

Peter went to bed, and Bridget and the sleeping Declan were left alone.

Remembering Peter's warning, Bridget checked the pillows again so Declan would sleep safely, but she had no intention of dropping off. She had spent all-night vigils before – her very first at Lough Derg, praying about her vocation – she would watch over Declan, and pray for a solution for him about this mysterious letter, and a solution would be provided. She would not let her sister's husband come to harm.

Sister Bridget watched her sleeping brother-in-law. Declan. He was still very handsome. He had always had that drive in him, even as a young lad on the island. She and he had always tied at the top of the class, but there was no money for university for people from their background. At fourteen they both had to leave school. Bridget had a job minding the doctor's children across the sea in Roundstone. Declan worked on the family smallholding, but he knew where he was going aged sixteen.

'I'm off to England,' he said, the day after his sixteenth birthday. 'My uncle has work there and I'm going to make my fortune, and then I'm going to come back and marry you, Bridget.'

'You think so, Declan?' Bridget had laughed, smiling up at him.

'I know so,' he had said standing, tall and confident, by the gate.

'We'll see,' Bridget had said, her parents openly listening and smiling proudly in the background.

'He's a good match,' her mother said later that night. 'He has drive, Bridget.'

'He's SO handsome too,' said nearly twelve-year-old Mary, adoringly.

'Handsome is as handsome does,' their mother rebuked. 'He's a good Catholic boy, Mary – that's what is important.' Mary's face fell. She hated disappointing her mother.

'You're right. He's very handsome too,' whispered Bridget, comfortingly, when her mother's back was turned, and winked so that her sensitive little sister would smile again.

Declan wrote as soon as he got to London. He wrote every week without fail, telling Bridget about life in England, how his uncle was pleased with his hard work on the sites, the different characters he worked with, the dances where no girl was as pretty or as good a dancer as her. Bridget's sixteenth birthday came and a restlessness was filling her. The babies she was minding were sweet, and she cycled from her day work along the shore road in the evening to do extra work in the kitchen in the big hotel, before cycling back over the bridge home. That was where she had first encountered fine cooking, thought Bridget, even before Fairbridge. The blue mountains, the sea and the sea birds calling, the rocky shore and roads, the stone walls, the cows in the fields and her father with his dogs rounding up the sheep on the mountains, the fuchsia bushes with their red flowers, the smell of peat turf fires rising from cottage chimneys, they were all as dear to her as they had always been, but it was hard to settle.

'You're missing Declan,' her mother said, sympathetically, catching Bridget sighing one night, quickly putting what she was reading in her apron pocket.

'She's reading that last letter from him again,' she heard her mother say in an undertone to her father. 'She's got it bad.' Her father had grunted approvingly.

But it hadn't been Declan's letter she had hidden. Someone had left a Vocations prayer card in the porch of Our Lady, Star of the Sea, and Bridget had picked it up after Mass. She found herself reading and praying it surreptitiously during the day, and the more she prayed it the more the longing grew. She went all the way to Lough Derg on pilgrimage with the doctor's wife and did the vigil – they thought she was praying to be married, but the call she felt was to something different.

Eventually she came out with it as she and her mother were finishing milking the cows one Saturday morning. Bridget leant her head against the brown cow's back, and pulled on the teats, so that the warm milk spilled into the cold tin bucket.

'Mother – I think I have a vocation,' she said carefully, her breath coming out in clouds as she talked. 'Praying at Lough Derg made me sure.'

The rhythmic sound and splash of milk into her mother's bucket stopped suddenly, then started again.

'What do you mean?' came her mother's voice.

'I think God is calling me to be a nun, Mother. I have a yearning . . .'

'Sure, aren't you promised to Declan? He's doing so well over in England – writing to you every week, and saving up for a fine home for you.'

Her mother came round to her, carrying the bucket of foamy warm milk.

'Have you spoken to anyone about this?' she said.

'No, you're the only one,' Bridget had replied. She remembered them bringing the milk into the house, then untying the cows and letting them back out into the early morning fields. The stars were still in the sky.

'I thought you had an agreement with Declan?' her mother said, in a low voice, anxious Bridget's father would not overhear.

'I never said so.'

'He said he'd come back to marry you.'

'He was only joking, Mother. He'll have met someone else.'

But they both knew that wasn't true.

'So you were never interested?' said her mother, worriedly. 'I don't know what your father will say. He and Paddy Lynch were so made up. The two farms and everything.'

'I don't know. He's handsome. We had the craic together. We are friends. But I don't love him, Mother. I want to give my life to God.'

There was a silence. It was a relief to have it out in the open at last. Bridget looked over at her mother, her kind, strong, sensible mother, who was biting her lip.

'We'll go and see Father Brendan,' said her mother, decisively. 'We'll go and see him after Mass tomorrow.'

Father Brendan listened carefully to Bridget and her mother. It was a difficult one. He knew only too well how pleased the two families were about this match. He too had heard good things about Declan over in England. He was working hard for his uncle's firm, and the Irish parish priest over in Fairbridge, a friend of Father Brendan's, had written to say that the young man was a credit to his family and had joined the Knights of St Columba already. He would be a catch for any girl, and this pretty, modest girl before him would never bring shame on her family. She would make a good wife and please God, a mother, who would do her duties in the home, as the Constitution set down – a real Irish colleen for Eire.

But then there was the pilgrimage to Lough Derg, and the Vocations card. She told him she had been praying it every day for months, saying her rosary, and growing in a desire for the religious life. He had even seen her taking the little ones she was minding during the day into the church to light a candle – he had remarked upon it to the doctor. He'd thought it was a sign she would be a good mother herself. Now he wasn't so sure. And God's will had to come first.

'How long is it since you've seen Declan?' he asked.

'Six months, Father.'

'About as long as you have been praying the Vocations card?'

Bridget nodded.

'He writes her every week, Father,' said Bridget's mother. 'Without fail.'

'Well,' said Father Brendan. 'I think this must be meant. I had a letter only this week from my friend, the parish priest in Fairbridge, where Declan is. He told me that Fairbridge Finishing School is a very nice educational establishment which is looking for good, honest Irish girls, like Bridget here. Full board and uniform, to clean the young women's rooms and serve table. One afternoon off a week, and time off on Sunday to go to Mass.'

'We don't have the money to send her to England, Father,' said Bridget's mother, awkwardly.

'That's all taken care of. They pay the fares and it's taken out of the wages. Bridget can meet up with her young man and see how she feels about him in real life.'

'But Father, what about my religious vocation?' said Bridget, politely, but her frustration coming through.

'This way you can try both,' said Father Brendan. 'Young lady – Declan is a catch for any young woman. He will give you a secure future, and not only you, but your family. Your parents have no son, but once married I am sure he will treat them as if they were his parents. It may be that when you see him again your feelings will become clearer. He is a handsome man, and a man who has not lost his faith over in England, with all the temptations there are. I think going to see him in England will be a good idea, and you yourself will be staying in a highly respectable establishment.'

Bridget opened her mouth, but Father Brendan pre-empted her objection. 'As to a vocation to the religious life – I know there is an Order working in the parish – the Sisters of Saint Philomena. Talk to them about your vocation. You have no priests or Brothers or Sisters in your family, do you?'

Her mother shook her head, shamed.

'Well then, this way you can get to know some nuns. See them day to day. You'll not have a dowry, I suppose?'

Again, her mother shook her head, shamed. Bridget did not like to see it.

'No problem. You would be a simple lay sister then, not a choir sister. You would be doing the manual work in the convent, not the teaching and so forth. But you are not qualified to teach, of course.'

'I'd be giving my life to Jesus all the same though?' said Bridget. 'That's all I ask, Father.'

'You would of course. But you know, Declan told me before he left that he was going to England to make his fortune, but with every intention to marry and raise a family back here in Ireland. Anyone who would marry him would be a lucky woman. I'd say she'd get a fine house, and he would make sure her parents were well cared for in their old age . . .'

Bridget said nothing.

'So then, I'll write to my friend and get things underway. It's a very respectable set-up. It's owned by a Protestant – an ex-Colonel – but he shows great respect for his Catholic workers. He likes their morality. He says good practising Catholic girls cause him no worries at all. So you can go over to Fairbridge and talk to Declan and, if you still want to, meet the nuns. I'll send the letter tomorrow.'

And he did. Within three months Bridget was settled into Fairbridge House, and making friends with a girl from Cork called Rose, who later was to fall in love with a certain Thomas Amis at a dance.

Declan shifted in his sleep. 'I'm sorry, Mary,' he said, and slept again. The top button of his shirt was undone, his tie twisted, but there was no mistaking the quality of his clothes and shoes. His hair was neat, his fingernails were nicely shaped, the hand that fell outside the bedclothes soft, not calloused by manual labour. It was many years since he had got his hands dirty by work. His face, always handsome, had aged well. He was not a jowly man, and Bridget could still see the man she had gone to school with all those decades before.

'Now, what have you to be sorry about? You've come a long way, Declan, from when we went barefoot through the fields to school. You've done so well.' Bridget thought with pride of the big city house her sister had, with the state-of-the-art kitchen and the magazine-worthy interior decor, the children and Fran the adored granddaughter. And Bridget and Mary's parents, when life on the island got too much, had ended their lives in luxury, looked after by Mary in the granny annexe Declan had built. He had been a perfect son-in-law, thanks be to God. Bridget had never had to worry about them in their old age.

Mary had been blessed, wanting for nothing. Yes, there had been that cancer scare last year, but that was over now, and Mary had been to Lourdes. And the situation with Noel had been hard, but they were all speaking at last. Bridget had told Declan and Mary they mustn't judge. And she was planning to introduce them to Matthew and George – that would reassure them. Such good, kind men – such a help to the community. True, they weren't Catholics, so it was a little bit different from Noel – but there were always so many bad things happening in the world, she was sure the good Lord was glad to see some love about. 'Where there is love there is God.' The world was much nicer than people thought.

Thirteen

After walking Sarah home, Matthew went to George's for a nightcap.

'I'd love to stay, but I do need to go back, George,' said Matthew, reluctantly taking his arm away from George's shoulders and getting up from the sofa, where they had been happily sitting. 'I have to get on with planning that course in the morning.'

'I'll walk you back,' said George, and they set off towards Matthew's home. George, overcome with love, reached out for Matthew's hand and squeezed it. Matthew jumped at the unexpected contact – they never held hands in public – then, as nobody else was about, he relaxed and squeezed George's hand back.

'I love you, Matthew,' said George.

'I love you too,' said Matthew, and they smiled at each other, joy and desire and amazement in their eyes.

They continued holding hands for a few steps until a car drove past. The front window was wound down and an empty drink can thrown at them, with a shouted curse. It hit Matthew, who put his hand to his face and crouched down, then the car drove on fast.

'Oh, my darling! Are you hurt?' said George immediately, putting his arm around Matthew and tenderly inspecting his face. There was a small cut. Matthew was shaking, and George felt him recoil.

'I'm fine, honestly,' said Matthew, straightening up, but still shaking.

'Are you OK?' came Em's voice. She and Chris ran up behind them.

'Matthew! I heard what they said.'

Em, dressed up in a sparkly dress for New Year, tucked her arm into his and George saw, with a pang of envy, that Matthew visibly relaxed, but still swayed a little on his feet.

'You've had a shock. Come on – let's get you home. We're staying in Mum's house just around the corner. She's always got some whisky in.'

Within a few minutes George and Matthew were ensconced on Em's mum's sofa, an old black Labrador lying at their feet, Em's mum pouring out glasses of medicinal whisky from her sideboard. Em came in carrying a black and white kitten.

'Here, hold Kylie – she will make you feel better,' she said, and the little kitten walked from one lap to another, eventually settling on Matthew's. George stroked the little kitten, longing to be able to hold Matthew, who he could feel was still very tense.

'We should phone the police,' said Em.

'No – no – please don't,' said Matthew quickly. 'I'll be OK – really.'

'But it's not right,' said Em, indignantly. 'I heard what they called you. It was hateful. And they threw that can. I'll ring 999.'

'No – please!' said Matthew, half-rising. 'I don't want to talk to anyone. I'm fine, really.'

'Really, Em, let's leave it. Thank you,' said George, concerned to see Matthew begin to shake again. 'It was dark and we didn't get a good look at the number plate or even the car.'

'But . . .' Em began.

'I think if they don't want to, love . . .' said her mum, handing George and Matthew their drinks.

'But why should those bullies be allowed to get away with it, Mum? It's not fair. They were just holding hands. Chris and I went out tonight and held hands without getting things chucked at us and being sworn at. It's just wrong. They shouldn't be allowed to get away with it. Matthew could have got seriously hurt.'

'Em,' said Chris, catching her eye and nodding towards the kitchen. Em followed him there.

'Em – they don't want to make a fuss,' said Chris, lowering his voice.

'It isn't "making a fuss" – they were attacked, Chris – you saw it,' whispered Em, furiously. 'It's not "making a fuss" to report that. It was horrible what they shouted. Poor Matthew and George. And they could have badly injured Matthew when they threw that can.'

'I know Em. I don't think it was right either, but we have to leave it to them.'

'But we should tell the police! Surely you agree?'

'Yes, the police should know and should help them, and I'd like to say they will, but they're not always the best in these cases. Honestly, Em. Even if they were, Matthew clearly doesn't want to talk about it. None of us can identify the car. Please – drop it. I know it's horrible, but you can't fix everything.'

Em frowned. 'I just thought you'd care.'

'I do! I feel as bad as you about it — but we just can't go against what Matthew wants,' said Chris, and her laidback husband expressing hurt and anger finally got through to Em.

'Sorry Chris. I didn't mean it. I know you care. I just feel so helpless,' said Em, wiping an angry tear from her face.

'I know,' said Chris, and gave her a hug. 'But it's not about us, it's about George and Matthew, and they need our support.'

They went back into the sitting room, where her mum was chatting easily with the men. Matthew looked tired but calmer, and had stopped shaking. Kylie was now asleep in his lap. It was George who looked most agitated and upset.

'If you don't want us to report it, would you like us to walk you back?' said Em.

'No, thank you,' said Matthew.

'I'll walk you home,' said George, determinedly.

'No,' said Matthew. 'You go home, George. I'll be fine on my own.'

George opened his mouth to object, but Matthew lifted the sleeping Kylie and put her on George's lap.

'Please, George,' he said, and got up. He still looked pale and shaken.

'Well,' said Em's mum, reaching for her coat and the dog's lead, 'If you don't mind, I'd like a bit of company walking Prince. I saw you on the telly, doctor, on *Antiques Roadshow*, and I want to ask you about a music box my Pete gave me . . .'

'Mum!' protested Em. 'Matthew has had a shock — he won't want to be talking about music boxes!' but her mum turned to wink at her whilst Chris gave her a surreptitious nudge.

'Oh, I will enjoy this dog walk. It's lovely to talk to a real-life TV celebrity!' said Em's mum, cosily steering a rather bewildered Matthew out the door. 'So, my Pete gave me this box and I think it might be antique . . .'

'Honestly! I'm sure Dad got that box from Woolworths!' said Em, as the door shut behind them, but Chris shook his head and the penny finally dropped.

'I could have walked him home,' said George, angrily. 'Why should the thugs win?'

'He looked very shaken,' said Chris, gently. 'I think he just needed to get home quietly without any more problems.'

'I've understood that, thank you very much,' snapped George. 'I'm not a fool.' He gently moved Kylie, got up and walked to the door.

'Do you want . . .' started Em.

'No, I bloody do not,' shouted George. 'I'm a grown man, Em. I can bloody well walk home on my own,' and he walked out, slamming the door.

'But he wanted to walk Matthew home,' said Em, hurt. 'Why couldn't he let us do the same for him?'

Chris sighed, and held her close, smelling the shampoo in her hair as he hugged her. 'It's very hard for them.'

'I don't understand why people can be so horrible,' said Em, sadly. 'They love each other – you can see that.'

A quarter of an hour later there was the sound of a key in the door and Prince pottered in, followed by Em's mum.

'Well, Prince didn't expect that extra walk. Good thing the poor old boy is deaf and fireworks don't bother him. Good boy!' she said as the old dog sank to the floor. 'Matthew's home. The light was on and he said his sister was in, so he won't be alone. Poor man. It shook him up. Where's his friend – George, isn't it?'

'He's gone home,' said Em. 'I didn't know Dad gave you an antique music box?'

'I don't think it is, love. I think it was from Woolies, but it was the only thing I could think of on the spur of the moment,' said her mum, taking off her scarf and coat and hanging them up.

Chris gave Em, who was looking very sad, a hug. He shuffled her under the mistletoe, making her laugh, and gave her a big smacking kiss. Em relaxed and giggled and kissed him back wholeheartedly.

'Here – you two – get a place!' laughed Em's mum.

'We have, Mum, thanks to Sister Bridget!'

'Never in a million years thought you'd end up in a convent, Em!' said her mum. 'Your dad would laugh!'

George walked furiously home, swearing under his breath, glaring at any cars passing him, daring them to stop, but they just went to and fro as normal. He was surprised to find his hands shaking as he put his key in the door, and when Sebastian, his big beautiful black cat, ran purring to greet him, he burst into tears. Sebastian followed him up the stairs and wound himself in and out of his ankles.

'Oh God. What would I do without you?' said George, and picked him up and hugged him. He poured himself a Spanish brandy and sat in his chair, with Sebastian curled up on his lap, looking over at a framed photograph on the bookcase of a smiling, kind-faced handsome Mediterranean-looking man. Miguel had been the love of his life. They had met and lived together in Spain, and George had been devastated when Miguel died two and a half years previously.

He reached over to hold the photo in his hands.

'What am I going to do, my darling? You're with your angels up in Heaven, but down here people can be hell. I know your prayers brought me Matthew and a new chance for love after you died. Please don't let those thugs split me and Matthew up. Put in a word for us, please. I don't know what I will do if I lose him as well.'

Just saying it out loud made him feel better, and although his flat was cosy and warm and there were no drafts, the angel chimes shifted slightly and made a soft noise. One of Sebastian's ears twitched, he woke and stretched, and then put his front paws high up on George's chest and stared up at him with his beautiful green eyes. George bent his face down to him, and Sebastian reached up and gently touched his wet pink nose to his, then, pushing his head down and up against George's chest, he purred deeply into him and kneaded him with his paws until George felt the tensions slowly disappear.

'Thanks, Sebastian. You really should consider a career in therapeutic massage,' George said, stroking him. Sebastian curled up and went to sleep, job done. George looked at the phone on the table beside him, hesitated for a moment and then picked it up and dialled a number.

A woman's voice answered.

'Sarah? It's George.'

'George! I was just going to ring you. Are you OK? Matthew told me about what happened tonight. I'm so sorry.'

'How is he?'

'Very shaken. You know. It wasn't just what happened tonight, it brought back very bad memories for him. He's worried he hurt you, not letting you walk him home, but he just couldn't cope . . .'

'No – he hasn't hurt me. I understand. It's not him I'm angry with. Can I speak to him?'

'Of course! I think he'll be relieved.'

There was a pause, and then Matthew came on the phone.

'Hello, George? I'm so sorry. I just couldn't . . .'

His voice sounded so uncertain that it made George feel heartbroken and angry all over again.

'Matthew – don't worry. *Illegitimi non carborundum*. Don't let the bastards grind you down. See, I might not be an academic but I know Latin too!'

Matthew gave a little laugh.

'See you tomorrow. Are we still going to the cinema?'

'Um. Can you come over here instead? I don't feel up to going out,' said Matthew, sounding close to tears. 'I'm sorry.'

'Don't worry at all. I'll bring a film. I'll come at seven – OK?'

'Thank you. See you then,' said Matthew.

'Don't worry. Everything will be all right,' George said, with more confidence than he felt. 'We love each other, that's what's important. We'll work it out. Now, sleep well my love.'

He looked over at the photograph as he put down the phone.

'I said it, but I don't know if I believe my own words. I'm relying on you and your angels and saints to back me up here,' he said ruefully. 'You have to put in a word. We can't do this on our own.'

He could have sworn he heard and saw the angel chimes move again in the non-existent draft. An unexpected sense of peace came over him. After such a shockingly miserable end to a lovely evening, with all the worries about Matthew being re-traumatised by what had happened back when he was a young, sensitive university student, George went to bed with a strange feeling of hope, and a conviction that what he had said to Matthew, as an attempt to comfort, was actually deeply true. Maybe the New Year held hope after all.

NEW YEAR'S DAY
Monday January 1st 1996

Fourteen

Declan woke in the morning to the sound of the door closing, his head pounding, and himself on a sofa bed in an
unfamiliar room. He turned his head and saw, with a shock,
his sister-in-law, dressed in her habit, asleep in the armchair
opposite him. He looked at his watch. It was six fifteen a.m.,
New Year's Day. He had missed the party. What would Mary
be thinking? He sat up and swung his legs to the side of the
bed. The letter he had held all night dropped to the floor and
he picked it up and put it in his pocket. He buried his head in
his hands, giving an involuntary groan. He was unaccustomed
to this feeling of panic, of being out of control.

He felt a hand on his shoulder.

'How are you feeling, Declan?' said Bridget, awake and
alert as soon as she heard him stir.

'What am I going to do? I've got to talk to Mary. How can
I put things right?'

'Mary knows you are safe – don't worry. First things first. I'll
go and get you some towels and toiletries and you can have a
shower and freshen up if you like,' said Bridget. 'We have

supplies at the B&B for people who have forgotten things, so I can bring you a razor and a toothbrush. Then I'll make you breakfast in the convent kitchen, and we can talk about whatever this is all about. It'll all be fine.'

Bridget knocked gently at the bedroom door to tell Peter the shift was over, but there was no answer. 'I'll let him sleep for a bit longer,' she thought.

'You must tell him,' said Father Hugh, pouring out another mug of tea for Peter. He had rustled up a full English, but was still in his pyjamas and dressing gown. Father Hugh had only just woken up when Peter rang the doorbell at six o'clock. 'It's only fair. You need to explain. You can't just do something like that and then keep quiet.'

'I don't need to do anything more. I only told him the truth. He's not sorry. He's only concerned he is going to Hell,' said Peter, bitterly. 'I just can't forgive him. My job is to look after a sick man, not run about helping a rich one. I have enough on my plate.'

'Mercy is good for the soul, Peter, as you know. What exactly can't you forgive him for?'

'You know well what it is,' said Peter. 'We've seen the results on the streets of London. People like him taking advantage of innocents like Jimmy.'

'Is that all? Are you sure it's not something else as well?' said Father Hugh, looking him straight in the eye.

Peter glared back.

'It's been fifty years, Peter,' said Father Hugh. 'You are sixty-six. Don't you think it's time to let her go?'

Peter shrugged, his defiance suddenly deserting him. 'I thought I had,' he said, sadly. 'I thought I had.'

*

Peter walked into the convent kitchen at seven thirty to find a sober and clean Declan sitting at the kitchen table with Sister Margaret, and Sister Bridget over at the sink.

'Peter!' said Bridget, 'Happy New Year! Good morning! Join us! Sit down and have some breakfast.'

'No, thank you,' said Peter. 'I have to go and relieve Katy and check on Jimmy.'

'I'll go and get the breakfasts served, Bridget. You concentrate on Declan,' Margaret said.

'Well now, Declan,' said Sister Bridget, 'have you your return ticket home?' Declan fumbled in his jacket and found an open return from the airport.

'We'll call on our friend George this morning and I am sure he will find the times of the flights back. Then we'll ring Mary and tell her when to expect you. I'll join Sisters Margaret and Cecilia for Morning Prayer now and you can ring Mary from my office, put her mind at rest.'

'I can't . . . I can't speak to her yet,' said Declan, his voice breaking.

'I tell you what. I'll ring her now and tell her you had a good night's sleep and you're safe and well and going to Mass with me and you will ring her after.'

'Tell her I'm safe, anyway,' said Declan, bitterly, and put his head down on the table and sobbed.

'Stay here with Declan, Bridget. Katy and Cecilia and I will get on with prayers and the B&B. We might see you and Declan later at Mass? We will pray,' said Margaret, and left them alone.

'My heart's not in the best of shape, Bridget,' said Declan. 'I told Mary I was going to play golf, I didn't tell her I was really going to a medical appointment. You see, I have a golfing friend – a consultant in private practice – he had me come in straight away, even though it was a Sunday and New Year's Eve.'

'I'm so sorry to hear that, Declan. But you are still only seventy, and you look very fit. They can do wonders nowadays. The doctors are very skilled.'

'Colum said he will do his best all right, and I have money for the surgery, but I should still set my affairs in order. He said I could have years, but worst case scenario is it could be any time. He has made me a hospital appointment for this week. And this letter arrived at Christmas – I don't know what to do.' He passed it to Bridget.

Bridget opened the letter:

Dear Mr Lynch,

Many years ago, when you were over in England, you worked with your mother's brother in the building firm he owned, and later left to you. You knew from the beginning he did not pay his workers fairly: no National Insurance, their wages paid in cheques which he offered to cash in the pub that he owned, knowing few of them had bank accounts. Your family took advantage of lads who had nowhere to go after work, who were homesick and needing comfort, which they looked for in the drink. And every drink they bought with their wages put more money in your uncle's pocket. You went along with it. Your countrymen trusted you, and many of us, like my friend JJ, were innocent boys from the country. When hard times came, because your family had not paid the men's National Insurance, they could get no support, and many of them ended up destitute on the streets, many addicted to alcohol or sick from asbestos they were exposed to at work, or worn out from working in all weathers, with no sick pay if they got ill. You even laid them off with no pay if there was snow, and only took them on again when the snow had gone. My anger has grown seeing your business and fortunes go from strength to strength, the pictures of you in the paper. You are the big man with your fine house and family, giving to church and charity, playing golf with priests back in the homeland, whilst the men your family exploited are too ashamed to return home.

My best friend JJ, the sweetest soul on earth, has spots on his lungs from contact with asbestos in the jobs he did for you. He is frail, probably now in his last months on earth, and living them out in hellish accommodation. I have just come back from visiting him. He has nothing, not even enough to cover the cost of a funeral, or to be buried in Ireland. What he does have, however, is a pure soul and a tender heart, and I have no doubt he will have a high place in the Heaven he longs to see. I cannot say the same for you.

Do you even remember JJ, who was not only your countryman, but your classmate? Who followed you from Ireland because he trusted you, and even now won't have a bad word said against you?

He may forgive you, but I certainly don't. And I don't expect you remember me, either. I can't sign myself a well-wisher, because I certainly do not wish you well. You put yourself first without a thought for the ones you hurt, you have ruined lives, and may you, like Dives who ignored the poor man Lazarus, rot in Hell. It can't be worse than what JJ is in now.

'Oh, that's not a nice letter at all, Declan,' said Bridget.

'But Bridget, the problem is it's true. It's true.'

'Don't say that, Declan. There must be a mistake. This is horrible.'

'We did do them a great wrong. I have known that for years, but I didn't want to accept it. They say our sins catch up with us. They have. We did cash their cheques in our own pub – keeping it in the family, I suppose,' he laughed bitterly. 'We told ourselves we were helping them, but we knew we made more money that way. And some of them did get too fond of the drink. We knew that too. They were innocent lads – some from my own school. I knew them well, and I let them down. I lived with my uncle, but they had no real homes in London when they worked for us. The signs on so many rental places said No Irish, No Blacks, No Dogs, so they were lucky to get anything. The landladies turfed them out in the morning, and wouldn't let them back until the night. There was nowhere to go but the pub, and we made sure it was a home from home. And I thought we were looking after them, but it's true – we paid no National Insurance, and they spent all they had in our pub, so they were left high and dry when they were old or couldn't work. I don't know who sent this, but I even know who he is talking about – it's JJ Kelly. You remember him? There was no harm in him. And Bridget – I knew he was in trouble with the drink, God forgive me. I even saw him on the streets in London a few years ago, drunk. I took Mary and the children to London for the weekend and I didn't want them to see him. I didn't want them upset and the weekend ruined. But in truth, I didn't want myself upset. I literally crossed over to the other side of the road. But I knew it would catch up with me.'

Bridget was shocked to the core. JJ Kelly. He had been in their class. A gentle boy. His family had not heard of him for years, and prayers were still being said for his return, but he had been presumed dead for decades.

'But Declan – are you saying you knew where JJ was, and you told nobody?'

'What could I do? I couldn't be sure it was him. He was in an awful state. He might not have wanted to be found.'

'But even if there was a chance – his family wanted to know where he was. His mother and father died heartbroken. Mary told me his mother said she was looking forward to meeting him in Heaven. And this means he was still alive, on the streets of London all that time, the poor thing.'

'Bridget – I am sorry. I am sorry.'

'Does Mary know about JJ being on the streets? Does she know about how you paid the men?'

'Of course not. You know Mary. She's so kind. She'd have worried herself sick. She would have given all our money away to help them, and then where would the family be? Where would she be? She's not been well, Bridget, and she had all those years looking after your parents and the children. I wanted us to have a good retirement. And I wasn't sure it *was* JJ.

'But now I want to put it right, at least help him out, but I don't know how to find him. How can I put it right before I die, and not hurt Mary and the children? I don't want her to see this letter. If it was just me I would give everything away, but it isn't. I can't drag them down too.'

'Hush now. God is a God of mercy and forgiveness,' said Bridget. 'Whatever you did, we will talk it through later, but I can tell you now, there is nothing that cannot be sorted out.'

'Do you really believe that?' said Declan, desperately.

'I do,' said Bridget, with total certainty. 'And God has it all in hand. I think Peter is the answer to your prayer. He has contacts in that world. Poor Jimmy has had a similar life. He might have come across poor JJ. Those are the men who can help you find him, for sure. It's all meant. May I have your permission to share the letter with him and Father Hugh?'

Declan nodded.

'So, I'll ring Mary now, and then Father Hugh and George,

and then we will go to Mass and hopefully meet up with Father Hugh and we can get this sorted. It will all be fine, Declan, trust me.'

'Thank you, Bridget,' said Declan, tearfully. 'What would I do without you?'

'How is he?' said Mary. 'I haven't been able to sleep.'

'Try not to worry, Mary,' said Bridget. 'Declan will tell you everything when he gets home. We're sorting it out today, and hopefully we can get him back to you tonight.'

'But why can't he speak to me now?' said Mary.

'He's a bit emotional, Mary. He wants to speak to you face to face. But everything will be all right. Trust me.'

'Thank you, Bridget, what would I do without you?' said Mary.

Thank you, Lord, prayed Bridget, as she put down the phone. *Thank you that I can help Declan and Mary. Please bless them, and help me get through to Father Hugh and may he and Peter sort it all out, and find JJ, and may George find a flight home today for Declan. Our Lady, Holy Mother of God, pray for us on your Feast Day.*

Fifteen

'I can't believe we're going to have our own flat at last!' said Em, hugging Chris. Her childhood bedroom that they had been sharing for the last nine months looked unnaturally tidy and uncluttered now that all their stuff had been packed up and was in the car. She picked up Kylie, who had been peacefully sleeping on the duvet, and kissed her, bringing her downstairs, whilst Chris good-humouredly lugged down a last heavy suitcase.

'I'm going to miss you two,' said Em's mum, giving them a hug, as Prince stood, his tail wagging.

'Oh, Mum,' said Em, bursting into tears as she got into the car.

'Don't be daft,' said her mum, wiping her own eyes. 'What are we like? You're only going around the corner! It's lovely – you're starting the New Year in your first married home together – even if it is in a convent! I'll be over lots – you never know – I might join the nuns myself! They'd have to take Prince though. I don't know if they have dogs in convents.'

'If that's the only thing holding you back, Mum,' laughed

Em, 'that shouldn't be a problem. After all, they've already got a kitten!' Em cuddled Kylie. 'Come on sweetie – you are going to meet your brother! Pangur is going to LOVE you.'

Katy and Margaret were waiting at the convent to help Chris bring the stuff into the flat. Em sat at reception to handle checkout, with Kylie in her little cat carrier, who was much admired by the departing guests.

Sister Cecilia was on her way to see if she could help, closely followed by Pangur, trotting after her happily. Suddenly noticing Kylie's cat carrier perched on top of the reception desk, he stopped, arched his back and puffed out his fur, his tail straight up. He hissed and spat.

'Goodness Pangur – whatever is the matter?' said Sister Cecilia, and then frowned as she noticed Kylie, who was also now standing up in her carrier, back also arched, spitting down at this intruder.

She swept him up in her arms.

'What is going on?' she said to Em. 'Can you stop your cat doing that?'

'Oh, it's just because they don't recognise each other,' said Em. 'Come on you two – be nice. Say hello to your sister, Pangur.'

Pangur hissed and Sister Cecilia snapped. 'He is obviously terrified. I have NEVER seen him like this,' she said. 'Would you please keep your cat under control, or I really don't see how this can ever work.' She swept out, without having said a word of welcome, and having completely ruined Em's day.

Father Hugh said that he would be very happy to see Declan at nine a.m., before New Year's Day Mass at ten, and George, initially a little surprised and grumpy to be rung early on New

Year's Day, was disarmed when he realised it was Sister Bridget on the phone having a family emergency, and agreed to open up the shop at eleven for them to help her brother-in-law get an urgent flight home. Bridget considered whether she should ask Peter to come to the meeting too, but his standoffishness that morning made her pause. Maybe it would be best to let Father Hugh talk to Declan first, she reasoned.

'You know, Declan, we can talk to Father Hugh together, but then I think I'll leave you and you can go to confession,' said Sister Bridget, as they left the house to walk to church. 'Won't that be a lovely start to the year?'

'But what if I can't find JJ? Can I be forgiven if I can't make things right?' said Declan, fearfully.

'I'm sure you can,' said Sister Bridget. 'God sees the intentions of your heart – I'm sure Father Hugh will agree.'

Father Hugh did. He listened to Sister Bridget about Declan's health worries, took the letter from Declan's shaking hands and read it, looked at his distraught face, and felt an immense compassion for him.

'I'll see you in the church, Declan,' said Bridget, leaving them together. 'I think Declan wants to go to confession, Father.'

'Is that right, Declan?' said Father Hugh, as Bridget left. 'Don't feel under pressure now.'

'No, no, I want to go to confession.'

Father Hugh, still sitting in the kitchen, reached over to where he had already hung a purple stole, ready for this, and put it around his neck.

'It's just . . . how can I go to confession when I don't know how to put it right? What can I do?' said Declan. 'I don't even know where JJ is.'

'We can pray for guidance about that – but first Declan, the main thing is you're sorry?'

'I am, Father. I'm very ashamed. And I want to put things right before I die.'

'Well then, Declan,' said Father Hugh, full of kindness, 'God, the Father of mercies, through the death and resurrection of his Son, has reconciled the world to himself and sent the Holy Spirit among us for the forgiveness of sin, through the ministry of the Church. May God give you pardon and peace, and,' at this Father Hugh made the sign of the cross, 'I absolve you from your sins in the name of the Father and the Son and the Holy Spirit. Amen.'

Declan gave a great shuddering sigh, tears pouring down his cheeks as Father Hugh blessed him, and Father Hugh marvelled yet again at the palpable sense of peace in the room after a good confession.

'I want you, as a penance, to spend some time every day now, thanking God for his forgiveness and unconditional love for you, praying for the men who were hurt, and asking for guidance about anything God might ask you to do.'

'I know already,' said Declan. 'I'm going to make recompense. I'm going to give some money to charity – the London Irish Centre and the Irish Chaplaincy in London for a start. I'll donate to homeless charities. And if JJ is still alive, I will track him down and make sure he lacks for nothing. I'm going to put things right.'

Declan smiled for the first time, a smile full of amazed relief. He looked like a huge weight had been lifted from his shoulders.

'Thank you, Father,' he said.

'No problem, Declan. I'll see you over in the church for Mass. And as you told me about the letter before confession, with your permission, I will make some enquiries about the whereabouts of JJ. I am very hopeful we can track him down.'

'Really, Father? That would be such a miracle!'

'Well, with God, anything is possible,' said Father Hugh, smiling and letting a tearstained but happy Declan out the door, ready to go next door to the church. 'Happy New Year!'

He looked at his watch. *I have time before I leave today. I'll give him a ring now and ask him over here after Mass. The sooner this is sorted the better. Lord, help me get through to him. He's a tougher nut to crack than poor Declan.*

Chris went back to reception and found Em hugging Kylie, who was wriggling to get free as Em was crying quietly all over her.

'Em – what's the matter?'

'Pangur and Kylie hissed at each other and Sister Cecilia was so horrible. She said Kylie was terrifying Pangur and that it wasn't going to work! What are we going to do, Chris? I can't give Kylie up. We're going to have to move back to Mum's. I can't bear it! We're going to lose our first home on the day we moved in, and on New Year's Day too!'

'Em – we are not going to lose our home. Sister Cecilia has no idea about kittens, and she isn't the boss anyway. Now, I'll take Kylie to the flat and unpack, and you go and wash your face. Is there anyone else to check out today?'

'Yes, I think there is a family.'

'Well then, check them out, and then come and find me in the flat. It's Moving Day and this is our new home. Sister Bridget, not Sister Cecilia, gave us this flat, and Kylie and Pangur will soon be the best of mates. Don't worry, Em. Everything will be all right.'

*

When Margaret, Cecilia and Katy got to the crowded church for New Year's Day Mass, Margaret was delighted to see the change in Declan, sitting in the pew with Bridget. He looked peaceful in himself. She exchanged a smile with Bridget, who whispered joyfully, as the bell for the start of Mass went, 'He's been to confession with Father Hugh.' Margaret felt a rush of love and gratitude for Bridget, who couldn't bear to see anyone in distress without fixing things, and towards the quiet, humble priest who was walking up the aisle at the end of a procession of male altar servers and Father Stephen.

I might have problems with the structures of the Church, Lord, Margaret prayed, *but I am very glad you called Hugh to be a priest.*

Father Hugh sat in Mass, trying to listen to Sister Cecilia reading out, but distracted by worry. It had all gone wrong, and it was his fault.

'I suppose he cried and you gave him absolution?' Peter had said, bitterly, after Hugh had rung and explained what he wanted Peter to do. 'It was that easy for him? All those men, coughing their lungs up on the streets of London and other places, their lives ruined, but a few magic words from you made Declan's soul as white as snow?'

'Hey — that's out of order,' said Hugh, stung. 'You know very well that's not how it works.'

'How *does* it work then?' said Peter.

'He is sorry. He wants to make things right. He wants to find JJ — and we both know how easy that could be.'

'To make him feel better about himself? Let him stew,' Peter snarled.

'But if it could help JJ?'

'What could Declan possibly give him now to make things right? Can he give health to a man whose body has been wrecked? Can he bring him back in time, so he can see his family in Ireland again? Can he raise the dead so JJ's family, who died not knowing whether he was even alive, can come back and hug him? Any money he gives will just be bribery – blood money, tainted by all the lives he ruined.'

'You don't know what it will do for JJ. Declan was shattered by that letter. We must help him put things right,' said Hugh, uncharacteristically angry, still hurt by the sneer, and shocked by the cold rage in Peter's voice.

'Get lost, Hugh,' said Peter, and slammed the phone down.

Forgive me, dear Lord, Father Hugh prayed. *I shouldn't have lost my temper. I shouldn't have spoken to him like that. I forgot it was you, not me, who forgave Declan and brought that peace into the room. I wanted it all sorted out before I went on retreat today. I thought it would be a wonderful way to start the New Year, and I knew that Peter could help Declan to meet JJ, but I ended up ordering him about and I know I had no right, especially knowing his history. I am sorry for my pride and arrogance. Please bless them all. Please sort this out.*

'Is Sister Bridget about?' said Chris, who was waiting in the hall for the Sisters to come back from Mass. Sister Cecilia walked past him without saying anything.

'She's gone with her brother-in-law to see George at the travel agents. Is everything all right, Chris?' said Margaret.

'Not really. Em is very upset. Sister Cecilia saw Pangur and Kylie meeting each other and claims Kylie terrified Pangur and that she wasn't sure if things were going to work out. Now Em's worried that we are going to be asked to leave, or give up Kylie, and she is crying in our flat.'

'Oh no!' said Margaret. 'I'm so sorry, Chris. Poor Em.'

'I know what it's like when kittens meet,' volunteered Katy. 'Did they hiss at each other and fluff their fur up?'

'Yes. I told Em I was sure this was normal and they would get used to each other, but apparently Sister Cecilia swept Pangur up and went off very angrily.'

'I think Sister Cecilia isn't very used to cats,' said Katy. 'I can try and talk to her.'

'That would be good,' said Margaret. 'Thank you, Katy.'

'I'll go and find her now,' said Katy, leaving Chris and Margaret alone in the hall.

'Chris, we are so grateful to you and Em. You are making the grounds absolutely beautiful, and Em is a wonderful receptionist, and we are only too glad to give you the staff flat. We want you to be happy here and I don't want this to spoil a special day. Please tell her – and I don't need to check with Sister Bridget about this – that she isn't to worry. Pangur and Kylie will get used to each other – they are brother and sister after all! And Sister Cecilia will get used to seeing two cats around the place.'

'Thank you, Sister. It's just . . . could you speak to Sister Cecilia? I know it's difficult, that she's very old and everything, but she is never very friendly to Em, and I think this was the last straw. Sorry to say this – but would you mind saying something? Em says she always seems to be cross with her and now Sister Cecilia seems to hate Kylie, and she doesn't know what to do.'

Margaret sighed. 'I understand, Chris. It is a little tricky – I honestly don't think Sister Cecilia means to be like that, but that's no excuse. I will talk to Bridget and we will think of a way to approach this. But in the meantime, can you assure Em we are very happy with her work, and we just want you all to feel welcome.'

'Thanks, Sister. Sorry to complain, but I just thought it was good to sort this now. I'm not bothered about Sister Cecilia myself – but it is really getting Em down.'

Right, Margaret prayed. *I have no idea how to handle this, Lord. Please may those kittens play nicely and Sister Cecilia accept them. We need Em and Chris to feel welcome. I need Sister Cecilia to appreciate them and understand she really needs to think about how she makes other people feel a bit more – but you know her, and you know that's not easy to get across. Please help!*

Sixteen

'I'll drive you to the airport, if you like,' offered George, once he had found the plane times. It was obvious Bridget's handsome Irish brother-in-law was having a crisis, and New Year's Day public transport would not get him to the airport in time for the afternoon plane he wanted to catch.

'Would you really?' said Bridget, delighted. 'That's so kind, George.'

'I've got nothing on this afternoon – and I'd actually like your advice, Sister, on the way back. If we leave now we should get there in plenty of time. Do you need to pick up any luggage from the convent?'

'No,' said Declan.

George kept his face professionally expressionless – years of dealing with the general public had taught him to hide his feelings more than was natural for his personality. Sister Bridget needed help for her brother-in-law – that was good enough for him.

'Thank you very much,' Declan added.

He looks worn out, poor man. Wonder what is going on?

'Fine – well, let me pop upstairs to get my car keys and I'll take you now, then. The car is round the back. Do you need to let the other Sisters know, Sister Bridget? Shall I give them a ring?'

'That would be grand, George. Thank you so much! What would we do without you?'

Sister Bridget and Declan waited in the car park for George. The sky above seemed leaden, and there was a feeling in the air that snow might be on the way. Declan shivered.

'We'll soon get you home to Mary, Declan,' said Bridget. 'And we'll be praying for your appointment this week.'

'I'm going to talk to Mary about it,' said Declan. 'I want to give money to the Irish Centre and the Irish Chaplaincy in London, and any other charities that might be helping anyone I have hurt. I am so glad I went to confession, but I'm still so ashamed. What will she think of me, Bridget? I've let her down. She doesn't deserve this.'

'Don't worry about Mary,' said Bridget. 'She loves you, and she's a very good woman. She will want to do what is right. You have to tell her about your health worries too, Declan.'

'I will. I might wait until I see my friend the consultant again, so I can talk to her about treatment. There is no sense in worrying her about everything at the same time – she gets too anxious about things anyway. He wasn't hopeful, but he said to meet again soon, and I am sure he will come up with some positive solutions. I can pay whatever is necessary. I think first tonight I will tell her about the letter and finding JJ and ask her what I can do about it. I feel I have to get this settled.'

'I've had an idea,' said Bridget. 'The cottage you rent out! Maybe you could give him the cottage on the island – so he would have a home to go back to at the end of his days,' said Bridget.

'But you wouldn't have it to stay in, then,' said Declan. 'I know the Sisters enjoyed the retreat you had in it – I've always liked that we could offer that to you, especially as it was your old home too.'

'Oh, don't worry about me,' said Bridget. 'JJ must be the priority.'

'I can never thank you enough for all you have done for me this New Year,' said Declan. 'I know Mary will feel the same.'

Barely had Father Hugh set off for his retreat at St Beuno's in North Wales, leaving Father Stephen in charge for the first time since his arrival the previous summer, than the phone rang at the presbytery.

There was a sound of someone putting coins in a call box.

'Is that Father Hugh of St Philomena's Parish, Fairbridge?' said a rather loud, posh man's voice.

'No, I'm afraid he is away at the moment. I am Father Stephen, the curate.'

'Well, you'll have to do, I suppose,' said the voice. 'Look, my late sister went over to Rome – crossed the Tiber as they say. All smells and bells and went a bit overboard on statues. Good quality. No cheap tat. Long and short of it is, she died.'

'I'm sorry to hear that.'

'Thank you. She had a good innings. Anyway, she wanted a Catholic church dedicated to St Philomena to get the statue of St Philomena she had, so you'll do. I'll have someone pop it over this afternoon – three p.m.? It's rather heavy, but you don't have to worry about that. They'll put it in the church for you. Just tell them where you want it to go.'

'But . . .'

'No, don't thank me. It's in the terms of her will. I won't get a penny until I have homes in Catholic churches for all of them. I got rid of St Francis and St Antony easily enough, and a couple of the Virgin Mary, but Philomena was a tricky one, the last I have to get off my hands. Start the New Year off right. I'll be glad to see the back of her, no disrespect intended, Father. Very good quality, just too big for a home.'

'But . . .'

'Splendid then. I'll have my men deliver at three. It's a real work of art – it just has to go. Terms of the will. I must run. Happy New Year!'

And before Father Stephen could get a name, the phone line went dead. Whoever had rung from a phone box was obviously keen not to be traced.

Maybe it's a hoax, he thought. *A New Year's Day practical joke. People just don't go around giving away valuable statues to churches. Do they?*

He looked at his watch. He supposed that he should be back for three p.m., in the unlikely case that a valuable statue of St Philomena would turn up. It gave him time to visit Bridie.

'Come in Father,' said Bridie, wheezing slightly as she opened the door to her flat. 'I was just saying the rosary.'

Father Stephen did not comment on the fact that a Norman Wisdom film was on the television, and a cigarette was smoking in an ashtray with a picture of the Pope on it on the table beside Bridie's comfortable armchair. There was indeed a set of rosary beads on Bridie's chair, and Father Stephen had no doubt she had been using them. He was used to her unconventional devotions now. Bridie was like nobody he had ever met during his seminary training.

An extrovert widow in her seventies, Bridie lived alone, but not out of choice. Bridie was not a big fan of silence or solitude, but she bravely put up with it when she had to, helped by the ever-present TV, a chatty mechanical honorary member of her family, and the crowds of crucifixes, pictures and statues of saints and Our Lady all over the flat. Bright comforting images of present and extended heavenly family members rubbed shoulders, school photos of her grandchildren and her children's wedding photos hung alongside pictures of the Sacred Heart of Jesus, St Francis, St Don Bosco and holy Padre Pio, who was just waiting to get his official title of saint. An old black and white photo of Bridie and her beloved English husband Bob when they were married during the war was on the mantelpiece over the electric fire, completely at home next to a statue of Our Lady of Lourdes in a plastic grotto appearing to a kneeling St Bernadette.

Our Lady did appear to be the favourite heavenly family member. She was everywhere. Little statues of Our Lady in various costumes and headdresses from her different apparitions could be seen all over the flat – fair skinned and dressed in white as in Fatima and Knock, or blue and white as in Lourdes, or, excitingly, brought back by Father Hugh from a holiday in the USA, a statue of a beautiful brown-skinned Mexican Our Lady of Guadalupe dressed in pink, blue and black.

'How are you, Bridie?' Father Stephen asked, gratefully accepting a mug of tea and a ginger nut biscuit.

'Not too bad at all, Father. Hoping for a win on the bingo this week. I'm asking Our Lady to help.'

Father Stephen had a disconcerting vision of Our Lady at bingo with Bridie. A year before he would have felt it to be bordering on the sacrilegious to imagine such a thing, but St Philomena's was changing him. After experiencing bingo run by Sister Bridget he could now imagine all sorts of saints enjoying the fun at the church hall. He would include Bridie amongst them. He never failed to feel better after a while in her company. Yes, maybe for the sake of her health she should give up cigarettes, and maybe cut down on the ginger nuts too, but there was something luminously good about this kind woman in her cluttered, colourful flat. Something, he had to admit, that was missing from the sour, pious Maura Ryan. He sighed. No wonder the Wednesday rosary group at Bridie's had taken off and Maura's hadn't.

'Everything all right with you, Father?' Bridie asked.

'Well,' said Stephen, deciding to omit his concerns about Maura. 'I had a phone call today about a statue of St Philomena being delivered at three p.m. at the church. An anonymous donor. But I don't know if it is a prank. Father Hugh has gone off for his silent retreat so I can't ask him. He didn't mention any arrangements about a statue to me.'

'Well, that's very exciting!' said Bridie. 'You'll have to let us know all about it tomorrow. Now, would you like to stay and have a bite with me? I can make you a nice ham sandwich.'

Father Stephen left Bridie's feeling better about everything, even if his clerical clothes now smelt a bit of cigarette smoke. A good walk in the fresh air would help with the smell. It was definitely worth it. It wasn't so much what Bridie said, or the copious amounts of tea, or the never-ending sandwiches and cake – it was just the tangible sense of peace and love you got from her presence. Bridie did not have much money, and was not in good health, and she was well aware that life could be full of sadness, for herself and others, but she always counted her blessings and tried to look for the best in people and, looking at the world through her eyes, Father Stephen never failed to feel more positive himself.

Snow began to fall from the grey sky. It was very beautiful. Father Stephen felt so lucky and so blessed to be a priest in this parish of St Philomena, in the university town of Fairbridge, with a kind, supportive parish priest and lovely parishioners like Bridie to remind him of the goodness of God.

His positive feelings lasted until three p.m.

The doorbell rang, and two men stood there, snow now falling heavily.

'Delivery of a statue for you. Sign here please.' Father Stephen signed the paper held out to him. 'Where do you want it?'

Father Stephen looked behind them to what was standing on the pavement, and his heart sank. This was not a window-sill or mantelpiece statue, or even the size of a little roadside shrine such as you saw in Ireland or Italy. This, being snowed on as he watched, was a huge, larger than life, church-size statue, and it would have to go in the church itself.

'I don't know if I can take it, actually. It's much bigger than I expected. I think you'll have to take it back,' said Stephen.

'No. You've signed for it, you see. We can either leave it here or put it somewhere – your choice. But you can't send it back.'

'But who even sent it?' said Father Stephen, desperately. 'Can I not speak to them?'

'No. They wish to remain anonymous, and you have signed that you accept the statue and will not attempt to contact the donor. Now. Shall we leave it on the path, or put it in the church?'

'Well, we can't leave it on the street, of course,' said Father Stephen, thoroughly flustered by now, and led the way into the church.

St Joseph's chapel was the nearest.

'Could you put it here?' he said, but the moment they put the stone statue next to the little wooden statue of Jesus' step-father, carrying a rather modern toolbox, it looked wrong. St Philomena towered over him, like some stone goddess.

'Oh dear. I wonder . . . I am sorry – but now could you move this wooden statue for me?' said Father Stephen. The men took pity on his panicky indecisiveness. They weren't churchy people, but even they could see the two statues didn't work together.

'No problem,' said one. 'Where do you want it?'

'Well, er, could we try it over here, in this side chapel, behind the candle stand and next to the statue of Our Lady. Joseph and Mary were husband and wife after all,' said Father Stephen.

'Oh yeah! Like Christmas. Joseph and Mary!' said one of the men, approvingly. 'My boy was Joseph in the school play this year,' he continued, as he put Joseph next to his wife. Both wooden statues in the same modern style, they were a perfect match. The man stepped back. 'I like it. Makes sense. Married and all.'

'Yeah, they look good together,' said the other one, overcome with a need to reassure this young vicar. He felt a bit guilty about the whole anonymous delivery thing, but the bloke had been insistent that the statue should not be returned to him.

'Thank you so much! I do hope the parishioners feel the same!' said Father Stephen, fervently, if rather optimistically.

Sister Bridget and George had left Declan to catch his plane and were driving back to Fairbridge, and George had just told Sister Bridget about what happened after the New Year's party.

'Oh George, that's terrible!' said Sister Bridget, in distress. 'I'm so sorry. Poor Matthew – was he very hurt?'

'He wasn't badly hurt physically – just a bruise and a little cut – but it could have been so much worse. The worst thing is though, that it has brought back all his trauma from his twenties – when he was bullied at Oxford. I know this might seem like an overreaction, but Sarah and I are so worried. He has already told me he can't cope with us going out as a couple. I've got a bad feeling. I'm worried if we don't get him out of the house soon, he is going to get worse and not want to go out at all – Sarah said that was what he was like when he was young.'

'But he'll have to go out to teach, won't he?' said Sister Bridget.

'No – that's the problem. He has taken this term as a sabbatical to plan his new course on the Irish artist Paul Henry. He has already taken out lots of books to study. He can hole himself up and go nowhere for weeks. I don't want him to do that – and I want him not to be scared to be seen out with me.'

'Well, would it help if you both came out in a group first? There is a group going to the panto tomorrow afternoon, and I know that there are two spare tickets. We were going to see if the theatre would take them back, but you and Matthew could have them. It's the Guild of St Stephen outing, but we opened it up to the parish, and there's about thirty of us. There's safety in crowds, as they say. It's "Sleeping Beauty" – just a bit of fun. I know Matthew might prefer something more intellectual . . .'

'No, that sounds perfect!' said George, enthusiastically. 'Thank you! Can we sit with you?'

'Of course! We'll have ice cream, and boo the villain, and hopefully poor Matthew will relax and forget those horrible people. And let it be a gift from us, George, for all the support you have given us this year. Matthew has helped us so much valuing and selling those Jack Mortimer paintings we were given, and you've advertised our B&B in your agency. You're such supportive friends, always cheering us on – and you have just driven all the way to the airport on New Year's Day!'

The snow, which had been falling lightly, began to fall more heavily, and George switched the headlights on.

'Thank you, Sister Bridget,' he said. 'What would I do without you? What would any of us do without you?'

Some hours later, Declan put his key in the door and stepped inside. A phone call from the airport meant that Mary was expecting him, and she was waiting, ready to hear what he had to say.

Tuesday 2nd January 1996

Seventeen

Lizzie and Mary arrived at the shop at the same time.

'Hi!' said Lizzie, spontaneously hugging Mary. 'Happy New Year!'

'Happy New Year to you! You're looking very pretty,' said Mary. 'Are those new earrings?'

'Yes,' said Lizzie, and something about the way she said it stopped Mary asking her who had given them to her. There was an excitement about her that made Mary worry, but she knew better than to bring up the subject of Lizzie's married lover. Mary had enough to worry about in her own life, anyway.

'How about you? Did you have a good New Year, Mary?' asked Lizzie.

'Well, not exactly,' said Mary, and to her own consternation, she started to cry.

Father Stephen had just finished Tuesday morning Mass and was rather depressed to find Maura waiting outside for him, with a small deputation behind her of other regular Mass goers, who all looked rather excited or concerned. Maura had been glaring at him during Mass, so he wasn't surprised that she had something to say. He noticed, with relief, some friendly witnesses, the Sisters in their pew, watching but not taking part.

'You have moved St Joseph into Our Lady's chapel!' said Maura, outraged. 'You NEVER see St Joseph and Our Lady together!'

'Well, that's not true . . .' began Father Stephen. 'Look at the crib.'

'They can be together for the crib,' conceded Maura, 'but NEVER normally. It's just not right,' she continued, looking around for support.

'Maura,' said Father Stephen patiently, 'yesterday, after Father Hugh went off on his silent retreat, we were unexpectedly given a very valuable statue of St Philomena by an anonymous donor, and so just for the time being I have put her in St Joseph's chapel, and I thought that St Joseph could join his wife on earth for the time being. It's just a week, until I can ask Father Hugh what to do.'

There was a satisfied murmur from most of the congregation, who started to drift away, Bridie clearly saying, 'Well, it's just until Father Hugh comes back. What harm does it do at Christmas, after all?' but there was an audible sniff from Maura, still standing her ground. 'So, St Philomena has a chapel to herself, but the Mother of God does not?' she said, almost spitting the words out in her anger.

'Well, I don't think of it that way,' said Father Stephen, taken aback by the intensity of her anger.

'You should! We simply cannot have a Lady Chapel with a St Joseph in it,' declaimed Maura, passionately. 'It's just not done. Father Hugh would agree.' She glared at him.

'I'm sorry to interrupt,' said Sister Margaret, coming to the rescue. 'But I need to speak to Father Stephen alone. On an urgent matter. Excuse us. Maura, Father Hugh will be back in a week, and the statue may well have gone by then anyway.'

Margaret ushered Father Stephen into the sacristy and closed the door.

'Don't let her bully you,' said Sister Margaret.

'She must know that I only have the greatest of respect for Our Lady,' said Father Stephen, bewildered by the ferocity he had just encountered. 'I can't understand why she is so set against Our Lady sharing with Joseph.'

'It's very interesting,' agreed Margaret. 'To be fair, it does seem strange seeing Joseph in the Lady Chapel! Somehow, it's not the same as the crib. I'm not sure why. Maybe Maura's strong reaction could be seen as a desire for Mary, as the Virgin Mother, to be given her own space, not being defined by her relationship with a man? A sort of feminist manifesto?' Father Stephen looked at her. 'Sorry – that's not helping,' said Margaret. 'Look,' she continued, reassuringly, to the pale young priest, 'it is much more likely, knowing Maura, that she is already angry because you dropped out of her rosary group, and you went to see Bridie yesterday, oh yes – and Maura is in charge of the candles in Our Lady's chapel.'

'I don't understand! And how would she know I visited Bridie?' said Stephen.

'Bridie and Maura are arch enemies. And I heard Bridie boast to Maura this morning that you had paid a home visit to her yesterday.'

'Oh dear. That wasn't helpful. Why did she do that?' said Father Stephen.

'Father Stephen, Bridie may be a saint, but she is not an angel,' said Margaret. 'Parishioners are human beings, and there are all sorts of power struggles and past histories. Bridie and Maura had a bitter argument over the candle stands last year. And in the end Father Hugh put Maura in charge of the candle stand in Our Lady's chapel, which Maura counted as a win, and Bridie got the new candle stand in St Joseph's. So of course, Bridie flexed her muscles a bit when she got a visit from you on New Year's Day and Maura didn't. And on top of that, basically, the Lady Chapel is Maura's domain, and you have invaded it without her permission.'

Father Stephen put his head in his hands. 'What am I supposed to do? How can I please everyone?'

'You can't. People like to moan. If it wasn't this, it would be something else. Surely they taught you that at seminary?' Father Stephen looked so miserable that Margaret took pity on him. 'Look – don't worry. I have an idea. St Philomena would look great in our grounds. I'm surprised we haven't got a statue of her already. We can take her!'

'Really? She is very heavy,' said Father Stephen, hope and despair struggling for supremacy.

'No problem – I can get Peter and Chris to come and help. Chris has a van. We can load it up. It might not be today . . .'

Margaret noticed the look of dread on Father Stephen's face – it was obvious he was not looking forward to facing an angry Maura again the next day. 'No – don't worry – we will get this sorted today,' she said, mercifully. 'St Philomena will be out of the church by tomorrow, and St Joseph will be back in his place. Come back with me and let's talk to Chris and Peter.'

'Thank you!' said Father Stephen. 'I am not very good at conflicts like this.'

'He wants to give your cottage away?' said Lizzie, outraged, handing Mary her coffee. The shop would not be opening for another half hour. 'But it's yours. Does he not know how important it is to you?'

'It's not his fault. He is so upset by the letter, and he is so ashamed of what he did. He went to confession, and for his penance he has to try to put things right.'

'I get that, but why does it have to be with your cottage? It's not your fault.'

Mary sighed. 'I'm his wife.'

'So what?'

'I'm his wife. We share everything. We're together for better or for worse. I've had the better, now I've got to put up with the worse.'

'The better? How have you had the better?' said Lizzie, exasperated. 'You're basically miserable, Mary. That cottage is literally the only thing that's really yours. Otherwise, you are just the nice housewife in his big house, lonely and bored out of your mind, doing good left, right and centre, pushed around by your children and family. You cared for your parents for years because your sister was too busy being holy to help.'

'That's not true!' said Mary, wounded.

'It is true. I'm not going to stand by and let you give up the one place where you can be yourself. I've seen your paintings. Why on earth did he decide that your cottage was his to give away, anyway?'

'Because JJ came from the island too. Bridget said that if Declan could track him down and give him the cottage, it would mean JJ could come home to the island as a homeowner and show his family he had made something of himself.'

'Why has your sister stuck her nose in? She's a nun, isn't she? It's not her cottage any more. It's none of her business. And if this man is still alive, he *didn't* make something of himself – his life was ruined by your husband, not you, and your sister can't pretend everything is all happy ever after.'

'She just wanted to help,' said Mary, surprised by Lizzie's anger. 'You didn't see Declan. He is so upset and feels so guilty about it all. He begged me to help. I had to promise him last night that if we found JJ, we would give him the cottage. The person I'm most worried about is Deirdre, if she doesn't have the cottage to rent out any more. They are in terrible debt.'

Lizzie swore. 'Sorry, Mary. But honestly! Stop worrying about your family and start worrying about yourself. Don't just let your husband get you to do his penance for him. Get him to sell his car or his golf clubs or cash in some shares, for goodness' sake. And get Deirdre to tackle her husband. There's no reason why they should have money problems. You should keep that cottage and you should be painting in it, full stop.' She swore again.

'Don't get so angry!' said Mary.

'I just can't bear it. You're being such a doormat,' said Lizzie, furiously. 'How can your husband be so selfish? It's so pathetic.'

'At least he is my husband, and not someone else's,' snapped Mary.

Lizzie opened her eyes wide with shock.

'Lizzie – I'm sorry, but I haven't come here today to have my family criticised like this. You might think I'm a pathetic do-gooder, and a put-upon wife—' said Mary, shaking with anger.

'I didn't mean it like that.'

'—and maybe you're right – but you don't have the right to swear and shout at me. I told you how I felt about the cottage because I thought we were friends. I'm sorry you think I'm so pathetic, Lizzie, and you have such a low opinion of my life choices and my husband and family and sister. I happen to love them. And don't lecture me about my marriage when you show no respect for your boyfriend's one. Now, I'm sure you can find another bored housewife who just comes here because her life is so hopeless to fill in for me today. Tell them I went home sick, I don't care. But I am going home.'

Mary took her coat and bag and left the shop, leaving Lizzie shocked and angry and more than a little upset.

'I have never seen such disrespect!' fumed Maura, left alone in the church. 'Imagine giving a saint her own chapel but making Our Lady and St Joseph share! If I didn't have a bad back I would move things myself. I shall be writing a letter to the Bishop tomorrow if that statue is still there. That young man is not fit to be a curate. I feel sick, I really do.'

She was beside herself.

'Help me, Lord. I know I have a bad back, but give me the strength to do what is right.'

Maura looked around to check nobody was about and, greatly daring, got behind St Joseph's statue and pushed it. First of all it didn't move, but then suddenly, it did.

'Thanks be to God!' Maura said, triumphantly, and in her elation gave it another firm shove.

It shot forward, and then, in slow motion to Maura's appalled eyes, he toppled over and crashed to the ground. St Joseph's head fell off, and rolled a little way away, his kind, patient expression unchanged.

'What have I done?' said Maura in a panic. She carefully set the headless torso up again and pushed it back to where it had been next to Mary. She balanced Joseph's head on top, but it obviously wasn't secure.

'Superglue!' thought Maura, and rushed over to Mr Abidi's corner shop.

'Now, you must take great care using this,' said Mr Abidi. 'Be very careful to read the instructions.'

'I will,' promised Maura. 'It's an emergency. I've broken something and I need to fix it quickly.'

'You must stay calm when using superglue,' counselled Mr Abidi, taking Maura's money and ringing in the purchase, handing back the change and the glue. 'It's hospital for you if you stick yourself. Can I help at all? I am practised at using it.'

'No, no. Thank you,' said Maura, and rushed off.

'That lady was not calm,' said Mr Abidi to himself, worriedly.

Back in the church Maura managed, with now shaking hands and fervent prayer, to superglue St Joseph's head back on to his torso, but, standing back to admire a job well done, she realised she had somehow managed to stick the first and second fingers of her right hand together. Mr Abidi's warning came back to haunt her.

'Oh no! I have to go to hospital!' she cried, and rushed outside, just in time to bump into Sarah Woodburn, district nurse, walking past the church on her way back from a call.

'Please, can you help me?' Maura begged.

Eighteen

Declan was surprised but pleased to see Mary back so soon.

'I thought you had to be there all day,' he said.

'There was a mix-up,' said Mary. She felt a bit guilty about walking out on Lizzie, but she still felt so upset and angry at Lizzie's contempt. If she felt so patronising about volunteers, let her try to do the job by herself then. She was paid, after all. Mary had never ever let her down, and she was so hurt that Lizzie obviously just saw her as a pathetic bored rich housewife. She thought they were friends.

'I'll make you tea. Sit down,' said Declan. He was looking anxious and insecure in a way that Mary had never seen him before in their marriage. He was always so untouchably sure and confident, so in control.

'Mary – I just want to say thank you,' he said, bringing the teas to the table. He had put some biscuits on a plate – a simple enough thing, but never something that would occur to him to do normally.

'For what?'

'For listening to me last night. For reading the letter and not getting angry or judging me or walking away.'

'Declan! I'm your wife! We're together for better or worse,' said Mary.

'I hope I have given you a good life,' he said, uncharacteristically self-doubting. 'I know I've taken you for granted. I've focused too much on money and not enough on the right things. You've always done enough praying and good works for both of us. You're a saint, Mary, and I don't deserve you.'

Mary winced. Another person commenting on her doing good. 'I'm not a saint, Declan—'

'Yes, you are, Mary. I should know – I'm your husband. But I'll make it up to you. I'll make it up to JJ and the other men too. I'll make it up to God.'

'All God needs is to know you are sorry. And you've been to confession, Declan.'

'But I haven't done my penance. I need to put things right. I WANT to put things right, Mary. And . . . if anything should happen, you will still find JJ for me and give him the cottage?'

'What do you mean, if anything should happen?' said Mary.

'Oh, don't mind that. I meant nothing by it. Don't worry. I just meant . . . you know, for insurance. That you support me in this . . . I know you do, Mary. You're wonderful like that.'

'I wanted to talk about that, Declan . . .'

He got up and paced the room. 'I just want to make things right. If I could see him home with his head held high . . . I'm just praying to God to help me find him.'

The afternoon performance of the Fairbridge 1995/96 pantomime 'Sleeping Beauty' was due to start at two, and the altar servers and parishioners had gathered to meet in the lobby at half past one. Father Stephen had been entrusted with the treat funds, and he and Cuthbert, the senior altar server, were taking orders for interval ice creams. Katy was crossing names off the list. Sister Bridget and George and Matthew had arrived, and were chatting happily.

'Maura has not arrived yet,' said Katy. Father Stephen heard Maura's name and tried not to wince. He felt as if, even though she hadn't yet arrived, he could feel her glaring at him even with his back turned. *Don't be paranoid, Stephen.* Why on earth was Maura coming to the parish pantomime outing? He could not imagine her enjoying it. He could not imagine her enjoying anything, to be honest. *Forgive me, Lord, for my lack of charity. Please help her.* He was grateful that one of the smallest altar servers decided at that moment, to the mortification of his parents, to drop a box of popcorn all over the carpet, so he could turn back and be kind rather than bitter, and focus on calming everyone down and reassuring the embarrassed parents and the tearful and overexcited little boy. The theatre staff were quick and efficient at sorting it out, and soon the whole group had been ushered into their seats. Everyone except Maura. The announcement came:

'Ladies and gentlemen, boys and girls, please take your seats for this afternoon's performance of "Sleeping Beauty".'

'I'll stay in the lobby and wait for Maura,' said Margaret to Katy.

The pantomime had still not begun when Maura arrived, looking unusually upset.

'Are you all right, Maura?' said Margaret.

'Yes, yes,' said Maura, but Margaret noticed she kept her hands in her pockets. They took their seats quickly. Margaret was on the end, next to Maura who was next to Katy, who was next to George and Matthew, who was next to Sister Bridget, who was next to Cuthbert and Father Stephen and the altar servers and their families. The theatre was full of excited children chatting. Suddenly the lights dimmed, to excited 'oohs', the orchestra struck up, the red velvet curtain rose on a beautiful palace, and the show began.

It was a lovely pantomime. The opening scene was a colourful and joyful royal christening, with cheerful songs and scene setting – suddenly, however, a wicked fairy, left out of the invites, cursed the baby princess to death by pricking her finger on a spinning wheel, and the good fairies used their wishes to change the future death of the princess to a long sleep. The panicked parents decided the safest way to protect their beloved daughter would be to destroy all the spinning wheels in the kingdom. Margaret glanced at the others in their seats and was struck by how enthralled everybody, young and old, looked. Even Maura looked like she was caught up in the story.

There was plenty of time given to Sleeping Beauty growing up with her friends in the palace, with lots of song and dance by the talented actors. The Dame, the palace cook who was always keen on nipping out of the palace to go shopping, was very funny, and the handsome prince, in pantomime tradition a woman, was a wonderful lovelorn singer. The scene changed again, this time to the tower with a lone spinning wheel and a wicked fairy, who, in spite of the audience's pleas, rehearsed in readiness by the Dame before she went shopping, enticed the princess to try to spin, to prick her finger and fall asleep. The props and scenery were amazing as the enchanted forest grew over the castle, and then it was the interval.

'There's a very strong smell of nail polish remover,' said Katy to Maura and Margaret. 'Can anyone else smell it?'

'No – I have a bit of a cold,' said Margaret. 'I hope it's not spoiling the panto for you?'

'Oh no! I'm really enjoying the panto. It's just an odd smell, that's all. Maura – would you like an ice cream? I don't think you were here when they were ordered?'

Maura shook her head. 'No. Thank you. I don't want anything.' She kept her hands in her pockets.

'Is everything all right, Maura?' said Margaret again, concerned. Why had Maura arrived so late, and why was she keeping her hands in her pockets? And why was she looking so anxious? Disapproving or angry would be more normal, but this was a more vulnerable Maura, and Margaret felt a sudden and new sympathy. Maura wasn't a happy person.

Sister Cecilia woke with a start. She had been reading a very interesting book on Catholic nobility and philanthropy in the Victorian era, but somehow seemed to have dropped off. She looked at the clock in the library. It might be a good idea to check on the last load of washing she had put in after lunch. There were tablecloths and table napkins she could hang in the boiler room.

'Come, Pangur,' she said. But Pangur wasn't there. The library door was slightly open.

She went outside and called 'Pangur!' and he appeared out of nowhere.

'Where have you been?' she said, a little severely in her relief, but Pangur took no offence, rubbing himself against her and purring.

'Oh, he found you!' said Em at reception, as Cecilia and Pangur passed on the way to the laundry.

'What do you mean? I was not lost,' said Cecilia. 'I was in the library all the time.'

'We had a little visitor, didn't we, Kylie?' said Em fondly to her little cat, curled up in a basket by her feet. 'Pangur suddenly appeared out of nowhere, and they had a brilliant time charging up and down the corridor. They are great friends now. Isn't that good?'

'Hmm,' said Sister Cecilia, and swept on by.

Em sighed. 'Count to ten, Em,' she said to herself, remembering Chris's advice, as Sister Cecilia and Pangur went through the door to the laundry. This job, so lovely in every way, definitely had its drawback, and its name was Cecilia.

Declan insisted on finding a midday Mass to go to. Mary had never seen him so serious and intent. It was as if all the energy and focus he had used to make him a successful businessman had suddenly switched into repentance and prayer. It was still repentance and prayer Declan-style, however.

'I'm taking you to lunch now, Mary. To the finest restaurant in the city,' he said after Mass, after he had lit many candles and spent a good ten minutes in silent prayer, unheard of for him. 'This is the start of a new life for us. I'm going to leave no stone unturned – I'll hire a detective if need be – and I know God will find JJ for me and I can give him the cottage – I just have to trust. And from now on, I'm going to be the husband you deserve. I'll retire – leave the running of the business to Tom – he has a good head on his shoulders. I'll take you anywhere, get you anything you want.'

Mary had a quick vision of the cottage, and had to close her eyes with the thought of how much she longed for it, and its impending loss – the only thing she really wanted – but it was impossible to bring it up with Declan in this state.

'We'll start again, Mary. I'll take you on cruises. I'll come on those pilgrimages with you. I want to make it up to you. And

I want to do something for the homeless Irish in Britain – you can help me there, I'm sure. We'll start a foundation together. You can help me.'

He insisted on taking her to the shops and buying her an expensive dress and coat and shoes she didn't really want, and then on to a restaurant where he talked non-stop of his relief about the confession and his determination to step back from work and dedicate himself to charity, but he looked so handsome and happy it was hard to resist, and impossible for Mary to interrupt. Declan always made things happen, whether you wanted them to or not.

Back at Fairbridge Theatre, Father Stephen distributed the ice creams, people disappeared to find the ladies and gents and in spite of the queues, everyone was back in time for the curtain going up on the second half. The Dame, who happened to have just popped out to the shops and so wasn't in the castle when the spell fell, was still awake and able to give some good practical advice to the prince, so they got through the undergrowth, and organised some community singing. The bad fairy tried to stop them, so that gave plenty of chances for the audience to boo and hiss. St Philomena's altar servers and their families did the parish proud.

'It's oddly therapeutic,' said Matthew to Bridget and George, as they booed loudly, and they laughed. Maura, next to Margaret, kept tight lipped. This pantomime was too noisy for her tastes. When the prince managed to get through to the tower room where the princess had pricked her finger and lay sleeping, the whole theatre, however, fell silent.

The prince, the principal boy, gently kissed the princess on the forehead. The princess woke up and sang a beautiful song about not being afraid any more when she had someone to love, and Matthew, to his mortification, sitting between Sister Bridget and George, started to quietly cry.

Both Sister Bridget and George automatically reached out on either side to hold Matthew's hands, but Sister Bridget let go to rifle in her handbag for a handkerchief to give him.

Nineteen

'Ah, Chris,' said Sister Margaret as she, Sister Bridget and Katy walked into the lobby of the B&B with Father Stephen. 'Do you have half an hour? We need a statue moving from the church and brought here to the garden.'

'OK, Sister,' said Chris, cheerfully. He liked the variety of his job.

'I'll go and ask Peter if he can help. Katy – can you come with me? I imagine Peter would like someone to sit with Jimmy.'

'I'd be so grateful,' said Father Stephen fervently.

Peter was very willing to help Margaret and Stephen, and he and Chris set off with Father Stephen in Chris's van, leaving Katy to sit with Jimmy. She brought the book of paintings Matthew had given them for New Year with her.

'Would you like a nice book?' she said.

'Ah now, I'm not a great reader, to be honest,' said Jimmy, who was secretly longing to put the TV on for a game show.

'It's the paintings I like in this book,' said Katy, dropping the book on his lap. 'Would you like a cup of tea?'

All was silent in the flat. Katy went to the kitchen, boiled the kettle and made the tea, finding some Mikado biscuits Mr Abidi stocked in the corner shop for his Irish customers, and putting them on a plate. Jimmy had a sweet tooth, and everyone took every opportunity they could to build him up. She came back into the sitting room to see Jimmy gazing at the book, tears running down his face.

'Jimmy! What is the matter? Are you in pain?'

He shook his head. The grief in his face was terrible to see.

'I'm sorry,' he said, as the tears poured down his cheeks. 'Sorry to be a trouble. I don't know why it has hit me so hard. Seeing Connemara. It's taken me by surprise.'

'Stay there!' said Katy, unnecessarily, and rushed out to get Sister Bridget from reception, where she was petting Kylie and cheering Em up by thanking her and praising her for all the work she was doing.

'I don't know what we'd do without you, Em. You're wonderful with the guests, and so cheerful all the time,' Bridget was saying, when she caught sight of Katy's face.

'Something has upset Jimmy,' said Katy. 'Please come!'

Jimmy was still weeping silently when Bridget arrived. She squatted down in front of him and took both of his hands in hers.

'Go and ask Em to send Peter back here as soon as he gets back,' said Bridget.

She looked into Jimmy's blue eyes, which were brimming with tears. They were the eyes of an elderly man, with a particular sweetness and innocence which also reminded her of a boy. A very sad boy. With a shock of recognition as she looked at the book on his lap, Bridget understood exactly who he was.

*

Declan fell asleep in the armchair when they got back, and Mary changed out of her new smart clothes, which she hadn't really wanted, and into a more comfortable dress. She cleaned the kitchen, rehearsing how to bring up the subject of the cottage. And also, how to somehow head Declan off from retiring and giving control of the family company to Deirdre's husband. Declan had no idea about their money problems. Handing control of so much money to a compulsive gambler would be a disaster, and it couldn't happen. Deirdre had sworn her to secrecy, but she had to realise this had gone too far. In a way, it would be a relief to tell Declan. He could make hard decisions, which Mary never could. She should have told him before, but Deirdre had inherited her father's strong will. Mary sighed. She had been so angry with Lizzie, and she was still hurt, but she knew Lizzie had meant well. She was right. Her family did push her around too much. She had to talk to Declan about the cottage.

Lord, it's a terrible thing that poor JJ ended up on the streets, and Declan is right – we do need to find him. Please help us. But also, please help me and Declan. I don't think I have the energy to run a foundation for the homeless with him. I feel so selfish. Lord, I don't want to be selfish, but I am tired. Please help Deirdre and Tom. And I want to keep the cottage. I want to paint. I am sorry to be greedy. Please can you help me give it up?

'What's happening?' said Peter as he walked into the flat and saw Bridget holding a crying Jimmy's hands.

'I know this man, Peter! His name is JJ! We know each other from childhood,' said Bridget, looking radiant. 'Thanks be to God! This is an answer to prayer!'

'Leave it, Sister,' said Peter, urgently. 'Jimmy looks very upset.'

'No, you don't understand,' said Bridget, ecstatically. 'It's a miracle. I really do know this man. He is from the island I am from. He has had a very unfortunate life, God help him. He was sent to an industrial school when his parents died, where by all accounts they did not treat him the way they should, God forgive them, and then he was not treated well by the Irish firm he worked for in England. The man who owns the firm now wants to find him, so he can put things right. JJ – would you like to see Ireland again?'

Jimmy – now JJ – nodded, tears running down his face.

'JJ – I will take you there myself, then,' said Bridget, squeezing his hands reassuringly. 'Peter will come, won't you? I have to tell you the good news! There is a lovely house on the island with your name on it waiting for you. It's my old family home – my brother-in-law Declan bought it from me – you won't recognise it. He's done it up beautifully now – all mod cons and central heating. Extended it – three good double bedrooms. A house to be proud of – and it's yours now. You're a man of property now. You'll be snug as a bug in a rug. TV and everything. Declan wants to give it to you as an apology for all the wrong his family firm did.'

'I don't understand. Sure, it was my own fault, Sister. Nobody made me drink but myself. Nobody owes me anything,' said JJ, shaking his head.

'That's not how Declan sees it. He has been to confession and he wants to – he has to make amends – to you and the other men he wronged. They paid you in pubs, they didn't pay National Insurance. You had nothing to fall back on. That was wrong and he is very sorry. That's why he wants to give you the house.'

'On the island you say?' asked JJ, his eyes filling with tears again. 'He is giving me a house on the island?'

'It's my parents' old house, JJ. Do you remember it? Declan extended it. It's lovely. And there is the stable too – he converted it and my sister used it as an art studio.'

'Could it be a chapel, do you think?' said JJ, slowly.

'I suppose so. Yes, thinking of it, the stable would make a beautiful chapel. There are big windows looking out over the fields and to the sea.'

'And no pubs on the island?'

'No.'

'Thanks be to God then, Sister,' said JJ. 'It would be a grand place for men like me, in trouble with the drink, to go and dry out – just the sea and the mountains and the chapel.'

'It sounds lovely,' said Katy.

'And it's mine – forever?'

'Yes, thanks be to God! It's all meant – Peter bringing you here. You're meant to go back to Ireland, and back in style too, JJ, with your head held high.'

'He's not well enough to travel,' protested Peter.

'I am,' said JJ.

'We get sick people to Lourdes, and I think JJ will feel better as soon as he breathes Irish air. We can get him to Ireland – Declan will pay for everything. JJ – can I take you back to Connemara?'

'Yes, Sister Bridget. And I want to go to Gurteen,' JJ said.

'You want to go to Gurteen, to visit your family's graves?' asked Bridget. 'Of course you can, JJ. Of course you can! Now, I am going to ring Declan to tell him the good news you have been found, and I will ask my friend George to help organise the best of travel for you. What a wonderful way to start the New Year! Thank God!' And Sister Bridget bustled off.

*

203

'They have found him!' said Declan, putting down the phone and shaking his head in disbelief and happy shock. 'Oh Mary, Bridget has found him! Our Lady intervened! I didn't even have to hire a detective. I can put things right. God has answered our prayers.'

'Who?' said Mary, unnecessarily, already knowing the answer. As Declan held her in his arms and wept with relief, she prayed for the strength to cope with what that meant.

Katy met an ecstatic Bridget, fresh from her call to Declan, outside the flat.

'Peter asked us to leave them alone for a while, as the news has given Jimmy, I mean JJ, a big shock.'

'Oh, is he all right? Can I talk to him?' said Bridget, immediately concerned.

'I don't think so. I think Peter wants some space. He . . .' Katy didn't quite know how to convey Peter's barely concealed fury. He had talked to JJ with such tenderness, but when he turned to Katy he had been curt in the extreme.

'Please leave. And don't let Sister Bridget back here tonight,' he had said. How could she tell Bridget that? Luckily, Bridget wasn't listening.

'Declan is made up!' said Bridget, happily. 'He said he told Mary all about JJ and she is totally supporting him, and they had just prayed the rosary. It's a miracle. I can't wait to talk to Mary myself. I wish I had asked him had he told Mary about his heart,' Bridget added thoughtfully, as they walked back to the kitchen. 'I can't talk to her about it until I know he has told her.'

'Why wouldn't he?' said Katy.

'Ah, he's very protective of Mary. She's had problems with her nerves. And there was the cancer. She's gentle. She's always needed looking after.

'I just hope he's told her. I want to be able to support her through that. She'll worry. That's how she is made. I might give it a day for this to sink in and then quietly ring him tomorrow. He does need to tell her the bad news as well as the good.'

'Have you seen Pangur?' said Sister Cecilia to Em as she passed her on the way to the laundry. She was not pleased to have Em smilingly point out two kittens, tangled up together, asleep in the basket.

'Look, Sister, aren't they sweet?' said Em, hoping to end the day with a smile from Cecilia.

'I don't know if it is suitable to have kittens at reception,' said Cecilia, frowning.

'But the reviews have said how lovely Pangur is – and the guests this morning loved seeing them together. They were playing so much that they tired themselves out.'

'I hope they weren't disruptive,' said Cecilia, disapprovingly. 'Come, Pangur,' said Cecilia. 'We have laundry to do.' Pangur's ears twitched and he opened his eyes and yawned, stretched, and, leaving his sister asleep, pattered over to Sister Cecilia, who could not resist a smile, which, however, she only gave to little Pangur. Em only got a nod.

'Honestly, the way she said it – "I hope they weren't disruptive",' imitated Em indignantly to Chris, back in the flat. She cuddled Kylie as she did so. 'She glared at me, as if Kylie was leading Pangur astray. It really wasn't nice, Chris.'

Chris smiled at her. 'I know she's not easy, Em. Imagine Sister Margaret and Sister Bridget having to live with her!'

Em sighed. 'I feel as if I do. She always seems to be passing on her way to somewhere, looking disapprovingly at me.'

'Come on, Em. Don't let Sister Cecilia get you down,' said

Chris. 'We've got our own place together at last, and we can save up. You're great at your job – you're even in the papers you're so good at it, and I love mine. I think I can really make these gardens beautiful, and make the vegetable patch and the orchards more productive. Kylie's happy, Pangur's happy. We love each other.' He put his arms around her and gave her a kiss.

'No, you're right. I just hate her blaming Kylie for things when she has done nothing wrong.'

'Kylie's not bothered!' laughed Chris. 'Don't let her spoil our evening. How do you fancy fish and chips as a treat?'

George was waiting in the queue at the fish and chip van when Em and Chris turned up.

'Hello. Thanks a lot for the other night,' he said. 'I'm sorry I snapped at you.'

'Oh, don't worry,' said Em. 'It was such a horrible thing to have happened – and I'm sorry I was bossy. How is Matthew now?'

George grimaced. 'Not good, I'm afraid. He just won't go out anywhere with me, as a couple. Sister Bridget helped me bring him to the pantomime today, but that was in a group. It was fun, and I thought it might help him get used to being out, but he is convinced that in the lobby, at the end when we were leaving, a woman glared at us as she passed us and muttered we were disgusting – I don't know if he's just getting paranoid.'

'That's so sad,' said Em. 'All because of those people in the car.'

'No, it's his past history, I'm afraid. He was bullied badly for being gay when he was a student. I'm getting fish and chips for me and him and Sarah because he just won't go out with me tonight in case anyone else says anything.'

'Could you get away from Fairbridge altogether and have a holiday?' said Chris, as George's order was handed over.

'That might be a good idea . . . thanks Em, thanks Chris.'

'Love to Matthew and Sarah – and enjoy your fish and chips, George!'

As George set off home he bumped into Sister Bridget and Katy.

'Ah, George! Just the person I was thinking of!' she said. 'We're buying fish and chips for Father Stephen and us all, as we've had a bit of excitement. Can you help us organise a trip to Ireland? We'll be taking Jimmy back there soon. Only his name isn't Jimmy! It's a real detective mystery! I'll tell you all about it tomorrow – can I pop over?'

'Sounds fascinating – I'd love to hear all about it,' said George.

'And how is Matthew?' said Sister Bridget.

'Actually, not great.'

'Oh no – was it the panto that upset him?' said Bridget, immediately concerned.

'No, that was very moving, that's all. We loved it. Thank you. Matthew is convinced someone passed us in the lobby when we were leaving and glared at us and said we were disgusting. I think he's being paranoid, but he won't even come out to a restaurant with me now.'

'That's terrible. I'm so sorry.'

'Chris and Em just suggested maybe we should go away for a holiday together, but I don't know where would be best. I don't want things to get worse.'

'George! Hold that thought. I'll pray about it tonight, but I think I have an idea!' said Bridget, her face suddenly full of excitement. 'God is good! See you tomorrow. I have such a great story to tell you, and I think it might help Matthew, too! After Mass – would eleven be OK?'

'Yes. See you tomorrow,' said George, his spirits lifted, as they always were, by meeting Sister Bridget. She seemed to have the rare gift of always making things better.

Wednesday 3rd January 1996

Twenty

Father Stephen went to pray in the church before Mass, and gratefully lit candles in front of both the Lady Chapel and St Joseph's. It was strange that it had caused Maura so much consternation to see them together in one chapel, but he was relieved the big stone statue of St Philomena was no longer there, complicating things. He hoped the morning Mass crowd, and in particular, Maura, would appreciate how fast it had been moved. He went and prayed for some minutes in front of the crib, where Mary and Joseph were allowed to be together. If he was a braver priest, he might preach a sermon about that one day – about our expectations for the saints and their family lives. He certainly wanted to talk to Father Hugh about it when he came back.

'Look, Maura – the statues are back in their places!' said Sister Margaret, as they came into the church at the same time. 'That's good, isn't it?'

'Yes,' said Maura, but she sounded more unsure, more muted than usual. Something was definitely still up. And Margaret noticed her hands were still in her pockets.

Sister Cecilia went over to Saint Joseph's statue and narrowed her eyes. 'That statue has been damaged! Look – there is a crack around St Joseph's neck that wasn't there before.'

'Are you sure?' said Father Stephen. 'I have just lit a candle in front of it, and I didn't notice.'

He went up to the statue.

'Well, I have to agree. It does look as if it has been knocked over. But whoever did it has obviously tried to fix it, and made a good job really. I certainly didn't notice this morning.'

'But who did it?' said Sister Cecilia. 'It must have been the men who delivered the statue in the first place and moved everything about. They should pay compensation. The parish isn't made of money.'

'Well, I don't actually know who the men were who delivered it, but I was with them in the church and there were no accidents. I was there last night too when Chris and Peter moved it out of the church to take it to the convent, and I know they didn't knock anything over either,' said Father Stephen.

Margaret turned to say something to Maura, but saw, to her surprise, that she was way over on the opposite side of the church, her head leaning on one hand, the other still, strangely, in her pocket, praying fervently.

'The solicitors are closed so we can't sign over the cottage to JJ today, but I thought I'd go to Mass and we could go to see the Bishop this afternoon about setting up the foundation,' said Declan over breakfast. 'I was going to ring him to arrange a round of golf anyway. If he is free this afternoon, I am sure he will be pleased to see us. I'll get him some whisky, that always goes down well.'

'I . . . I have to do a shift at the shop today,' said Mary, suddenly desperate to talk to Lizzie and to avoid the Bishop.

'Oh all right. We can tell the Bishop together later this week. I also have some medical things to sort out this week, just with Colum. Nothing to worry about, Mary, just for insurance. But the main thing is we're agreed. We'll do this together, Mary.' He put out his hand and took Mary's in his, and suddenly kissed it, something he had never done before in their long marriage.

'I feel like a new man, Mary! The relief! That letter about JJ, and the curse, I don't mind telling you I was worried. That's why I had to go over to Bridget, to ask her help. I couldn't put all that burden on you.'

'I would have listened too, Declan,' said Mary, hurt.

'I know, Mary, but you're not as strong as Bridget,' said Declan, as if that was an indisputable fact. 'And it has all worked out, thank God,' he blithely continued, not noticing Mary's hurt expression about his comparison of the two sisters. 'I can't tell you how good I feel that I went to confession, Mary. Father Hugh is a great man. I have a lot of penance to do, but I know with you by my side we can do great things, and I hope that God will forgive me. A lot of men's lives have been ruined and I am going to dedicate the rest of my life to putting that right. That, and treating you the way you deserve. You and me together, Mary, we're a winning team. I need you. I want to be more like you. You'll go straight to Heaven. You could never hurt anyone.'

'Oh Declan. Don't talk like that. You know God has forgiven you,' said Mary.

'I can't tell you how much it means to have your support and understanding, Mary.'

*

'Oh Mary!' said Lizzie, as soon as her friend arrived at the shop half an hour later. It wasn't opening time yet, and Lizzie rushed to open the locked door to let Mary in. 'Thank you for coming back today. I want to say – I'm so sorry about yesterday. I shouldn't have said those things about your family.'

'I'm so sorry too – you spoke a lot of truth and I didn't want to hear it. I've got to talk to you, Lizzie.'

'What's the matter, Mary? You look awful.'

'I tried to talk to Declan about the cottage, and how I want to get back to painting, and to Connemara. You are right, Lizzie. I do need to do that. Going back to the cottage . . . it stirred things up. I love it so much.'

'I know you do, Mary. And your paintings are so lovely, too. You have got to take yourself seriously. Remember what the tutors said.'

'I wanted to talk to him. Make him understand. But then lots of things happened. My sister rang us – she actually found the homeless man Declan wants to give the cottage to, and he is someone from our island and I just . . . I just couldn't say anything, he was so excited, and it is good to help poor JJ. He's had a terrible life.'

'Oh, Mary,' said Lizzie, sympathetically.

'Then yesterday Declan told me he wants to retire and pass on the business to Deirdre's husband Tom and he thinks I am a saint and he wants us to start this big foundation for the homeless together, and meet the Bishop, and he is so determined and focused, like he always has been, and I just can't say "no", and I still haven't told him about Tom's gambling. I feel so fed up and trapped and weak,' and Mary burst into tears.

*

When Sister Cecilia got back from Mass she was very angry to find two little cats creating mayhem in the library. Pangur was chasing Kylie up a curtain, and Sister Cecilia's notes were scattered on the floor. She swooped down on Kylie and plucked her off the curtain, then, ignoring the kitten's purring as she held her, dumped her on the desk at reception, where Em was.

'Your cat has got into the library and messed all my papers up. Kindly keep her under control,' said Sister Cecilia, then marched back to the library, where she was expecting to see Pangur. But he wasn't there. She turned and went back to reception. Em was on the phone to a prospective guest, and tried not to be put off by Sister Cecilia's impatient presence.

'Where is Pangur?' she demanded, as soon as Em had put the phone down.

'I don't know!' said Em. 'Kylie is here with me, as good as gold. Look.' The little black and white cat was now curled up, fast asleep.

'Humph,' said Sister Cecilia, ungraciously, and went off in search of him. But he was nowhere to be found. He was not in the library, and not in the kitchen, nor in the laundry.

Sister Cecilia went out into the garden and heard a mewing. She looked up and saw Pangur on a branch halfway up a tree, looking down, obviously stuck and scared.

'Pangur!' she called out in distress, looking around for a stepladder. 'Stay there and don't move!'

She went to the shed to fetch a ladder, and propped it against the tree. She firmly planted the bottom rungs in the soft ground.

'I'm coming, Pangur!' she called, hitching up her habit a little, and starting to climb.

'Sister! What on earth are you doing?' came Peter's voice,

and he and Chris ran to hold the ladder steady. Sister Cecilia had already reached high enough for Pangur to step on to her shoulder. Cecilia started the descent. The rungs of the ladder were wet, and her foot slipped halfway down, and she fell, but luckily Peter caught her in his arms, like a dancer, and quickly put her on her feet again. Pangur was still gripping tightly to her shoulder.

'Sister! That was incredibly dangerous!' said Peter, crossly.

'I'm sorry,' said Cecilia, uncharacteristically meekly. 'Thank you both.' She had picked Pangur off her shoulder and was stroking him, but Chris noticed her hands were shaking.

'Come in and have a hot tea and sugar for the shock,' he said.

'I'm so glad Peter caught her! She could have really hurt herself. She looked as light as a feather, though,' Chris said to Em later over lunch. 'Like a little bird. I know she is being a pain about Kylie, but honestly, she is mad about Pangur. I don't think she should have climbed that ladder – but you have to admire her – ninety-one years old and up that ladder as fast as she could go. She could have really hurt herself but she didn't care.'

Em sniffed. 'I'm glad that she is OK, and I know she loves Pangur, and I love him as well, but I want her to love Kylie too. I'd be happy if she just *liked* me!'

'She will, Em, don't worry. Who couldn't love you both?' said Chris, tickling Kylie under the chin, who purred, and giving his wife a hug.

Mary found sorting out the new donations very calming. There were some unopened presents, still in their boxes, and she hoped that nobody would notice that their presents to friends and family had been recycled in this way. Some people clearly didn't enjoy jigsaws as much as their nearest and dearest imagined, and one Christmassy scented candle looked as if it had first been given many years before. On impulse, Mary put a pound in the till and decided to take it home and burn the candle herself. Christmas wasn't over yet. Everybody, including a candle in a rather bashed box, should have a chance to shine.

Sinead and Rory came in.

'How did your grandmother enjoy the Kylemore Abbey jigsaw?' said Mary.

'She loved it!'

'Wait a minute – I found another one. It's brand new, never been opened. Roundstone Pier. Connemara again. Near where I'm from, actually.'

'That's amazing. You two really have to get together and talk about Connemara! She'd love that.'

'Definitely. Has she been back recently?'

'Not for years and years. She lost her only brother, and I think she had a hard time in an orphanage there so it makes her sad to visit. She never took my dad, and we've never gone as family, but it's funny, I think she still has happy memories from when she was a child. I know she loves seeing it on TV and on jigsaws and stuff like that. I want to take Rory there one day. So beautiful. I love those mountains. I'll take it!'

'And Rory – did you finish *Bananas in Pyjamas*?' Rory nodded. 'I've got a lovely one with puppies and kittens – would you like that?' said Mary and, popping another pound in the till, handed it to the little lad, who smiled shyly and hugged it closely.

'Oh, thanks a million,' said Sinead. 'You're too good, Mary.'

*

'You ARE too good,' said Lizzie, after Sinead and Rory had left. 'You can't keep buying things for the customers.'

'Well, I have enough money, Lizzie,' said Mary. 'I complain about poor Declan, but I don't lack for anything.'

Lizzie tilted her head and looked at Mary wryly.

'You're looking different today, Lizzie,' said Mary, changing the subject. 'I'm trying to work out what it is. Is it your eye shadow?'

'Mary,' Lizzie blurted out. 'Aidan asked me to marry him last night.' She said it with a mixture of pride and pleading in her eyes. Mary's heart sank.

'But – he is married already!' she said, as gently as she could. She loved this young woman so much, and she couldn't bear to think of her being hurt.

'I knew you'd say that – but he has separated from her – and I thought you'd like to know . . . he is getting an annulment. They said he had good grounds. They were only eighteen when they married. They were so young. They didn't know what they were doing.'

'I was only sixteen when I married Declan!' said Mary.

There was an awkward pause.

'Please don't let us row about this,' said Mary. 'I'm just old fashioned, I suppose. I've always thought marriage is for life – for better or for worse. But I do know there are such things as annulments. That's a good thing if you get one. You can marry in church then.'

'He's lovely. He is so gentle and kind, Mary. And he says I make him happy.'

'I'm sure you do, Lizzie. I don't know what to say. I just want you to be happy too.'

'I am,' said Lizzie. 'Could you give me a hug, Mary?'

'Of course,' said Mary, glad to have got through this difficult conversation. She couldn't bear another argument.

'Have you managed to talk to Deirdre yet?' said Lizzie.

'Not yet. And I need to talk to Declan about the cottage before he signs it away. We've got enough money – I am sure we can do something for JJ but I want to keep the cottage. I will talk to him tonight.'

Twenty-One

'So, George, it's all a wonderful answer to prayer!' finished Sister Bridget happily, updating George in the travel agents that afternoon about the Declan and JJ saga. 'We need to get Jimmy – or JJ as we know him from home – checked out to see if he is well enough to travel, but he is desperate to get over to Connemara, and I know it will do him a power of good to be back on Irish soil after such a long exile. And I was thinking – the cottage sleeps six. How about if you and Matthew join Peter and JJ and Margaret and me? We could all have a little Irish holiday together. It would help Matthew to get out and about, and after all, we would never have found JJ if Matthew hadn't given us the Paul Henry book! You two need a break after what you have been through – God used you as part of the miracle too! I am sure Declan will pay for us to hire a minibus to get us from the airport – and I know you can drive one, so it would be a great help for us, too!'

'You are AMAZING, Sister Bridget!' said George. 'I know that Matthew wants to go to Connemara to plan a tour of Paul Henry country for his students. This is perfect!' He gave her a hug. 'You always seem to make things better, honestly, you're an angel!'

'Well, I don't know about that!' said Bridget, but she looked very pleased.

On the way back from George's Bridget popped into Mr Abidi's. Inspired by Sister Bridget and the elderly Irish immigrant parishioners of St Philomena's, all living near his shop, he had, with a mixture of kindness and business acumen, built up a special Irish section in his shop. He stocked soda bread, barm brack cakes, Tayto crisps, red lemonade, and Mikado and Kimberly biscuits. Sister Bridget bought a cake and crisps and lemonade and biscuits.

'Are you having an Irish party, Sister?' he asked.

'I am. It's a celebration – we are bringing an old man back to Ireland soon and he hasn't been home for years!' she said. They beamed at each other, both knowing what it was like to live far from where they were born, and to long for home and home comforts.

'In that case – the barm brack is on me!' said Mr Abidi, generously. 'And how are you, Sister? Do you need a check up at the GPs I wonder?'

'Why? Do I look as if I do?' said Bridget, a little surprised.

'Only joking!' said Mr Abidi. 'It's just that Bahnaz is starting at the surgery today. Our little girl, a GP in Fairbridge, thanks to the finest education you Sisters have given her! We have much to thank God for!'

'We do indeed, Mr Abidi,' said Sister Bridget. 'We do indeed.'

George's mum re-read the card from Julia that had come that morning. She would be coming in a fortnight to stay. Julia would love to come to bingo, and she was looking forward to tasting this amazing nun's cake. It would be great to have a reunion after all these years.

As she put the kettle on she found herself unusually humming a cheerful tune. She had a fortnight. She would get Matthew and George to help re-decorate – smarten the house up. Julia was always a kind girl, but she had married a rich man, and she would be expecting a certain level of accommodation. The food would have to be tip top. They would go out to restaurants, of course, but she knew that Sister Bridget's bingo and cake would be the things Julia would never forget. And nobody else she knew would know a nun.

'So, what are you most looking forward to about going back to Ireland?' said Katy to JJ, who, after the initial shock, was looking very happy, and with a new energy and strength in him that seemed to have grown overnight with the good news.

'I'm looking forward to going to Knock, to thank Our Lady for bringing me home, and then I'm looking forward to seeing the mountains and the sea and the rocky shore, and to sitting in my own home, thanks be to God, and to seeing the fuchsia bushes and the dry-stone walls. I'm looking forward to the peace, Katy. The wild flowers and the little birds and the hares, and I'd like to share that peace with others who aren't as lucky as me.'

Katy looked at JJ with deep admiration. He had no idea about his own humility, about how amazing he was.

'Will you have family there we can contact?'

'Ah, none,' said JJ, a look of sadness on his face. 'I only had a sister, God bless her, and I lost touch with her long ago. It was better for her. I was sending her money every week as she was growing up, but when she wrote to tell me she was engaged, I was already in trouble with the drink. When she got married, I let her go. I knew she'd be better off without me. I didn't want to bring shame on her then, and it's too late now, after all these years.'

'Maybe it's not though,' said Katy.

'Ah, you're a good girl, but we'll leave it. If she is still alive it will be too much of a shock to her. No, I'll go to Gurteen and visit my parents' graves. Maybe God will be good to me and let me see my sister again, but I don't know where she is or even if she is alive, and I don't remember the name of the man she married, or what her name is now.'

'We could ask? Make enquiries?'

'No, thank you. I won't be greedy. If she is alive and the good Lord wants me to see her, that would be a mercy, but I won't disrupt her life after all these years. I'd like to get some new clothes, though, and a haircut, and new shoes. Would that be possible, do you think?'

'I'm sure it would,' said Katy. 'I know that Peter was saying you would need a check-up from the GP before you can go to Ireland. Maybe we can sort all those things out this week, if you feel up to it?'

'I do, Katy, thank God, I do. I can't believe how Sister Bridget has changed everything in one day, God bless her!'

'I know. She's amazing!' said Katy. 'It's so clear God works through her. I love these Sisters so much!'

'You'd make a grand one yourself,' said JJ.

'We'll see,' laughed Katy. 'I'm thinking about it anyway. There's no guarantee they would take me, of course.'

'They'd take you, of course they would,' said JJ, confidently.

*

223

Mary let herself into the house. Declan was playing her CD of Nóirín Ní Riain and the monks of Glenstall Abbey, and she could smell that he had lit one of her beeswax candles.

'Hello?' she called.

'Hello, love, come in here,' replied Declan from the lounge. 'This CD is beautiful, isn't it?' he said, as Mary came in. 'I've been listening to Taizé songs, and the St Louis Jesuits. I've sorted so much out and I have had such peace today, I can't tell you. I never bothered with this type of music before, but you always knew what was important, Mary. I have so much to learn from you.'

'Oh Declan,' sighed Mary. 'I need to talk to you.'

'First of all, Mary – I've been out, and I have this to give you.' He went behind the sofa and brought out a huge bunch of flowers, and a small jewellery box.

'Oh Declan! What is this for?'

'To thank you. To thank you for being the best and most beautiful and saintly wife a man could ever ask for. I see that now. I'm so sorry for being so wrapped up in the business all these years, and for taking you for granted. Everything is going to be different from now on. And I have a great surprise for you!'

'What?' said Mary.

'I've booked a pilgrimage. You'll love it. It's not until later this year – but it's the trip of a lifetime, to thank God for our Golden Wedding Anniversary. We'll be going to the Holy Land, no expense spared. And there's more – I have brochures for pilgrimages to Fatima, to Lourdes, to Medjugorje. I've seen one to Mexico too – did you know Our Lady appeared at Guadalupe?'

'Thank you, Declan,' said Mary. 'But—'

'And we are going out tonight with Deirdre and Tom, to

the new restaurant at the Bay. I'm going to tell them about what happened, about what went wrong, but about our happy ending, and your sister finding JJ, and about my plans to hand over the business to Tom.'

'Yes – about that,' Mary tried to say, but Declan was in full alpha-male flow and, as usual, was not listening to her.

'And, of course, this new path God has called us to. I'm going to hand over the reins of the business to Tom, but I thought Deirdre might help us with the foundation. She has a head on her shoulders. Open the box, Mary.' He got down on his knees as he presented it, which totally shocked her. It was something he hadn't even done when he asked her to marry him. The monastic music carried on in the background.

Mary opened the jewellery box. It was a huge diamond eternity ring, and not Mary's style at all.

'It's just a small token of my appreciation for you, Mary. This is just the beginning.'

'But Declan, I don't need – I don't want – all this money spent on me,' said Mary.

'I know, I know,' said Declan, fondly. 'And most of the money will go on the foundation, of course. But I wanted to do this now, after all these years. To show the world how special you are to me.' He looked at his watch. 'The taxi is coming in half an hour Mary. I need to ring Colum about the appointment tomorrow. Put on the lovely new outfit we got you – Deirdre hasn't seen it yet – and put on the ring.' He gave her a big hug and a smacking kiss, and went off to the study.

Mary sat in the lounge with her unwanted ring and flowers, as Noírín Ní Riain and the monks sang on, and the beeswax candle spread its perfume. She felt strangely disconnected from it all. This adoring religious man was the husband she had always wanted but had never had. All those lonely years, at the start of her marriage when he had worked late, she would have been ecstatic if he had brought her flowers, had presented her with a ring, said those things. But now, now, after all these decades of trying so hard to be a better wife, to silently make it up to him for the disappointment she knew they both shared, but never mentioned, that she was not Bridget, she was tired. All she could feel was her heart breaking at the thought of losing the cottage, and being steam-rollered by Declan and his new fervour. Even her meditation music and candles, which she had so often used over the years to help her feel peaceful and pray, had been taken over by him, and she was surprised to find herself resentful. She had wanted him more in her life for so many years, but now he was, she felt overwhelmed, and wished she could send his organisation and drive back to work, where it belonged.

And where was God in all this? She had been a good and dutiful wife all these years, but he had not given her the courage to speak out when she needed. God was just standing by and letting her lose the cottage she loved so much, and her painting, which brought her such joy. God, to whom she had prayed faithfully all her life, was ignoring her. He had obviously now chosen Declan for a great work, and there was no arguing with Declan's powerful, successful, energetic God of Charitable Foundations and Bishops and Nuns and Good Works. Of course poor JJ was a lost sheep, and needed help. That was clear. She understood that. He had clearly had a terrible life. And Declan had had a great conversion. She had said so many prayers for him to have exactly that – to have an experience of God, to care less about money, to want to pray with her. So why wasn't she happier that her prayers for him had been answered?

But didn't God want to help her, too? Why, yet again, did she have to fit into other people's lives, other people's vocations? Bridget had followed her faith. Now Declan had found his, too, but she was losing hers. But that was an unbearable thought. Her faith was what had kept her going all these years.

She switched off the music, and was about to blow out the candle when she thought better of it. She could not give in to despair, though it was hard not to. She looked at the crib, and the Holy Family. She was glad they always kept the crib up until the sixth. She missed it every year when it was tidied away. Jesus was born far from luxury, a totally dependent baby. Our Lady had not had it easy, and had been there for her during the cancer scare, during all the ups and downs. She could at least ask for her intercession now.

> Hail Mary,
> Full of grace,
> The Lord is with thee.
> Blessed art thou amongst women,
> And blessed is the fruit of thy womb, Jesus.
> Holy Mary, Mother of God,
> Pray for us sinners,
> Now, and at the hour of our death,
> Amen

She blew out the candle and went upstairs to get ready to go out.

Thursday 4th January 1996

Twenty-Two

'What a wonderful evening!' Declan enthused, just past midnight on Thursday morning, as they got ready for bed. 'That went so well. Tom and Deirdre were made up about the business. It's good to hand over to the young ones. Oh Mary, I love you so much! Why did it take that letter and all it brought to make me realise? I don't deserve you. Thank you for supporting me all these years, and now for joining me in this great work. We're going to change the world Mary, you and me together. You have the wisdom and I have the drive.'

Mary turned her back to him, trying not to cry. It was all so unstoppable. What was the point of telling him what she wanted? She took off the big sparkling ring he had foisted on her, and put it in her jewellery box. She had never wanted things like that. There was a time, back on the island, when she was young, when a shy admirer had given her a grass ring he had made. Now THAT had been what made her happy, back then when things were simple. But Declan – he didn't see her at all.

'Mary?' he said. 'Shall I stay with you tonight?' Declan had got into the habit of sleeping in the spare room in past months, as his snoring had got so much worse he had even woken himself up. He was grateful for that now – it had led to the checkups which had uncovered his heart problems.

'I'm a bit tired, Declan,' she replied. 'And you drank wine. I do think you might snore tonight.'

'Good night then, Mary. I'll see you in the morning,' and he reached over, took her hand and gently kissed it again, that unfamiliar romantic gesture the New Year had brought. 'I couldn't have a better wife. I love you.'

'I love you too, Declan,' she said, getting into bed and closing her eyes. 'Sleep well.'

He left to sleep in the spare room, closing the door gently behind him.

She lay awake for a while. Then, just as she thought she might have to get up and make herself a hot drink, she was asleep.

When she woke, she knew immediately that something had changed. There was an absence in the house. She got up and put on her dressing gown. The birds were singing, and she felt strangely afraid. She knocked gently on Declan's door, and when there was no answer, she pushed it open. Declan was in bed, lying on his back, his eyes closed, rosary beads in hand. He looked more relaxed than he had for years, handsome as ever and at peace, and there was a half-smile on his face.

The Sisters had just finished Morning Prayer when the phone rang. It kept ringing until Sister Bridget picked it up.

'Oh Bridget,' came her sister's sobbing voice. 'He's dead! Bridget – Declan is dead!'

'Oh Mary – oh, poor Declan. I am so sorry! What happened?'

'I don't know. I don't know,' she wept. 'He just died in the night. I woke up and went to see him. He looked so peaceful, Bridget. He was smiling, with his rosary in his hands, and he was cold already – there was nothing I could do. He must have died soon after he went to bed.'

'May the Lord have mercy on his soul. Poor Declan. At least he was prepared. He made a very good confession, Mary. But I'm so sorry the consultant could do nothing.'

'What consultant?' said Mary, her voice rising slightly.

'I thought he had told you. He was going to tell you,' said Bridget, hastily. 'He just didn't want to worry you.'

'I don't understand. So he was ill and you knew he could die? YOU knew he could die, and I didn't?'

'He knew he was very ill, Mary. But you know Declan. He had hopes there would be a treatment, that he could get it fixed. The consultant . . .'

'Was it Colum from golf?' asked Mary. 'He said he was going to see him today.'

'I don't know what consultant,' repeated Bridget. 'I just know that at New Year Declan came to me, very upset about the letter – you know about the letter? – and he told me he needed an operation on his heart.'

'Yes, I know about the letter, and about JJ and the cottage. He told me that at least. After he told you, of course. But I knew nothing about an operation on his heart,' Mary said bitterly. Then she started crying again. 'Bridget – Declan is dead. Declan is dead. What am I going to do?'

'Mary – listen to me. What is happening now?'

'Deirdre is coming over. The doctor is on his way. Why didn't you tell me my husband was so ill, Bridget?' said Mary, suddenly angry. 'I could have been with him. I might have saved him. And I might have had a terrible argument with him last night.'

'But you and Declan never argued. You were a model couple,' said Bridget, bewildered. 'You didn't argue last night, did you?'

'No, we didn't. But we nearly did. I nearly argued with him. I nearly argued with him on his last night on earth. And then I would have had to live with that for the rest of my life.'

'Mary – you're in shock. You *didn't* argue with him – that's the main thing. I am so sorry he has gone, but at least he died at peace. He had such a good death, Mary, thanks be to God. He went to confession here, he died with nothing on his conscience – and he knew we had found JJ, thanks be to God, so we can give JJ the cottage and let him come home and honour Declan's wishes. We can do that for him at least.'

'*I* can do that for him. Not you, Bridget. It wasn't your cottage.'

'It was my home too,' said Bridget, bewildered.

'But we bought your share out. The Order got the money years ago. Declan gave the cottage to me.'

'Mary – you're not yourself. I'm sorry I even mentioned it today. What are we arguing about a cottage for, today of all days? You shouldn't be on your own. When will Deirdre come?'

'She's at the door now. I have to go.'

'I'll come over today to help you. You'll be wanting a wake – I will sort that.'

'No. I'll let you know when the funeral is. Don't ring me – I will ring you,' and Mary put down the phone.

Bridget looked at the receiver in her hand, shocked beyond words. She put it back on the cradle, her hands shaking, and went to find Margaret and the others.

'May the Lord have mercy on him,' said Father Stephen, as the Sisters told him before Mass. 'I'll sign a Mass card and I can say Mass for him on the sixth.'

234

'Shall we cancel bingo today?' asked Margaret, looking at Bridget, who although calm now, had cried her heart out back in the convent when she had told her the news.

'No – no, we mustn't. It's too short notice. They depend on me. Poor Declan. I can hardly believe it. Sure, it was a wonderful death really. A blessing. He went in his sleep, with his rosary in his hands.' said Bridget. 'No, we'll carry on as normal. Mary said she will let me know when the funeral is. Until then it will be business as usual.' Margaret and Katy exchanged glances. Bridget was obviously in shock.

'I really think we should postpone bingo this week,' said Margaret, firmly but gently. We had it at New Year. People will understand. You can put up a notice, can't you, Katy?'

'Of course!' said Katy.

'Maybe you are right,' said Bridget, her voice shaking. 'Thank you both. It's just a week. I think people will understand. We will have to tell JJ today too.'

'So JJ, Declan is in Heaven now, but his dying wish was that you should get the cottage,' said Bridget, back in the flat. 'It might take a little time to transfer the deeds, but there is no reason, once the doctor says you are fit enough, for you not to go and stay there as soon as you like. We can all go, it will be lovely. It's what Declan wanted.'

'May the Lord have mercy on him. Thank you, Sister,' said JJ.

'You're looking better every day, JJ,' said Bridget, smiling. 'Thank God.'

'Peter is going to take me out to get my hair cut this morning,' said JJ. 'I feel stronger now I know I am going home. I'm like a new man.'

*

Father Hugh spent the last day of his retreat in silent prayer for the parish. It had been a wonderful, restful time. The bed had been comfortable, the food had been amazing, the garden and countryside and the chapels full of beauty and consolation, and his spiritual director kind and wise. He was determined to return with a little more concern for his body as well as his soul – Jesus was God incarnate, after all, and Declan's ill health had shocked him. He had also found he wanted to pray for so many people in the parish, and that they had effectively come along with him on retreat. He had been able to offer them to God. He had prayed for the Sisters and Katy. He had prayed for Stephen at the beginning of his life as a priest. He had prayed for Thomas Amis, for Em and Chris, for George and Matthew, even George's difficult mother, and Maura, always so miserable. In particular, Declan, and the countrymen he had let down so badly, kept coming back into his mind all week. He had thanked God for Declan's good confession. He had prayed for humble, gentle, Jimmy, for his health and future, and, most of all, Peter, and the bitterness in his soul. 'How can Peter find peace?' he had prayed every day. On this last day he had watched the light dawn on the Welsh hills, and thought of the poet Gerard Manley Hopkins, and the Holy Spirit brooding over the 'bent world' with 'warm breast and with ah! bright wings,' and, although he had no answer, as yet, he had the sense that it was all in hand.

Friday 5th January 1996

Twenty-Three

'You can't be serious!' said Deirdre, sitting in Mary's kitchen, her coffee forgotten with the shock of what her mother had just said. 'You are going to give our cottage to a stranger?'

'I do know him. We both knew him,' said Mary, patiently. She looked tired but determined. 'Your father talked to me about it before he died, and I agreed.'

'But . . .'

'Look – Deirdre – it's not easy for me. But I promised your father. He felt he had treated this man very badly when he was young.'

Deirdre laughed in disbelief. 'Dad must have murdered this JJ's entire family to justify giving him a cottage in Connemara!'

'I think he certainly believed he had ruined his life,' said Mary.

'But why can't you just give him some money? You have money in the bank, Mum. Why don't you offer him money instead of our cottage?'

'It's because he was from our island. We grew up with him.

He's old, and has no family, and this way he can spend the remainder of his life on the island.'

'Oh – OK then. Well, why not let him go there for a while for free? Why do we have to give him the cottage?'

'It was your Aunty Bridget's idea, and your father agreed. Your father wanted to give it to him so he could go back to the island after all those years with his head held high – a man of property.'

'But Dad's dead now.' Mary winced at the baldness of the statement, but Deirdre, who was very agitated, just carried on. 'You're in charge now, Mum. You can decide for yourself. It's OUR cottage.'

'Actually, Deirdre, it's MY cottage,' said Mary. 'Your father and your aunt had no right to give it away. But I agreed. I promised him I would do that, and I am not going back on my word.'

'But what about me?' shouted Deirdre.

'What about you?'

'Dad's dead and it will all go to you, won't it?'

Mary took a shocked breath in. Declan was barely a day dead, and already his only daughter was talking about the will.

'You will have all the money,' continued Deirdre, unaware of her mother's reaction. 'You can afford to lose the cottage and give it to a stranger. You won't miss it – you never used it anyway. But I've lost everything. I've got nowhere to go.'

'What on earth do you mean, Deirdre?'

There was a pause. Deirdre bit her lip, then flushed.

'Tom has gambled all our savings away, Mum,' said Deirdre. 'He told me the other night, after Dad said he was handing over the business to him. He said he was so relieved when Dad said that, because he is in debt, and he had thought that to pay the debts we would have to sell the house, but that if he is left to run the business he could release cash to get us out of trouble in the short-term, and he had a plan to pay the business back. He seemed to think I'd be pleased to hear that!' she laughed bitterly. 'I told him there was no way he was going to run Dad's business into the ground. I told him I was leaving him – that I was going to the cottage with Fran. But now Dad is dead and,' she said bitterly, 'there's going to be some old derelict drunk there and I am the one who is going to be out on the streets.'

'Oh Deirdre!' said Mary, getting up out of her seat. She gave her a hug. 'I am so sorry. I had no idea. But you know you are never going to be on the streets. Tom may be in debt, but I am certainly not. I have plenty of money to go around. Your father made sure of that. And you could never have just taken Fran out of her school here and moved her to Connemara. You'll just have to come here, that's all.'

'But what am I going to live on?' wailed Deirdre. 'I had some independence renting out the cottage. You took that away from me.'

Mary recoiled, taking a step away from Deirdre in her hurt.

'Deirdre, I can't believe you said that. Your father has just died. I don't want this conversation now. That cottage was never yours. I should never have let you rely on its income. You need to at least try and sort things out with Tom and get him some help. We knew he had a problem – we stuck our heads in the sand. We should have told your father. I should never have promised to keep it a secret.'

'But—' Deirdre started to speak, but Mary spoke over her, needing to be firm and in charge because she felt that if she stopped, she would just collapse.

'So, first things first, Tom needs help and he certainly will NOT be running the business. I'll get some advice about what to do about that.

'You and Fran can stay in my house as long as you need,

and I will never leave you destitute – but you also need to go out and get yourself a job. And NEVER call JJ a derelict drunk again. Do you understand? The cottage, and what happens to it, is not up for discussion.' Deirdre nodded, sniffing.

'Now – get your stuff and bring it back, and we'll sort this out together. I have to sort things out this afternoon about your father's funeral, but we'll talk about it more this evening.'

'Sorry, Mum. I just felt desperate. I don't think it's sunk in about Dad.'

'I know. It's a nightmare. I can't believe it myself. But Deirdre, like it or not, your father IS dead. We shouldn't be arguing about money – he isn't even in his grave. I don't want these rows. I just want to do what he wanted me to do – what I promised him I would do – and get through this awful time. I'm sorry you and Tom are going through a bad patch – but all marriages do.'

'Yours and Dad's never did.'

Mary made a grimace. 'You don't know everything, Deirdre. And maybe it would have been a better marriage if we had had more rows.'

'You can't mean that, Mum?'

Mary held back the tears. 'I don't really think I can cope talking about this with you, Deirdre. Not now. Let's focus on your immediate situation. You've been with Tom since you were at school together, and we have always loved him – and I think you love him still.'

'I do, Mum, but I'm scared. The other night – he was obviously just planning to use the business to keep funding the gambling.'

'Well, that's not going to happen, for sure. But we have to try and get him help. We should never have ignored it. He's in trouble and we can't let him go under.'

EPIPHANY

Saturday 6th January 1996

Twenty-Four

It was the day of the Epiphany, the day the three wise men followed the star and came to pay homage to the child Jesus in the manger. Cecilia, who had shooed Kylie away, but allowed Pangur to follow her, placed the three new figures in the convent crib on the dining-room mantelpiece first thing in the morning, before Mass and the tasks of the day.

As soon as they had returned after Mass, Bridget was relieved when the phone rang and she heard Mary's voice on the other end.

'So, just to tell you, Bridget, the funeral is arranged for this Friday. It will be midday at the cathedral, and there will be a reception back at the house,' she said, without any preamble.

'I will come over as soon as I can to help you with arrangements,' said Bridget. 'I just need to arrange cover at the B&B—'

'—no need,' interrupted Mary, with a strange little laugh. 'Declan has done it already. He did it as soon as he came back from yours, apparently. There was an envelope with instructions on his desk. "In case of death." He did everything in one day, apparently, when I was out volunteering at the shop – he contacted the undertakers and pre-paid for a funeral, chose the hymns and his coffin and even paid for the church flowers. He wrote down who he would want at the reception and what food should be served and the caterers to order it from. He didn't want a wake, or extra flowers from mourners, just a plain coffin and a donation to the Irish Chaplaincy in London. He even managed to speak to the Bishop, who apparently has already agreed to preside if necessary, and when I rang today to tell him Declan had died, he said of course he would make sure he was available for the funeral.'

'That's wonderful!' said Bridget. 'Declan is still looking after you after death.'

'Or still doesn't trust me to do anything properly . . .' said Mary, bitterly.

'Mary? Are you all right?' said Bridget.

'No, Bridget, I'm not all right. My husband is dead. He died suddenly. He was so worried about his health that he secretly organised his own funeral, and apparently everyone knew he was ill apart from me.'

'Well, he didn't want to worry you,' said Bridget.

'I can give you the keys to the cottage at the funeral and you can take JJ down there,' said Mary, changing the subject.

'Is it that simple?' said Bridget, delighted. 'What about the solicitors?'

'I am giving you the keys to the cottage, Bridget. JJ can go and stay there until he dies. Isn't that enough for now?'

'But Declan wanted to actually give it to him . . . to make him a man of property . . .' said Bridget, confused.

'Bridget. It was none of your business to suggest Declan gave MY cottage to JJ,' said Mary, suddenly absolutely furious. 'It was none of your business to know about my husband's health and his worries before me. So, it is none of your business to tell me what to do now.'

Mary's voice was cold and firm, unrecognisable from her normal gentle, warm, slightly anxious one.

'Of course. I understand. But—'

'Bridget – I don't want this conversation. I have enough to do. And I have worries about Deirdre and Tom—'

'Oh no! What worries?' said Bridget, but Mary continued, ignoring her.

'—I have to bury my husband, I have enough to deal with. You can come to the funeral. Take the keys. Take JJ to the cottage. Don't ask for more. I know what Declan wanted, I know what you want, but you both forgot it was *my* cottage. Everyone has forgotten it is my cottage. I am still deciding what to do.'

'But I told JJ already, that Declan was going to give him the cottage. He was so happy. And yesterday you seemed to say you *were* going to give it to JJ,' said Bridget.

'Yesterday was yesterday. Bridget – you have no right organising my life as if I have no say. I will decide what to do about the cottage. It's MY cottage, not yours. You've got what you wanted – I'm giving you the keys at the funeral. JJ has a home for life and I can't go there any more. Isn't that enough? Or do you want him to own it so that he can leave it to you? I know you Sisters are always worrying about money.'

Bridget was shocked and hurt by the bitterness. 'Mary! Of course not!'

'We already bought you out of the cottage years ago. We paid a fair price for your half and it went straight to the Order. So why did you think you had a right to suggest to Declan what to do with it?'

'Mary – I am sorry. I just thought – well, it's not as if you use it yourself. You've just been renting it out and you have enough money. Declan will have left you very well provided. You don't need the rental from the cottage.'

'Bridget! What right have you to comment on my money or what I do with the house? It's none of your business!' shouted Mary. Bridget recoiled from the phone, holding the receiver away from her ear.

'I don't want to argue about this now. You are very upset,' said Bridget, hastily.

'I am very upset?' repeated Mary. 'Yes, Bridget, I would say I am.'

'What time shall I come to the house?' said Bridget, uncharacteristically nervous.

'Declan ordered enough cars. All the Sisters can come if they want to. I can send you the money for the air fares. Declan specified that too. The funeral is at twelve. He wants to be cremated and his ashes scattered on the island. Which is funny, as he hasn't been back there for years.'

'Ah, he never forgot his home,' said Bridget.

'So, I will see you at the funeral,' said Mary, very formally. 'Let me know if the other Sisters are coming and how much you need reimbursed. I will pay for JJ and his carer to travel to the cottage too. Goodbye, Bridget.'

'Wait . . . Mary. What's wrong? I seem to have upset you. What exactly have I done?' said Bridget.

'What's wrong is that my husband is dead. What you have done? Well, you figure it out,' said Mary, putting down the phone.

Bridget looked at the phone in her hand with horror. How had it all gone so badly?

'Can you order some more floor cleaner?' said Margaret, knocking and entering the office without waiting. 'Is everything all right, Bridget?' she said, seeing Bridget's strained face. Bridget turned to her and burst into tears.

'I just don't understand,' said Bridget over coffee and the last of the panettone from New Year's Eve. 'I don't understand why Mary is so upset about the cottage. She has so much. Declan wanted to give it to JJ. He saw it as part of his penance – he wanted to put things right – to do it to be at peace. Mary never even went there – Deirdre was renting it out. And now I have to tell JJ he can go to the cottage but it won't be his. How can I do that? He was so happy. It was what Declan wanted. I never thought Mary was greedy. She will have inherited a fortune from Declan. She doesn't need the cottage the way JJ does, and she knows Declan wanted to give it to him.'

'Money can bring out the worst in people,' said Cecilia, solemnly. 'Greed is one of the Seven Deadly Sins.'

'Mary was never a greedy person,' said Margaret.

'That's true,' agreed Cecilia. 'She has sent me some lovely jigsaws.'

'And I can't imagine her getting so angry,' continued Margaret, thoughtfully.

'You should have heard her!' said Bridget. 'But you're right. Mary was never greedy, and she has never been angry with me like that, never. I can't believe it. She has always been my little sister. I've always looked after her, made sure she was all right. It was one of the things I thanked God for, that I had seen her settled with Declan before I joined the novitiate. I knew she needed looking after. We've always been such good friends – she's never been angry with me like that – never,' she repeated.

'Maybe it's because she has had a shock?' said Katy. 'I mean, we can all do strange things after we have had a shock. She has just lost her husband, after all. I know when Mum died, I felt so angry.'

'That's true. Poor Mary. It's an awful shock. Nearly fifty years they were married. He was the best of husbands. He did everything for her – everything. She wanted for nothing. She will want for nothing. She is an extremely lucky woman. I don't know why she doesn't see that. Whereas poor JJ . . . I just am dreading telling him, that's all,' said Sister Bridget. 'I feel like I gave him the world and I am taking it away from him.'

'I'm sure it won't be that bad,' said Margaret. 'Don't worry. Let's get it over with and go and talk to him now. I'll come with you, Bridget. I said that I would sit with him before lunch. He is looking so much better every day, don't you think? He says it's the peace and having a good night's sleep that's helping.'

'So, JJ, I'm so sorry I spoke too soon,' said Bridget, over in the flat. Peter was there, having just made JJ a cup of tea. 'You see, poor Declan didn't get the chance to sign over the house before he died. But my sister wants to give me the keys next week and bring you down to the island as soon as the funeral is over on Friday, and you can stay there as long as you like.'

'But I can't make it into a retreat house or a respite home?' said JJ.

'Well, no,' said Bridget, blushing a little. 'Not yet, anyway. You see, my sister is very upset, and she has lots to do with the funeral, and worries about my niece, and so the paperwork might take some time.'

'But there will *be* paperwork?' said Peter.

Margaret could feel Bridget wrestling with her conscience, wanting to say 'yes' but knowing that would be a lie.

'At the moment, no,' she admitted reluctantly. Peter turned away, but Margaret was sure she heard a muttered 'typical' under his breath.

What's his problem? Margaret thought, crossly. *How rude! What's Bridget ever done to him?*

'I will talk to my sister again,' said Bridget, apologetically. 'I'm so sorry, JJ. I feel awful.'

'Ah no, Sister,' said JJ, immediately. 'Please don't worry. She has enough to deal with losing her husband. You have done so much for me already. Sure, it was only that I was so happy to go back to the island and thought it would be nice to share my good fortune with others. But it's very good of Mary to let me go and stay there at all for free – how long will that be for, Sister, do you know?'

'Well, as long as you want. As long as you need, but we'll go for a week to start with,' stuttered Sister Bridget.

'Realistically, JJ can't go over there on his own. I suppose I'll have to come along too,' said Peter.

'Thank you, Peter. If you are sure that's all right with you, I appreciate it very much,' said JJ. 'Even a week back on the island is more than I could have dreamt of. Thank you, Sister. And I'm very sorry for your loss. Poor Declan. May he rest in peace.'

'I'm so sorry,' said Bridget again. 'I'm mortified, really. I know that Declan wanted you to have that cottage.'

'Ah, Sister, you have nothing to say sorry for,' reassured JJ.

Peter said nothing.

'So – I will go to George's now and try and get the tickets booked,' said Bridget, trying to sound more upbeat. 'My sister will pay for them. That's a definite. Shall I make an appointment with the GP to check you are well enough to travel? Mr Abidi's daughter has just started there – we used to teach her,' said Sister Bridget. 'She's a lovely girl.'

'I have registered us already,' said Peter, unsmilingly. 'I can make the appointment and bring him to the check-up.'

'So, the problem is the funeral is on Friday. Would you like to go? I don't know if it will be too long for you JJ, with the journey and everything?'

'I won't be going to the funeral,' said Peter, flatly, giving no explanations.

'No, I think maybe we won't go to the funeral,' said JJ, looking at Peter.

'It might be a bit of a long wait,' worried Bridget. 'What can we do?' Her usual optimistic energy was notably lacking. She seemed to be unravelling before Margaret's concerned eyes.

'I wonder would George and Matthew be willing to come with us so soon? We'll need to hire a car.' Bridget looked flustered. 'What do you think we should hire?' She kept looking at Peter for some reassurance, but his face remained impassive.

'Anyway, JJ, Peter, we'll go and make arrangements and get back to you,' said Margaret, and putting her arm around Bridget's shoulders, guided her out of the flat.

Twenty-Five

'I'm very sorry about your brother-in-law, Sister Bridget,' said George, when she and Margaret went to book the tickets at his agency late that morning. 'It must be a terrible shock.' He was concerned by Bridget's pale face.

'I knew he was ill, of course, but it was still unexpected somehow. Declan was always so very alive . . . he was very successful, you know? He inherited his uncle's business, which employs so many people now. It will be a big funeral, that's for sure.'

'Well, we'll get you there, no problem,' said George.

'Thank you, but it seems very complicated. Peter and JJ aren't going to the funeral, but we want to take them to Connemara afterwards for a week. I thought . . . maybe you and Matthew would like to take the opportunity to come with us? But it's such short notice – maybe that's a stupid idea,' Bridget said, uncertainly, looking almost pleadingly at George.

'It's a wonderful and kind idea,' said George. 'I think it is just what Matthew needs. I am sure we can work something out. We can take JJ and Peter somewhere whilst you are at the funeral.'

'Knock!' said Margaret. 'I remember JJ saying he would like to visit the shrine. How far is it from Galway?'

George spread out the map.

'You could fly to Knock and drive to Galway in an hour, an hour and a quarter, I'd say. You could drive from Knock to the island in about two hours.'

Margaret and George looked at Bridget, but unlike her usual self, she looked utterly defeated by the logistics. Her normally cheerful face looked very sad and tired and she seemed lost in her thoughts, unaware that George had said anything. He exchanged concerned looks with Margaret.

'I think with the flight and everything . . . and then we have to drive to Connemara,' said Margaret. 'It seems too much for JJ in one day, to be honest. Don't you agree, Bridget?'

'What? Oh yes,' said Bridget, bringing herself back to the present.

'Well, how about going a day early – on Thursday – and checking into a hotel in Knock the night before?' said George.

'I suppose I can change bingo to the Wednesday,' said Bridget, worriedly. 'I think I can ring round and get the message to the regulars.'

'We can put a notice on the side of the church,' said Margaret, 'and announce it at Mass too. I am sure people will understand. I think we do need to travel on the Thursday and stay overnight, for JJ's sake.' *And for yours, Bridget.*

'We are not travelling at peak season, so I think we should be fine,' said George. 'There seem to be quite a few hotels and B&Bs there. I could ask for a later check-out time, so JJ could rest until you come back. Then JJ will only have the two-hour journey on the Friday.' *And arriving the night before will give you more rest too, Sister Bridget. You seem suddenly so much older and more vulnerable, with this bereavement,* George thought.

'That sounds wonderful, George,' said Margaret. 'Let me leave the convent credit card with you. Can I leave you to do all the arrangements?'

'Of course. I know Matthew has a sabbatical and nothing scheduled, so I will present this as Sister Bridget needing our help, and I know he won't be able to refuse. He can get some work done preparing his Paul Henry trip, and I can get him out of the house.'

'Thank you, George,' said Bridget.

'Don't worry, Sister,' said George, 'I'll sort it all out,' and he came round from behind the desk to give her a hug.

When they got back, Bridget was a bit subdued. They had soup for lunch, and then they went off to do their various afternoon tasks.

'What are you going to do, Bridget?' asked Margaret.

'I think I'll ring round the regulars and tell them to spread the news that bingo will be on Wednesday instead of Thursday. I'll make some cakes for the bed and breakfast,' Bridget said, bravely making an effort to cheer up. 'We could do with some now we have finished the panettone, and I thought maybe the guests would like a treat.'

'Good idea,' said Margaret, saying a prayer for Bridget. She found herself praying for her at every opportunity these last days. Declan's death, and Mary's anger, seemed to have fundamentally rocked her in a way that Margaret had never seen before, in all the years of living in community with her.

Lord, thank you that Bridget can make such delicious cakes, Margaret prayed. *I think, more than ever at this time, she needs to make people happy, and everybody loves her baking. Everyone except Peter.*

He's so nice to everyone else, including me, but he is really cold to her . . .
I don't know why.

'Margaret? Do you know if I have offended Peter in any way?' said Bridget, as if picking up on Margaret's thoughts. 'I keep offering him and JJ cakes, and JJ loves them, but Peter always refuses to take any for himself.'

'Maybe he just doesn't like cakes,' said Margaret. 'Some people don't. But everyone else loves them, Bridget, so I wouldn't worry.'

'You're right, of course,' said Bridget, trying to smile. 'I'll make some extra special ones for bingo this week, I think. People need cheering up.'

You do, Bridget, thought Margaret, affectionately, but she felt very irritated by Peter. If things didn't change, she was going to have a word with him. He was their guest, and Bridget had enough problems. She had just had a bereavement, for goodness' sake. There was no excuse.

Bridget went to the kitchen and started baking.

'Maybe, if Peter doesn't like cake, he might like a piece of flapjack for afternoon tea,' she said to herself. She put on the Daniel O'Donnell CD. 'I think this will be the last day for Christmas songs.' She switched on the oven. Then she greased a baking tray. It calmed her down. She melted butter in a saucepan and, with a wooden spoon, stirred in the oats, sugar and golden syrup, and poured the whole delicious mixture into two baking trays, pressing the mixture into the corners. 'Twelve for the twelfth day of Christmas,' she said, as if she was at bingo. 'Some for us and some for the guests,' as she scored each tray into twelve squares and popped them inside the oven. Then she greased three bread tins and measured out flour and sugar and yeast and warm water, adding it all to a big bowl and kneading for a while, and leaving the bread dough to rise on top of the oven.

The Kingdom of Heaven is like yeast, she reminded herself. It only needs a little to change everything.

The timer went, and she got the flapjacks out of the oven, and left them to cool. Then she measured out the ingredients for a lemon drizzle cake. 'I can bring Thomas over a slice. Maybe Peter likes lemon drizzle,' she said to herself, hopefully, as Daniel O'Donnell's cheery voice raised her spirits. 'I don't think I've offered him that before. I'll try him with the flapjacks first.'

The cake went in the already hot oven, the bread dough continued to rise, and Sister Bridget sniffed the flapjacks appreciatively, unable to resist removing two still warm slices and putting them on a plate.

'I'll just pop them over to Peter and JJ. Peter might still be there after lunch. There's nothing like fresh baking.'

Bridget knocked at the door, and Peter opened it.

'May I come in?' said Bridget, on impulse. Peter shrugged, and stood aside to let her in, not exactly welcoming.

'I've brought you some nice warm flapjacks to have with your tea,' said Bridget to JJ, once she was inside. 'They smelt so good I thought I'd bring them over right away.'

'Thank you, Sister,' said JJ.

'And you, too, Peter?' said Bridget. 'Can I tempt you to try some? I know you don't like cake, but . . .' She did her best twinkly Irish smile.

'No,' he said curtly.

'Well, now, I'll see you tomorrow, JJ,' said Bridget, quickly. 'Is there anything I can do for either of you?' said Bridget.

'We're fine. Thank you,' said Peter, and without quite realising how it had happened, Bridget found herself in the corridor again, the flat door shut firmly behind her.

She went to the kitchen and cleared up after lunch. She cleaned inside the fridge and swept the floor. Then she put two now cooled slices of flapjack on a plate for Chris and Em, but she was not her normal cheery self when she brought them over, and Em was worried.

'Sister Margaret – is Sister Bridget OK?' said Em, when Margaret walked in mid-afternoon, back from a visit to the local care home. 'She just doesn't look well.'

'I'll go and check. Thank you, Em,' said Margaret, heading off to the kitchen. There was a wonderful smell of baking, and fresh loaves of bread and a lemon drizzle cake were out of the oven. Daniel O'Donnell was singing happily, on the umpteenth play of his album, but Bridget was sitting at the table, her head in her hands.

'Bridget – what's the matter?' said Margaret. 'Is it Declan?'

Bridget raised her head, her eyes filled with tears.

'Declan is gone, and Mary is so angry with me, about the cottage, and me knowing about Declan being ill before she did, and there's something wrong with Peter. I made him some flapjacks and he looked at them as if they were poison. I just don't know what I've done to him, Margaret. I know I have disappointed JJ about the cottage, but he forgives me. But Peter – he really hates me, Margaret. He won't eat ANY-THING I cook. And I feel so tired. Sorry – I'm just being silly.'

Margaret gave her a hug. 'Bridget – go and have a rest. Katy is making her lovely vegetable lasagne tonight. Have a nap. You're exhausted.'

'Thank you, Margaret, I think I will,' said Bridget. 'I don't know why I am being so silly. Peter has every right to not eat my flapjacks.' She gave a miserable laugh. 'Listen to me, forcing my baking on people.'

'Well, I'm very glad you bake for us, and I for one can't wait to have that lemon drizzle later,' said Margaret, giving her another hug. 'Go and have a lie down, Bridget. You'll feel better for a sleep.'

She waited until Bridget had left, and then looked thoughtfully at the lemon drizzle cake. It smelt delicious. She looked at the clock. Four o'clock. Peter would probably still be in the flat.

'Hmm,' she said thoughtfully. 'I think it's time to tackle Peter.'

Twenty-Six

'Mary! What are you doing here?' said Lizzie. 'I didn't expect you back until after the funeral.'

Mary came into the shop with a bin bag full of clothes.

'These are Declan's. The dress suits have all just been dry cleaned.'

'Oh, Mary,' said Lizzie, and gave her a hug. 'Thank you – but isn't this too soon? You must be exhausted. Go home and have a rest.'

'Please let me stay, Lizzie,' said Mary. 'Deirdre has moved in, and if I'm at home all I have is Deirdre complaining to me about Tom and Tom ringing me or her, and Fran moping around the house. Noel is back in Switzerland until the funeral. He doesn't need to get caught up in Deirdre's drama. And Bridget keeps leaving me messages on the answerphone and I just can't ring her back. I'm still so angry with her. My family are driving me mad.'

'What's happening about the business?' said Lizzie.

'We have extended everybody's paid leave until after the funeral. Deirdre helped me send an email to everyone telling them about Declan's death, and the funeral. We have had lots of answers, so the cathedral should be packed. Poor Tom keeps on at me to give him the right to sign off financial deals, but I keep telling him that we are awaiting legal advice. I've been to see the solicitor Michael O'Driscoll, and told him I'm not keen for Tom to take over the running as yet, so he has suggested, after the funeral, calling the board together to discuss things. I don't know what to do, Lizzie. It's even worse than I suspected. Tom needs help, but he won't admit it, and he can't be allowed to have access to the finances, but I don't want that common knowledge. It's a good thing Declan was so controlling and did all of that himself.'

'Well, you've got some time then,' said Lizzie. 'Just let the funeral be over. You have enough to do.'

'But have I?' sighed Mary. 'Honestly, Declan prepared everything to the last detail. He even chose his coffin, and the undertakers have sorted out the crematorium. We have used the catering company so often that they know all about how to lay out the food. Honestly, Lizzie, just let me come and do some work. Please.'

'Well, if you are sure. We need to steam clean and price up lots of donations downstairs, or you could be on the till. What do you want to do?'

'I think I'll stay on the till until closing time and sort out another jigsaw, Lizzie, if that is OK. It will be nice just to put something together and make it all make sense.'

Two young women came in and bought some coats, and an elderly man asked for help choosing a novel which, he shyly explained, was for his wife who was ill in bed. Mary found a copy of *Light a Penny Candle* by Maeve Binchy and he went off happy.

Then Sinead and Rory came in.

'Mary! I was hoping you would be here!' said Sinead. 'Would you be able to visit my grandmother at all soon? She is delighted with the jigsaw, and she is very keen to meet you.'

'I'm a bit busy during next week, Sinead,' said Mary. 'But how about Saturday?'

She said nothing about Declan's death or the funeral. It would be good to visit someone who knew nothing about it.

'That would be great!' said Sinead, scribbling down her grandmother's address. 'How about ten a.m., a week tomorrow? I'll make sure I'm there to make you tea so you can have a good chat. Thanks so much, Mary. She will really appreciate a visit.'

'Peter, would you have time for a chat?' said Margaret, when he opened the door. As if to back up her request, there was a sudden rumble of thunder and a gust of wind blew rain against the windows of the flat. There would be no gardening for the rest of the day.

'Come in,' said Peter. 'Would you like a cup of tea, Margaret?'

'That would be lovely,' said Margaret. 'I've brought some lemon drizzle cake I made,' she added. Lord, I know that isn't strictly true, but you know why I need to say this – I will put this right, I promise.

'Grand. I'm partial to a bit of lemon drizzle cake,' said Peter, going through into the kitchen to make the tea.

Got you! thought Margaret, feeling rather like Miss Marple. She was glad to see that JJ had fallen asleep in his armchair, and was gently snoring. An empty mug and a plate with flapjack crumbs on the table in front of him showed he had had his tea. Her interrogation of Peter would be done without interruption.

She waited until Peter had smiled at her and taken his first bite of cake before she moved.

'That's delicious cake, Margaret,' he said. 'Compliments to the chef, as they say.'

'It was Bridget,' said Margaret. 'It was Bridget who made the cake. NOW what do you think of it?'

Peter opened his eyes wide and then shrugged. 'I don't know what you are talking about,' he said, pushing his chair a little back, and laughing rather unconvincingly.

'You do, Peter,' said Margaret. 'For some reason, you NEVER eat anything Bridget bakes, and yet you have just shown that you DO like cake.'

'What are we on? *Murder She Wrote*?' said Peter, trying to laugh it off. 'Is your name actually Jessica?'

'What's your problem with Bridget?' demanded Margaret.

'I don't know what you are talking about,' said Peter, but his gaze was a little too challenging. Margaret remembered that look all too well from years of teaching. Peter was lying, and she knew he knew she knew.

'We both know that's not true,' she said.

Please Lord, help, she prayed, and somehow, something shifted. There was a sudden change in the atmosphere of the room. There was peace, and there was pain.

Peter was silent for a moment. The room was getting darker, as raindrops fell like tiny pebbles against the windows, and JJ slept on.

'I knew her when we were young,' he said, slowly. 'She was older than me, but I grew up on the same island as her and her sister and JJ and Declan, and I came over to England to be with them, but she doesn't recognise me. Must be the beard. And how I've changed over the years. She's probably forgotten I even existed, to be honest,' he said bitterly.

'I don't understand. You behave as if she did you some great wrong. You weren't in love with her, or something?' said Margaret, bluntly.

'Not her!' said Peter. 'Her sister.'

'Mary?'

'Yes. I've loved her all my life. We were in the same class at school. I only came over to England aged sixteen because Bridget invited Mary to join her, and I couldn't bear to be parted from her. I didn't tell her what I felt – I was planning to make some money on the buildings and then ask her to marry me. We were both so innocent – we hadn't even officially gone out as boyfriend and girlfriend – but we were always a couple. Even as a young boy I knew I wanted to marry her – I even gave her a grass ring when we were children. She was always the one for me.

'She was so young. We were both so young. Even when we were both in England I thought I had time. Time to save, time to get things ready, to save up for a proper ring to put on her finger, diamond, not grass. Then suddenly, Bridget declared she was going to be a nun, and the next thing Mary and Declan were engaged, and it was too late. I had lost her.'

'But how was that Bridget's fault?' said Margaret.

'Mary was too young, Margaret. She was always a gentle girl, a very religious girl, unsure of herself. She idolised Bridget and Declan, and she would do anything to please her parents. Declan – well, you know yourself. Declan was a real force of Nature. An alpha male – and Bridget, for all her charm, or maybe because of all her charm, was the alpha female. She was bright and nice all right, but she always got what she wanted. They were the natural power couple – everyone expected them to marry – but in the end, Bridget didn't want

Declan. Oh no. She wanted the top man. Even Declan couldn't compete with God,' said Peter, bitterly.

Margaret winced at the bitterness.

'But Bridget always has to tidy things up so she is still in the right,' he continued, as if once he had started he didn't want to stop. 'She knew her parents had been made up she was marrying Declan, and they would have had a good son-in-law in their old age, so she kept it in the family, and conveniently matched her little sister off with her ex-fiancé. Only Mary wasn't like Bridget. She was quieter, more gentle, more easily dominated. But pretty too – prettier even, I would say, than Bridget, but without that charm.' He said the word 'charm' again with disdain, and Margaret bridled in defence.

'Peter – is all this shunning of Bridget because Mary married someone else decades ago? You do realise that Mary and Declan had a long marriage? Nearly fifty years! Ultimately, they must have been well matched,' said Margaret, carefully. She couldn't believe Peter had been holding this grudge for so long.

'You don't understand. Declan was what the family wanted, and she had a big crush on him. Mary was no rebel. Once she was married she was a good Catholic – she would never have left him. But she was never right for him.'

'But she was right for you?'

'I loved her,' he said simply. 'Declan just wanted a trophy wife. I've seen the photos in the papers over the years, the big man himself at different functions, with his lovely wife, and she never looked at ease, never. And he wasn't even faithful to her, especially in the early years – there were plenty of scandals and gossip, but Mary never left him. He didn't deserve her.'

Margaret shook her head. Nearly fifty years of unrequited

love and she didn't know whether to pity him or admire his faithfulness. 'Did you ever tell her you loved her?'

'How could I? Once Declan and Bridget decided she was wife material, I didn't have a chance. She was swept off her feet – her parents were delighted, everyone was pleased with her.'

'So the girl you loved married another man, and you've been blaming Bridget all these years?' said Margaret, still trying to understand.

'Not just any man. The man who ruined so many other people's lives by his greed, the man whose family got rich by exploiting their fellow countrymen in a strange land, and left them destitute on the street. I've spent my working life dealing with the destruction he and his uncle caused. I was in England picking up broken men from the streets and trying to help them, whilst he inherited a business and went home with money he should never have had. Oh yes, he went from strength to strength in Ireland, a pillar of the community.

'And yes, yes I DO blame Bridget, because she's one of those charming people who can afford to be nice because ultimately, they always get what they want in life.'

'Now, Peter, that's not fair,' began Margaret, in defence of her friend, but Peter was unstoppable.

'It IS fair, Margaret. She wanted to be a nun and for everyone to be pleased with her, and that's what she got. What she always gets. Nothing, and nobody else mattered. She didn't even know I loved her sister – I was just a young gossoon, a shy country lad when I arrived in England and she barely registered my existence, even though we were from the same island. She certainly didn't care about my feelings for Mary. It's no surprise to me that she doesn't even recognise me now.'

'But Peter . . . surely you can see this is so unreasonable? Bridget had a vocation,' said Margaret.

Help him, Lord. I can't believe he has let this eat away at him for all these years.

'I thought I had a vocation,' Peter burst out. 'First of all, to marry Mary, but when that couldn't be . . . I had a deep faith too, Margaret, like Mary and Bridget. Like you. My heart was broken, and I knew I could love no other woman, but I thought maybe God wouldn't give me Mary because he wanted me to be a priest. So I told everyone I was going back to Ireland to be a priest, went back home, convinced myself and Father Brendan I had a vocation (I never mentioned the extent of my feelings for Mary to him – and anyway, she was a married woman by then) and, in due time applied to the seminary.'

'And what happened?'

'They accepted me. Off I went, aged eighteen. Everyone was delighted. My parents were proud, and for a while I was at peace. I prayed and turned out to be a good scholar, and I was given opportunities I would never have had with my background. I was even sent to Rome for the last years of my studies. I'm an expert in Canon Law, you know?'

'I had no idea,' said Margaret.

'I loved Italy. I loved the people, the land, the language, the architecture. It was like a dream for a boy from the island. I never forgot Mary, but I could pray for her, and I was happy. There were some people – some tutors – I didn't feel at ease with – and have learnt since I was justified in that instinct – but maybe I was protected. I was still innocent and naïve, and thought the best of everyone, never one to gossip, so I was out of any cliques, and I was nobody's "favourite". I was ordained in Rome – my parents and sisters came over – and then I went back to Ireland for a year in a parish, and then they sent me over to England, to a big London parish. I met

267

Hugh when I was there – he was a curate in the next parish, and we became friends.'

'Oh, I didn't know that's how you knew each other,' said Margaret.

'I started working as a priest with the Irish men on the streets, and my eyes were opened. These were fellow Catholics. Trusting, naïve, inexperienced country boys like me, who had been cheated by savvier men like Declan, who nobody criticised because he was "in" with all the right people in the Church. And I started hearing stories from them, and even some of my fellow priests, about bad things going on in seminaries, and Magdalene Laundries, and Christian Brother Homes back in Ireland. I knew JJ had been at the home in Letterfrack, for example, and I had an idea it had been hard, but I met men who told me just how hard it was, and though JJ never talked about it, I could see how hurt he had been by them. And I just couldn't make it link up – my faith with all the abuse and the secrecy. And I started seeing Mary and Declan in pictures in the papers, and then they were at a big Church fundraising event over in London, and as soon as I saw her in the distance, I knew I hadn't forgotten her at all.'

'Did you tell Hugh?'

'Not so much about Mary – she was a married woman after all – but I talked for hours with Hugh about the Church. He IS a good priest, and a great friend. He has such deep faith – he always has had – but, I don't know, Margaret, mine just went. Nothing Hugh said could bring it back. I couldn't find God in the institution, and I found I didn't understand what had made me ever do so. All I could think about was how I had missed out on life with Mary, and I saw her with Declan, and how they had children, and how in spite of all his wrongdoing, Declan's career was going from strength to strength, and it seemed the God I had given up everything for was showering blessings on him. They were model Catholics, never missing Sunday Mass – they even met the Pope when he came to Ireland in seventy-nine, you know – and there I was, without Mary, without a wife, without children, working with broken men, and hearing more and more terrible stories about the Church I had given my life to, and I just wondered where God was in all this, and I just couldn't stand it any more.'

Twenty-Seven

'I started drinking,' said Peter. 'I couldn't stop. Hugh tried to help me, but it just got worse and worse. To be fair, in the end the Bishop offered help. They would have paid for me to go to a clinic – I wasn't the first priest with a drink problem – but I refused. I wanted nothing to do with them. I blamed the Church for everything. I walked out and spent some time on the streets myself. I hit rock bottom for a while. I knew my family in Ireland would be ashamed of me. But Hugh didn't give up on me. He looked for me, and got me to see I had a problem, and I went to AA. Hugh helped me get on my feet again, found me somewhere to live, and I ended up retraining as a social worker, and the rest, as they say, is history. I've spent my working life with the homeless, and Hugh and I have tried to help poor JJ, and that's why we've ended up here. I never expected to see Bridget and Declan ever again.'

The anger seemed to have gone out of the room. They both were quiet.

'Please forgive Bridget,' said Margaret, gently. 'She was just one person in your life, and it all happened so many years ago.

It's not fair to put all the blame on her. I know her. I've lived with her all these years. I can imagine how she tidied everything up, and how once she and Declan decided Mary was perfect for Declan, it was hard to stop it happening – but she was young. She thought she was doing the right thing. You were all young. You could have said something to Mary, Peter. Even when she was engaged. But you didn't.'

Peter nodded. 'No, I didn't,' he said slowly.

'And Bridget wasn't responsible for what happened in the seminary, or with Declan's business, or to the men on the street. She didn't abuse anyone. I know her. I know she is charming – but she is sincere – she really has spent a life trying to love God and be kind to people. You just have to go to parish bingo to see how much good she does. She knows how hard life has been – and often still is – for some of the people who go there. That's why she does her best to never cancel. She knows they rely on it. She doesn't ignore their pain. She plays Daniel O'Donnell and bakes them cakes to make them feel better, and safe, and to give them some fun and remind them of more innocent times, and it works – it cheers them up. Please, let go of this grudge against her. It's making you both miserable.'

Peter sighed. 'I'm not sure what is happening. I've been angry with her for so long, but now, suddenly here with you, I want to stop. But I'm still angry with Declan, even though he is dead, and I'm angry with Hugh, for giving him confession, so he died white as snow, after all the misery he caused. And believe me, he caused a LOT of misery.'

'But isn't it good, Peter, that Hugh helped him find mercy?' said Margaret, frowning, but her voice kind. 'Isn't that what we all, ultimately, need? Haven't you spent your whole life doing the same thing – helping desperate men find mercy?

You talk as if Bridget and Declan ruined your life – but it's so obvious how much Hugh respects and admires you. You have done so much good in your life, loved and helped so many. Look what you are doing for JJ.'

'Ah, JJ is a saint,' said Peter, and smiled. 'Being with him is an honour. He wanted to be called Jimmy so nobody could track him down and bring shame to his family. He has the sweetest soul in spite of everything he has been through. And I know he is praying for me, to find my faith again, to forgive and let go.'

'Peter. You are a good man. Even if you want nothing to do with the Church, it's obvious God has been and is working through you. But honestly, I have to tell you, you're being cruel to Bridget, and for both your sakes, you need to stop. She is devastated right now. Declan is dead and her only sister is angry with her and, it might sound silly, you refusing to eat what she bakes for you is the last straw. "Blessed are the Merciful, for They shall have Mercy shown them," Peter. "Forgive us our trespasses as we forgive those who trespass against us."'

'Thanks, Margaret,' said Peter. 'You've given me a lot to think about.'

'And pray, Peter. God is always there ready to listen.'

'Well, we'll see about that,' said Peter, wryly.

'And, for goodness' sake, eat Bridget's cake,' said Margaret, and smiled at him, as she got up and left. She had felt so furious when she arrived, but now only felt compassion and great liking for this quiet, principled man.

Bless him, Lord, she prayed. *Bring him healing of all his hurts. And make it all all right with Bridget.*

'I saw Peter at Mr Abidi's,' said Katy as they met for dinner. 'He was buying milk too. He sent a message to you, Sister

272

Bridget. He said to tell you he was going to take JJ to bingo next week, and he hoped he would win one of your cakes.'

'Really?' said Bridget, her tired face lighting up. 'We must tell him it is Wednesday, not Thursday.'

Thank you, God, prayed Margaret.

'That's good news that Peter and JJ are coming, isn't it, Bridget?' said Margaret.

'Very good,' replied Bridget, emotionally. 'What is Peter's favourite cake, I wonder?'

'Your coffee and hazelnut cake is my favourite,' said Katy. 'I've never tasted anything like it.'

'Well, he enjoyed a slice of your lemon drizzle cake this afternoon,' said Margaret, 'I'm sure he'd like anything you make. But he'll have to win it first!'

'*Nollaig na mBan Sona Daoibh* – Happy Women's Christmas to you all!' said a cheery woman to Sinead and Rory as they were leaving the shop, and Lizzie, who had just come up from the basement.

'I want that feather boa in the window. I'm going to wear that tonight, and put my feet up whilst the men wait on me hand and foot! That's a tradition I firmly believe in!'

'I'd forgotten about Women's Christmas!' said Sinead. 'I'll have to tell Rory and his daddy all about it!'

'You do that!' said the woman approvingly, as Sinead and little Rory left. 'Now, I hope you ladies have a good evening planned!'

'Sure, why wouldn't we?' said Lizzie, easily, passing the boa to the woman and taking a pound in exchange. 'Now, behave yourself tonight. Don't go wild and make a show of yourself! I don't want to read about you in the papers tomorrow!'

The woman laughed as if Lizzie had paid her the greatest compliment ever.

'Thanks a million, girls!' she said, winding the boa, still with the ticket attached, around her neck, and sailed out of the shop.

'Any plans, Mary?' said Lizzie, sympathetically.

Mary made a face. 'Well, there are only women in my home at the moment, unless Tom comes round again begging Deirdre to forgive him – but it's not very Christmassy. It's been nice to be out of the house this afternoon, and I'm not looking forward to going home, to be honest.'

'I know with Declan and everything this might be . . . but would you like to come back to my house for a drink when we close up, Mary?' said Lizzie. 'I don't have anything on – I thought I'd be meeting Aidan, but we both forgot it was Women's Christmas, and his mother took it into her head he should go and cook her a meal.' She made a face. 'I don't think she is quite ready to welcome another woman to join her – at least, not one she sees as breaking up her son's marriage. And before you say anything – I didn't, Mary. They were separated already.'

'You know what, Lizzie? I would LOVE to have a little bit of Women's Christmas with you. Even if there will be no men to wait on us!' said Mary, a great sense of relief filling her. 'I will ring home and tell them not to worry – but I tell you something – I'm not inviting them to join us!'

Lizzie's small flat was warm and welcoming. It was full of colour and sweet smells of incense. She had incense burners and pottery candle holders and statues on her mantelpiece, and bright rugs and throws and flourishing houseplants, and books – novels and poetry and self-help and psychology – in bookcases and on the coffee table. There was a tie-dye throw on the wall, and no signs of religious pictures like The Sacred Heart, or statues of Our Lady, but there was a St Bridget's Cross on the wall and little brass figures of the Buddha and of a beautiful many-armed Hindu goddess sitting on a lion on the mantelpiece. Lizzie noticed Mary looking at it.

'Aidan brought it back for me from India,' she said. 'The Goddess Durga – she is a beautiful divine mother and defeats demons.'

Mary smiled at her. 'I'd say she would be a good woman to have at your side, all right,' she said.

'I have a little statue of Mary by my bed as well, though,' said Lizzie, her eyes rather pleading. 'And Aidan says he is bringing me a statue of St Bridget.'

'Lizzie – thank you for inviting me here,' said Mary, sitting down on a bright red sofa amongst multicoloured bright cushions. The whole flat was so different from her tasteful house, and although her and Declan's home had hosted some expensively catered dinner parties over the years, for Mary this tiny flat felt so much more genuinely hospitable. She sighed deeply. 'I can't tell you how good it is NOT to be home. Deirdre is very upset about Declan, of course, but she can't stop going on about the cottage, and Tom keeps ringing, and Fran just stays in her room all the time. Declan micro-managed his own funeral so much I feel like there is nothing for me to do apart from turn up.'

'What will be done about the cottage?' said Lizzie, passing Mary a glass of wine.

Mary sighed. 'I haven't promised anything. At first I thought I had to give it to JJ – it was Declan's wish, but Deirdre was furious about that. Then I thought to myself, well, Declan was wrong, it wasn't his to give, and I said to Bridget that JJ could stay there as long as he wanted, but I wasn't going to give it to him outright, and Bridget was shocked. Sure, the poor man is at death's door, according to Bridget, so he won't be living there long, and I don't want him leaving it to Bridget. I could just imagine that happening. But I can't help feeling guilty. I did promise Declan I would give it him outright. I never got to take that back. And then I feel so angry with Declan for putting me in this position, and how the cottage was mine and it wasn't his to give away – and that's the worst thing of all. And then I feel angry with myself for being such a terrible wife – such a terrible widow.'

She took the tissues sympathetically handed her by Lizzie, wiped her eyes and blew her nose.

'Sorry. I'm not much company.'

'Ah, don't be silly, Mary! You mustn't judge yourself,' said Lizzie. 'Sure, you're still in shock.'

'You know, I've been very hard on you, Lizzie, about things. I'm sorry. And what you said about Aidan and his wife getting married too young, and getting an annulment – I keep thinking about it. I feel so awful, as Declan is not even in his grave, but I keep thinking – were *we* too young? It was a long marriage, but was it good? Surely if it was, I'd be heartbroken now, instead of angry. I feel so angry, Lizzie. I keep wishing I had had the guts to have that row with Declan and tell him I wanted to keep the cottage. Surely, if I was a good wife, I wouldn't be wishing I had rowed more with him? I've hardly cried at all since he died. It's like I am sadder about losing the cottage than losing Declan, and I am so ashamed.'

'I don't think feelings work like that, Mary,' said Lizzie, thoughtfully. 'I don't think it's the house instead of Declan – it's what the house stands for. It stands for all your hopes and future creativity. You're a great painter, Mary. And of course you miss Declan. I just think it's too early to be analysing all your feelings at the moment. Just get the funeral over – things will be better then. You can always go to bereavement counselling. I can get you names of good people I know.'

'You're a good girl, Lizzie. A good, wise woman,' said Mary. 'You're like a daughter to me. I can't think of a better person to celebrate *Nollaig na mBan* with.'

Deirdre was out when Mary got back home, and Fran was up in her room, listening to music. It was very loud. Mary lit a tea light in front of the crib. The Three Wise Men were there, visiting Jesus. Women's Christmas. Not really, judging from the crib at least. The shepherds were all men. Our Lady was the only woman in the scene, unless you counted the angel, who certainly appeared very feminine, although the only names of angels which sprang to Mary's mind – Michael, Gabriel, Raphael, were all very masculine. She tried to pray.

'Hail, Holy Queen, Mother of Mercy,' she began, looking at the young mother gazing at her baby Jesus, but instead of continuing with the prayer, she had a sudden conviction that she should go upstairs and check on Fran.

She knocked at the door, and eventually, after knocking several times, the music was turned down, and Fran opened the door, her face mutinous but tear-stained, her Goth eyeliner running and making her look even younger and more vulnerable.

'Hello, Fran. Just wondering if you would like some hot chocolate? I was feeling like watching something good on TV, and I would appreciate the company. I have *The Muppets Christmas Carol* on DVD. Your grandad used to enjoy that – do you remember?'

At that Fran's mutinous face changed, and she threw herself into her grandmother's arms, crying.

'Everything is horrible. Mum and Dad are so angry with each other and Grandad is dead, and . . .' she sobbed.

'Sssh, now. Everything will be all right, *alanna*,' soothed Mary, holding her grandchild in her arms, glad to be the comforter. 'Come downstairs and spend the rest of Women's Christmas with me.'

'I know it's Epiphany, but it seems a shame to take down the crib,' said Katy, thoughtfully, after Night Prayer. 'Didn't they use to keep it up until the 2nd of February in medieval times?'

'I'd be happy to do that,' said Margaret. 'I feel as if I still have things to learn from Christmas.'

'I'd like to keep it,' said Bridget, emotionally. 'We can move it out of the dining room and into the chapel. So much has happened I haven't had time to just be quiet and look at the crib.'

'Well, I see no reason why we shouldn't keep it here until the Feast of the Presentation,' said Sister Cecilia. 'Especially as it was the custom for the medieval church. Perhaps we can take down the Christmas tree though? Pangur and that other kitten have not been very good with it, and I have caught both of them climbing it several times this past week. A bauble was broken. I had to have words with Emily the other day.'

Oh dear, thought Margaret. Not more 'words'. Poor Em. Funny how you know that 'words' like that are never nice ones. And it's Em, not Emily, and Kylie, not 'that other kitten'.

'I do feel the new kitten is a bad influence,' continued Cecilia. 'Pangur never climbed Christmas trees before she came.'

'I think, to be fair, he did, Cecilia,' Margaret corrected gently.

Cecilia nodded. 'Perhaps. All I know is that when Pangur was on his own he was content to stay with me doing our tasks, working in the library et cetera, but now he seems to be always off getting into trouble. There are times when I do not know where he is.'

'But he always comes back, doesn't he?' said Katy. 'Look – here he is now!'

And it was true. Pangur was there winding himself around Sister Cecilia's legs, purring. Margaret saw her expression change, and her stern features relax into a besotted smile, which she quickly suppressed.

'Well, I'm off to bed. Good night, everyone,' she said, and set off upstairs, pretending to ignore the faithful little cat following her to bed, as always.

Sunday 7th January 1996

Twenty-Eight

The next evening, after the final Sunday Mass celebrating the Feast of the Baptism of the Lord, Margaret and Katy made a head start on changing the colours of the cloths in the church, on the altar, on the lectern and in front of the tabernacle, from white to green.

'It's strange that the time now after Christmastide is called Ordinary Time,' said Katy. They were in the sacristy, folding and putting away all the white cloths in the drawer. 'Really, it was anything but ordinary for Mary and Jesus and Joseph. They were running away from King Herod, escaping to Egypt. I don't call that ordinary. I'd hope not, anyway.'

'I think "ordinary", in this sense, isn't about things being run of the mill or unremarkable,' said Margaret. 'It's just about ordinal numbers as opposed to cardinal numbers, chronology rather than quantity – it means ordering or counting weeks until the next important season, like Lent, or Eastertide, or Advent and Christmas, but it doesn't mean that nothing important happens in between. In that sense, no day is ordinary, because every day is special.'

'Well, I like the colour green, anyway,' said Katy. 'Green for new growth. Like Gerard Manley Hopkins says in "God's Grandeur": "nature is never spent; / There lives the dearest freshness deep down things." I know he doesn't talk about green as such, but that's what I imagine dearest freshness to be.'

Margaret looked out the window. 'It's ironic that we're changing everything from white to green, and there is snow forecast for the next week. I hope it doesn't affect our journey to the funeral.'

On her way home, Margaret decided to call in at Mr Abidi's, in case the snow started suddenly and they ran out of things for the B&B. She bought some eggs and milk and bread and butter and flour for the Monday breakfast and went to the till, where Sarah was queuing in front of her.

'Thank you for putting the nail varnish remover on that poor Irish lady's fingers,' said Mr Abidi to Sarah. 'I told her when I sold it to her that superglue was very dangerous, but she was in a big rush. That was a very upset person, I said to myself after she bought it. I asked myself, was I right to sell it to her? I was very sorry to see she had the accident so quickly, but glad to see you come in with her.'

'She's fine. I got the nail varnish remover on her very quickly. It's a good thing you stock it.'

'I will never NOT stock it now,' said Mr Abidi. 'For as long as I sell superglue I will always sell nail varnish remover beside it. I should never have sold it to her in that state. Some purchases should not be done in haste. I said to Mrs Abidi that I will never sell superglue in a rush to anyone again, whatever they have broken.'

Even if it is a church statue, thought Margaret, with a flash of inspiration, suddenly absolutely sure who the upset Irish lady was, and why, exactly, she had smelt nail varnish at the panto-mime. She didn't want to ask Sarah or Mr Abidi for the name of the person who had got in a mess with the superglue, because the roles of nurse and corner shopkeeper both car-ried a certain duty of confidentiality – if not exactly of the confessional, very close to it. She knew Mr Abidi would never gossip about anything someone bought, any more than Sarah would talk about her patients' treatments. She realised, how-ever, that she didn't need to ask. *Peter was right, I AM Jessica Fletcher from* Murder She Wrote! she thought to herself. *Maybe I have missed my vocation! Would Father Hugh employ me as a parish sleuth, I wonder? What more mysteries can I uncover?* She smiled to herself, amused at the thought. 'Ordinary Time' didn't look like it was going to be that ordinary after all!

Ordinary Time

Twenty-Nine

The next few January days were very busy for the Sisters. It was cold, but there were no snow showers, and all the parents and sixth-form students, booked into the B&B for the open days at Fairbridge University, still managed to get there. Pangur and Kylie were a big hit, and comforted and amused the guests, young and old. When the nuns were at Mass the cats ran up and down the stairs and along the corridors of the B&B together, and at least there was no Christmas tree to tempt them any more, but when Sister Cecilia came back she was driven to picking Pangur up and separating him from Kylie, who then tried to follow them to the laundry, where her attempts to get in were firmly ignored by Sister Cecilia, or to the library, where she sat and mewed outside for her playmate until she was distracted by guests, who couldn't wait to fuss her. Em was both proud of how popular Kylie was with the guests, and annoyed at Sister Cecilia for her treatment of her.

'How could anyone not love you, Kylie?' she whispered, stroking her cat. 'Silly old Sister C.'

Pangur, for his part, was relaxed about being separated

from his sister. When he was with Kylie, he enjoyed it very much, but when he was with Sister Cecilia, he was very content. He had the gift of happiness in all situations, and Sister Cecilia let him pat her rosary beads when she prayed, and gave him catnip mice, and, when nobody was looking, had all sorts of toys for them to play with in the library. She even let him sleep on her lap.

Sister Bridget was very busy with the B&B all week, and a model host, but Margaret noticed she was getting more stressed as the days went on. She saw how Bridget asked if there had been any calls from Ireland, and constantly checked the answering machine for messages, and how her face fell when there were none. Margaret also noticed that Peter and Bridget were still awkward with each other, neither keen to talk when they happened to pass each other. Bridget looked nervous, but Peter was politer and smilier than normal, so Margaret's talk did seem to have had some good effect, although he was still not exactly chatty.

Thirty

And so Wednesday 10th January came, and in the morning Bridget made two bigger-than-normal chocolate and hazelnut cakes, and lots of fairy cakes. She chose a non-Christmassy Daniel O'Donnell album, and when they set off for bingo, she handed Katy and Margaret some pots full of flowering hyacinth bulbs to cheer up the hall. It might not be Christmas any more, but Bridget still wanted the evening to be special for her regulars.

They set up the hall as usual, and then they had two special visitors.

'We've come to bingo, Sister!' said a beaming JJ as he arrived in his wheelchair, pushed by Peter.

'Chris lent me his van. I thought we would come and see if we can win one of your famous cakes!' said Peter.

'Oh, you're very, very welcome,' said Bridget, fervently.

Margaret caught Peter's eye. They smiled at each other, and she noticed that he looked like some burden had been lifted from him. It wasn't only Bridget who was happier for this visit.

Bridget waited until everyone had arrived and settled until she personally went around the tables, giving out the pens and bingo cards.

Thank you, God, prayed Margaret. *Peter has made the first step. I think this afternoon will really help things move on. Poor Bridget has been so anxious. She really needs a rest. She's heading for a breakdown at this rate.*

Daniel O'Donnell worked his magic, and the regulars enjoyed a dance. Everyone looked very pleased to be there. Margaret noticed Maura from church and George's mother getting on very well, and wasn't quite sure if that was good or not. *That's either two difficult lonely people who will be nicer because they have made friends, or two difficult people who will be double trouble,* thought Margaret. *I think I might have to keep an eye on that friend-ship.* It was funny, she thought, once a teacher always a teacher. People were fundamentally the same, whatever age, and some people never grew out of trouble making, or taking their misery out on others.

It was time for Bridget to call the numbers. Margaret hoped she was the only person who was noticing the unusual strain and nervous tension in her voice. Bridget was almost feverish in the way she called the numbers until . . .

'HOUSE!' called Peter, sounding surprised. Everyone clapped the fortunate new player.

That's perfect! Thank you, God, prayed Margaret. *I would never have asked you to fix it like that, but I am glad you did!*

'Beginner's luck!' called the young Baptist minister good-naturedly, as Peter, looking tall and distinguished, with his grey beard, stood up, smiling.

'Come and choose your cake!' said Bridget, her voice, to Margaret's ears, sounding just that little bit higher than normal.

Peter walked to the front, choosing one of the delicious chocolate and hazelnut cakes.

'You're lucky mate – they look especially good this week!' someone else called. 'They must be bigger on a Wednesday!'

'Thank you,' he said to Sister Bridget. 'I'll enjoy that.'

Margaret beamed over at Bridget at the perfect conclusion to the bingo game, but was surprised and concerned to see how Bridget looked very upset, as if she was going to cry. She got up from her seat and went over to her.

'Bridget – are you OK?' she said.

Bridget shook her head. Margaret put one arm around her shoulders, then spoke into the microphone.

'Sorry everyone – Sister Bridget isn't feeling very well.'

There was a buzz of concern around the hall.

'I can take over,' said Katy, and went over to the microphone. 'Now everyone, I will take over for Sister Bridget, but you are going to have to help me, I'm afraid. What is it we say? "Eyes down for a full house"? So the first number is eleven – what is that?'

'Legs eleven!' shouted someone helpful from the back, and someone daring did a wolf whistle.

'Yes, well, moving swiftly on,' said Katy, blushing a little.

Margaret led Bridget to the back of the hall and into the kitchen. They could hear the crowd helpfully assisting Katy, who was bravely continuing to call the numbers. The crowd seemed to have warmed to her.

'Oh Margaret, I have done a very wicked thing!' said Bridget, bursting into tears as soon as they got inside the kitchen.

'I THOUGHT so! Didn't I tell you, Maura?' came George's mum's triumphant voice, as she stood with Maura in the doorway.

'Excuse me? This is a private conversation!' said Margaret, but George's mum continued:

'You fixed the bingo, using the trick you did at the party, didn't you?' she accused Bridget, her eyes fixed on her.

Bridget started weeping.

'Please leave us alone. Now. You should not be here,' said Margaret, angrily, trying to keep her voice low so nobody else would overhear.

'Did she or did she not fix the bingo?' said George's mum, refusing to be deflected. Maura stood beside her, looking delighted at the drama.

Margaret felt a wild fury overcome her. *God, help me!*

'How dare you?' she hissed. 'Do you want to ruin Bridget and close down the bingo with these very serious accusations? Do you?'

'No,' said George's mum, defensively. 'But it's not fair. I've wanted to win a cake for ages. Sister Bridget never has time to bake them or sell them. Bingo is our only chance. And now she has fixed it so your new friend could have his pick. That's not right. Maura agrees.'

Maura nodded.

'I think,' added George's mum, greatly daring, 'if Sister Bridget is giving cakes to her friends like that, I should get one too. I have a friend from school coming to visit soon . . .'

'Don't say ANYTHING, Bridget,' warned Margaret, then put her chin up and glared at the two women, a cold fury in her eyes that they had never seen before and were taken aback by.

'Let me make this QUITE clear to both of you. If either of you so much as breathe a word of these suspicions to anyone else outside this kitchen, then, so help me God, you will regret it. For a start, you will NEVER ever come back to bingo again, or ANY parish activities where the Sisters of St Philomena help out, and, let's face it, we help out at everything.'

'But—' began Bridget.

'Be quiet, Bridget!' snapped Margaret, and continued, her eyes fixed on George's mum.

'If you say anything about this to anyone, I will tell George and Matthew how you tried to extort a cake, with threats, from the kindest nun you could ever meet, who has helped your son and his partner so much. A nun who has been so good to them – and to you – and who is very upset and not her usual self because her brother-in-law in Ireland has just died. Shame on you!'

George's mum had the grace to look ashamed, and Margaret felt she had to make sure this was nipped in the bud.

'Furthermore,' said Margaret, in a flash of inspiration, 'I will also tell your son and his partner that you are best buddies with the woman who told them that they were disgusting for holding hands in the theatre lobby, which has made Matthew not want to go out in public with your son any more.'

George's mum turned on Maura. 'Is this true?' she said angrily.

'No, yes – I didn't know,' spluttered Maura. 'I didn't know who they were.'

'How dare you! My son can hold hands with whomever he wants,' said George's mum, furiously. 'YOU are the disgusting one!' She took a step away from Maura, and refused to look at her.

Maura opened her mouth to speak, but Margaret got in there first.

'And as for you, Maura – I have three things to say to

you – St Joseph, superglue and nail varnish remover. How ARE your fingers by the way?' Maura turned pale.

'So,' Margaret continued, pressing home her advantage, 'there will be NO further gossip outside this kitchen about fixed bingo games or anything like that. Do I make myself perfectly clear? Now go back out there and report that Sister Bridget is not feeling well, her brother-in-law in Ireland has died and she is very upset. That is ALL you will say. Agreed? Can I have your solemn promise? And remember, you only have baseless speculation and no proof – but I know things about you I will not hesitate to divulge. I am not bound by any seal of confession, you may be sure.'

Both women, not looking at each other, nodded.

'Now please, leave the kitchen and go back to your seats whilst I help Sister Bridget,' said Margaret. 'I want to never have to speak about this with either of you again.'

Margaret waited until the door closed behind them and then put out her hand to the wall to steady herself. She leant against it for a minute, feeling rather wobbly.

'Phew. I hope that worked,' she said in her normal voice. 'I feel a bit bad I had to drive a wedge between them like that, but I didn't want them egging each other on and spreading gossip. What on earth came over you, Bridget?'

'I'm so, so sorry, Margaret,' said Bridget, in a very small, lost voice which completely melted Margaret's heart. 'I don't know what came over me. I just wanted Peter to win the cake so much, and I remembered the party trick, and I gave in to temptation . . .'

'Come here,' said Margaret, taking pity on her. 'Let me give you a hug. Everything will be all right. Stay there, Bridget, whilst I make an announcement.'

Margaret made her way to the microphone. She noticed, out of the corner of her eye, that George's mum and Maura were not sitting together any more. *Good,* she thought.

'Sister Bridget is going home. She is not well.' There was a sympathetic buzz from the hall. 'As you know, she has had a recent family bereavement – the funeral is Friday – and everything has got too much for her. So I will take her home now, and if you can keep supporting our wonderful young Katy here, I will be back to help clear up at the end. I'm sure you will all want to wish Sister Bridget well as we travel to Ireland tomorrow.' Everyone clapped.

'Are you OK?' mouthed Margaret to Katy.

'Fine,' mouthed Katy back, and put her thumbs up.

Thank you God for Katy. She's a wonderful addition to our community, prayed Margaret gratefully. She went back down the hall to the kitchen to escort a tear-stained Sister Bridget home, as Katy started calling the next game.

'I'll have to go to confession about it,' said Bridget, as they walked home, arms linked.

'Well, I'm sure Father Hugh will be happy to hear your confession,' said Margaret, 'but I think the first thing you need to do is accept you are not well. You are so stressed and worn out. Why was it so important to you that Peter won the cake?'

'Because he said he hoped he would,' said Bridget.

'But everyone who goes to St Philomena's bingo hopes they will win one of your cakes. Peter only said he wanted to win it to show you he liked your baking, because I told him you were getting upset that he wasn't eating your cakes.'

'I didn't know,' said Bridget.

'I realise that. I should have told you I spoke to him. I tackled him about it because I could see you were getting very down,' said Margaret, 'and so I know he was trying to tell you he would eat your cakes, not hinting about winning.'

'I just wanted Peter to like me, I suppose.'

'But Bridget – you're seventy! You must have met someone who didn't like you before?' said Margaret.

'Not really, Margaret. People who don't like nuns, yes, but that's not personal, and I can normally win them round. But not me personally. Peter doesn't like me, Margaret, me, personally, and I don't know what I have done.'

I'll have to get Peter to talk to her directly. I can't just tell Bridget what I know, Margaret thought.

'I do feel I have let poor JJ down about the cottage. And Mary is so cross with me,' Bridget's voice wobbled. 'Everything is so awful, and I got fixated on Peter telling me he wanted to win a cake and I suddenly realised that was one good thing I could make happen. Only it wasn't good. Not the way I did it. What was I thinking? I must be going mad. Mad and bad.'

'Oh Bridget, you're neither. You're just really, really tired,' said Margaret, as they reached the B&B. 'I'm sending you to bed now. You need a good sleep before we go to Ireland tomorrow.'

'I haven't even organised about bingo next week,' worried Bridget.

'We'll ask Katy to help out again. The people will understand. They can do without you for a week,' Margaret reassured her, as she hugged her goodnight.

When Margaret returned to the hall everything was nearly cleared up. Maura had gone but her heart sank to see George's mother still there.

'May I have a word?' said George's mum, as soon as she saw Margaret.

'All right,' said Margaret, warily. 'Shall we go to the kitchen?'

Help me! I don't have the energy to put on another threatening show, prayed Margaret swiftly.

Luckily, none was needed.

'I wanted to say that I am very sorry,' said George's mum, after Margaret had closed the door and made sure the shutters were down and nobody was near enough to overhear. 'I don't want to hurt Sister Bridget. I don't care about the cake. I was being ridiculous. I am very grateful to her for being so kind to my son. And if that horrible Maura ever brings up the subject of the Christmas trick, which I very much regret telling her about, then I shall immediately deny I ever said anything and will happily tell anyone who asks that Maura is a liar.'

'Well. I don't think it will come to that,' said Margaret, hastily, remembering Maura's pale face when she mentioned the superglue. 'But I accept your apology. Sister Bridget is very tired and upset, but I'm sure once we get back from Ireland and the funeral, things will get back to normal.'

'When George's father died, I was not myself either. As far as I'm concerned, nothing happened in this hall. Please tell Sister Bridget that I am sorry. And that I am grateful to her for looking after George and Matthew, and getting them to Ireland together. And tell her that if Maura tries to cause any trouble about bingo I will crush her without mercy.'

Poor Maura, thought Margaret, surprising herself.

Later that night, alone in the chapel after Night Prayers, Margaret did not feel at peace.

What else could I have done, Lord? she prayed. *I couldn't have let it get out that Bridget had cheated. I had to threaten them. Bingo does so much good, for so many people. I couldn't let Maura and George's mother ruin everything. Bridget has done so much for the parish, and she has enough to worry about right now.*

But she left the chapel before she could hear an answer she didn't want to hear.

Thirty-One

In spite of the forecast, snow had not yet fallen in Fairbridge by the next afternoon when George and Matthew, Peter and JJ, and Bridget and Margaret set off for Knock. The pilot announced, as the plane started to descend, that it was 'a grand, soft day' and they were met, not with snow, but with wet misty weather, cold enough that they were glad to get into the heated people carrier George had hired and make the short drive to the warm, clean, bright hotel they had booked in the centre of Knock. It was a particularly bright and particularly Catholic hotel, full of religious pictures, and photographs of superstars associated with the pilgrimage centre – one of Pope John Paul II, who had visited there in 1979, raised the status of Knock Church to a basilica, and donated a golden rose, one of Monsignor James Horan, who was responsible for the building of Knock Airport, which opened in 1985, and one of Mother Teresa.

'"Jesus came to give us the good news that God loves us, and that he wants us to love one another as He loves each one of us." Mother Teresa, Knock Basilica, 1993,' quoted George.

'It's the truth,' agreed JJ, his face illumined with faith, and everyone with him was struck by how simply lovely he was, and what a miracle it was that his sweet nature had survived all the suffering in his life.

Please may he be happy on the island. Please may Mary be good to him, prayed Bridget. *He deserves it, Lord.*

'And look who's here, Sister Bridget!' said George. Next to a framed and signed picture of Dana, the singer, was one of Daniel O'Donnell, which appeared to be up there more because of the fandom of the hotelier, rather than any specific links with Knock itself, though the lady assured them that he had been there, and was a man of great faith.

'Sure, I love him!' said the lady running the hotel. 'My husband has bought me tickets for his concert in Dublin later this year.'

'He really is everywhere!' said George quietly to Margaret, who smiled.

They sat down for a hearty meal of cabbage and boiled bacon and potatoes, a menu choice popular with returning emigrants on pilgrimage from America.

'Would you like to hear Dana sing "Our Lady of Knock"?' asked the helpful hostess, and they ate ice cream and apple tart whilst listening to a recording of the hymn.

'I want to get up early and pray at the Apparition Chapel, before leaving for the funeral,' said Bridget to Margaret, when the hymn was finished.

'I'd like to join you,' said JJ.

'We will too,' said Matthew. 'George will be up, of course.'

'Are you sure?' said Margaret. 'I feel like we're imposing our religion on you. It must be the first time you've had to listen to a hymn when you were eating your dessert.'

'Not at all,' said Matthew, courteously. 'I feel it is all part of the cultural experience. We are, after all, at a pilgrimage site.'

'Well, you're very good,' said Margaret, and meant it.

In Fairbridge, Sister Cecilia had gone outside after lunch to find Chris, and ask his help in fixing a door which would not close. Chris was working in an outhouse, and Pangur followed her out into the garden as the first snow began to fall. He jumped and swiped at the falling snowflakes, shaking his paws in indignation as they landed on him, miaowing loudly, and followed Sister Cecilia back quickly into the warm convent.

'Sensible boy,' she praised him, and he stayed close to her the rest of the evening and night, as the snow fell faster and faster, and covered everything outside with a carpet of white.

In Knock on Friday morning, Bridget and Margaret got up early with George and Matthew and JJ and Peter, and they all went to the Apparition Chapel.

'This is, in fact, the original gable of the parish church,' said Matthew, consulting his guide book. 'It's somehow very moving that the apparition was seen, not inside, but outside the church, on this gable wall, on a wet dark August evening in 1879. Apparently it lasted for two hours, in the pouring rain, witnessed by the villagers of Knock. The statues are of the Virgin Mary, St Joseph, St John the Evangelist, and the Lamb of God on an altar surrounded by angels. They were carved in Italy in 1960, from Carrara marble, by a Professor Lorenzo Ferri, carefully replicating the apparition as described by the witnesses. The Pope blessed the statues in September 1979.'

'Thank you, Matthew,' said Bridget. She and Margaret knelt and prayed in the quiet chapel, and Peter wheeled JJ up beside the statues, whilst Matthew and George stood at the door. It was quiet and peaceful inside. Already rain had started to fall, but unlike the original witnesses, they were in the dry, sheltered from the elements by glass walls.

Thank you for this apparition appearing outside the building, prayed Margaret. *Thank you for being there for humble, ordinary people, living hard lives. And bless JJ, and bless Matthew and George, who really are outside the church, but are so kind to us. May they see you too – or at least, may they see you through us.*

And I am sorry again about how I spoke to Maura and George's mother. I know I was right to stand up for Bridget, but I don't feel good about the threats. I just don't know what to do. What if I go and apologise to Maura, and she takes revenge by telling everyone? Please help.

Please come with us to the funeral and then to the island, prayed Bridget. *Bless my sister, and grant eternal rest to poor Declan.*

'I'm sorry to tear you away like this and put a big journey on you, George,' said Bridget, as they drove off for Galway and her sister's.

'Oh, no trouble,' said George. 'Matthew is very keen to study the Irish stained glass in Knock parish church,' he said, 'So he is happy. And JJ has already sorted out Mass, and they are going to the basilica, and want to look at the museum. They have a full morning planned, and I'll be back for lunch. Mrs McShane back at the hotel says JJ can have a rest in the afternoon before we come and collect you. I did like that chapel – there was something about it – but I'm happier in a car than a church, to be honest. I'm enjoying being in Ireland, and glad to help.' George smiled at Bridget. The rain fell heavier against the car windows, and the three of them sat in easy silence, as the windscreen wipers rhythmically swiped from side to side, and the car sped on towards Galway and Declan's funeral. George thought of how recently he had driven Declan and Bridget from Fairbridge to the airport, and how quickly lives can change, and glanced over at the little Irish nun he loved so much. She looked terribly sad. He was glad she had Margaret as a support.

'Look at Kylie and Pangur!' said Em to Chris. 'Aren't they sweet?' The two kittens were sitting on the windowsill together, mesmerised by the falling snow, reaching up and patting the glass as if to catch the snowflakes. Katy and Cecilia had wrapped up warmly and strode out to morning Mass as usual. Nothing – not even a snow blizzard – would stop Sister Cecilia getting to Mass. Bad weather increased her resolution, and she and Katy had set off together in good humour.

'Rather you than me,' said Em, as they put on their wellingtons and gloves ready to go out.

'It's fun. I feel like we're real pilgrims,' said Katy cheerfully, and Sister Cecilia nodded in agreement as they set off into the flurries of snow.

Thirty-Two

The funeral was over. The church had been packed with the great and the good. Readings and hymns and a Requiem Mass, celebrated by the Bishop, with many other priests concelebrating, had been offered up for Declan's soul. Saints and angels had been implored to come to Declan's aid and lead him into Paradise. Only Bridget and Margaret and his immediate family had gone to the crematorium. Tom had joined Deirdre and Fran and Noel, and Bridget was touched to see Deirdre turn and cry in Tom's arms when the coffin went behind the curtain.

Please help that marriage, she prayed. She longed to comfort Mary, who was standing, stiff backed and composed at the front, but was glad to see Noel take his mother's hand.

Back at Mary's home, there were crowds of people, many of whom had come to the house in the days before the funeral to offer their condolences, waiting to continue to commiserate with Mary, to mourn, but also to celebrate Declan's life as a successful businessman. Organised and uniformed catering staff passed round drinks and excellent sandwiches and canapés.

Margaret found herself looking at the clock more and more, counting down until George and the others would arrive. Her heart ached for Bridget. Deirdre had been very unfriendly to her aunt, barely acknowledging her, and Mary herself had been self-contained, pale and polite, barely crying at the funeral and withdrawn at the reception. Bridget had not had a moment with her.

'We should start saying our goodbyes, Bridget,' she said, interrupting Bridget, who was talking to a very friendly Martin and Nola O'Dowd. Leaving Bridget to apologetically disentangle herself from the conversation, and move over to hug Fran, Margaret went and looked for Mary, and found her in the kitchen with a crying Deirdre.

'Mary – Deirdre – I'm afraid we have to be off,' said Margaret.

'Oh. Thank you for coming, Margaret,' said Mary, automatically hugging her. Margaret could feel how tense she was. She wanted to say so much, to intervene on behalf of Bridget and make peace between the sisters, but it didn't seem the right place, especially with Deirdre there.

'Don't be a stranger,' was all she could come up with, praying that her words would somehow reach through the suffering. She hugged her harder, and for a moment she felt Mary relax and return the hug.

'Goodbye Mary, Deirdre,' said Bridget's voice from the doorway. 'Thank you for the cottage key. We'll be taking JJ in a minute, just for the week.'

Margaret felt Mary tense up again, and released her from the hug.

'Goodbye, Bridget,' said Mary, making no effort to go towards her, leaving Bridget to come into the kitchen and exchange awkward hugs with her sister and niece. Then Margaret and Bridget made their way out. They saw, with relief, that the people carrier was already parked outside.

Bridget and Margaret got into the front. Bridget sat next to George, who automatically reached out and held her hands as the tears, which she had been keeping inside, flowed down her cheeks.

'I'm so sorry,' said Bridget, fumbling for a tissue.

'Don't apologise, dear Sister Bridget,' said George, and Matthew handed forward a clean and folded white cotton hanky.

'I think you were right not to go,' said Margaret, turning back and talking to Peter and JJ. 'It wasn't the time.'

Peter nodded. George looked in the mirror. 'Everyone ready? Shall we go?'

'I'm sorry to be a trouble . . .' said JJ, awkwardly.

'Don't worry,' said Peter, swiftly understanding. 'Is there a downstairs loo near the door, do you know? If we could just nip in without anyone noticing.'

'I'm sorry,' repeated JJ.

'No problem,' said Margaret. 'I'll help.' She got out and came round to the back seat. 'You stay there, Bridget, we'll be back in a minute. The door isn't locked so we can be in and out quickly.'

Margaret was glad to find the downstairs loo unoccupied. She stood on guard as Peter helped JJ inside.

Deirdre, hearing a sound, came out to the hall.

'Oh, Sister Margaret,' she said. 'Did you forget something?'

'No, our friend just had to use the bathroom,' explained Margaret, feeling rather embarrassed. 'I hope that's all right.'

Mary, hearing voices, came out. 'Oh, Margaret!' she said in

surprise, as the bathroom door opened and JJ and Peter emerged.

'Ah, so it's yourself, Mary, after all these years,' said JJ, completely at ease. 'I'm sorry for your trouble. Poor Declan, God rest his soul.' He reached out his hands and she came forward to take them, biting her lip. She was obviously shocked at how frail he looked, and, after hardly crying at all during the funeral, her eyes were now filled with tears.

'JJ! Thank you,' she said.

'No, thank YOU for letting me stay in the cottage,' he said.

'No . . . no problem,' said Mary, turning away so he wouldn't see her crying. 'You're very welcome.'

Peter and Margaret linked arms with JJ, guiding him out of the house and back into the minibus.

'Was that OK for you, Peter?' Margaret said quietly.

He nodded but didn't meet her eyes. 'She didn't recognise me,' he said. 'It's for the best.'

'Did you recognise her?' Margaret asked, and this time Peter looked back at her, and she saw the depth of pain in his eyes.

'Well, yes, I did,' he said. 'Yes, yes I did.'

Deirdre and Mary stood at the door and watched them go. 'So that's the famous JJ?' said Deirdre, looking cheered up. 'I see what you mean about his being frail. I don't mind him staying in the cottage now. And who was that distinguished looking man with him? His carer or someone?'

'I don't know,' said Mary, frowning. 'There was something about him . . . I felt like I recognised him from somewhere. But he would have said something if he knew me, I'm sure.'

*

Back in Fairbridge, the snow had stopped falling and Chris took advantage of this to go out in the garden to fix some fencing. Sister Cecilia was on her way to check the laundry, followed by Pangur, but on passing reception he suddenly saw Chris go out the back door, and as if he was in telepathic communication with Kylie, they both decided to follow him.

'Pangur!' remonstrated Sister Cecilia. 'He won't like it,' she said to Em. 'He went out in the snow with me the other day and couldn't wait to come back in.'

Em and Cecilia both went to the garden door to see what the little cats were making of the snow. At first, Cecilia noted with satisfaction that neither seemed to be enjoying it – they miaowed and stopped to clean their wet paws – and Cecilia expected them to turn back, but suddenly they both decided snow was fun. They began pouncing and running and leaping and bounding all over the snowy garden, chasing each other.

'They love it!' laughed Em.

'Well, Pangur didn't love it when he was on his own the other day,' said Sister Cecilia, in an accusing tone.

'For goodness' sake!' said Em. 'What are you saying? It's snow. They are having fun. Together.' She went back to reception before she said something she regretted.

Sister Cecilia was concerned to find that she couldn't easily see Pangur against the snow. She resented that it was easier for her to see Kylie's black markings. She put on her wellingtons and coat and set off into the garden, following the sets of footprints in the snow. She went right down to the bottom of the garden, to the convent graveyard near where Chris was fixing the fence, and found Kylie and Pangur charging around amongst the departed Sisters' gravestones, digging tunnels in mounds of snow, jumping and bobbing about. A little robin was perched on a snowy bush, watching them and singing.

'Pangur!' Cecilia called. 'Come inside!' He licked his little pink nose and came bounding towards her, closely followed by Kylie, who Cecilia ignored. She turned and went back into the house, two little cats at her heels.

'It's extraordinary,' said Matthew appreciatively, as they drove further into Connemara. 'The changing light on the mountains is exquisite.'

'It's beautiful, but this part is much bleaker and more dramatic than I expected,' said George as the mainly tree-less landscape opened up.

'Cromwell said "to Hell or to Connaught",' said Bridget. 'The land is very hard for farming, and you can imagine the suffering during the famine when the poor people were evicted from their homes and wandering without shelter.'

Margaret was surprised at Bridget's realism. She found herself rushing in to supply the glass-half-full cheerfulness that Bridget normally offered: 'But even in the winter it's breathtakingly beautiful.'

'You can't eat beauty,' said Peter, backing up Bridget.

'You can certainly understand the power and appeal of images of the homely Irish cottage and the turf fire,' said Matthew, as rain started to fall. 'The family home surrounded by mountains and bog land and sea, but with smoke coming out of the chimney.'

'When we get to the island and the cottage, you'll see how cosy it is,' promised Bridget, as the rain fell faster and heavier, and the landscape they had been discussing was hidden from view. Her natural instinct to tilt the world towards the positive was back in force.

'You'll see lovely wildlife too, when it clears up,' she continued, swinging further back to cheerfulness to compensate for the worsening weather. 'On the island you'll see wild hares, and birds, and wild flowers galore. It's a shame it's not spring or summer.'

'Oh it's a nice place to be, on a fine summer's day,' sang Peter suddenly, his voice strong and tuneful, 'watching all the wild flowers that ne'er do decay, oh the hare and lofty pheasant, are plain to be seen, making homes for their young, round the cliffs of Dooneen.'

'I hope you have brought your guitar, Peter,' said Matthew.

'I made sure he did,' said JJ.

They drove on until they got to the turning for the island, and then, as they started to cross the bridge, the rain suddenly stopped and the low evening sun came out.

'Oh look – a rainbow!' said Margaret.

'Sister Bridget – this is just beautiful,' said George, in admiration, as they passed little cottages and stone-walled farms, their fields leading down to the sea. 'How could you bear to leave it?'

'It was hard,' said Peter, gruffly, in the back. Margaret took a quick breath in and looked at Bridget, wondering if Bridget had noticed Peter's slip up, but she was looking out the window, past George, to the right-hand side of the car.

'Sure, we were young, and wanted adventure,' said JJ, peacefully. 'There was a poem in our school book, I remember, about how Ireland needed its youth to stay at home, but sure what future was there for us here, especially if we had no land, or had brothers and sisters older than us? We were young, and we wanted the craic over in America or England.'

'Take the right turn here,' instructed Bridget, and to the right and up the stony road they went, until the mountains and sea were in front of them, and down to the left were sloping dry-stone walls and fields, some with cows, and paths and, scattered across the landscape, little cottages, some with smoke coming out of their chimneys.

'Paul Henry would have loved to paint this,' breathed Matthew.

'It's the best view on the island all right,' said Bridget, proudly, her enthusiasm returning as she neared her old home. 'Now, if you turn right again here, down where that clump of trees is, that's the little road down to the cottage.'

Thirty-Three

Mary and Lizzie had left the cottage very clean and tidy, and everyone exclaimed with pleasure when they arrived, at the soft, welcoming furnishings, the art on the walls, bright cushions and traditional dresser full of mugs and plates. There were instructions left for guests on how to switch on the central heating, and when Margaret followed them it came on quickly. There was also a small bucket filled with sods of turf, and Peter got a small turf fire going in the wide fireplace, the smell of peat filling the room.

'It's like Heaven,' said JJ, simply, content to just sit and watch the flames on the turf, and breathe in the scent of his early childhood.

JJ and Peter had the small downstairs twin room with use of the converted bathroom. Upstairs Bridget and Margaret and Matthew and George each had an ensuite room, with two beds, like those downstairs, that could be connected into a double.

'What an amazing view!' said Matthew, when they reached their bedroom. Stone-walled fields and mountains and sea and sky were all that could be seen from the window.

George came behind him and put his arms around him. Matthew turned round, more relaxed than he had been for months, and they kissed in delight.

Miguel and all your angels and saints – thank you! thought George.

'Oh George, thank you for bringing me here,' said Matthew, his face alight with joy. 'JJ is right – this is Heaven.'

Sister Cecilia went back to the laundry to check if Katy had left any more washing. She was irritated to discover Kylie had followed her and Pangur there, but gave her no encouragement. Then, having put some tea towels and tablecloths in the wash, she turned and, followed by Kylie and Pangur, went back past reception, where Em was checking in a couple with a little girl, who excitedly pointed at Cecilia and said, 'Look Mummy – the lady has got cats following her EVERY-WHERE!'

'Come, Pangur,' she said, bowing her head in acknowledgement. She was indeed the lady with the cats – but only Pangur would be allowed into the library. She carried on up the stairs and, as she opened the library door, felt a tugging on the edge of her habit.

'Pangur – stop!' she remonstrated, and was very displeased to find not Pangur, but Kylie, who appeared to have set herself the challenge of trying to leap high enough to catch Cecilia's veil.

'NO!' said Cecilia, and picked her up firmly, going back down the stairs to reception and depositing her, purring, on the desk. 'Kylie is not allowed in the library,' she said to Em. 'Please keep her under control.'

Em counted to ten.

*

The phone rang at the presbytery and Father Stephen answered it.

'Hello – is it possible to speak to a priest about my mum?' a male voice said. 'She is a parishioner of yours and I am worried about her.'

After half an hour, Stephen put down the phone and went to the church to pray for Maura. What he had learnt from her son had moved him deeply.

'I know she is difficult, but she had a terrible childhood. She was an orphan, and brought up by some really strict nuns in Ireland, and they seem to have drummed into her that she was full of sin. She came over to England for work and met and married Dad, and he was the best person she could have met – he was so kind and relaxed and cheerful and adored her, and she was a different person when we were growing up. She could be a bit serious and anxious, but Dad could always cuddle or laugh her out of it, and she was a really loving mum and so happy with Dad. We had a really good childhood. But then Dad died five years ago, and she met up with some really strict people on a pilgrimage, and it all seems to have triggered something in her. She's a nightmare now. She comes to visit us and she just lectures us and upsets the children – she's always complaining that none of us pray enough and that we're going to Hell, and she comes armed with leaflets about damnation or some conspiracy against the Pope. But we know she is lonely, and we all keep trying and hoping the next visit will be easier, but sooner or later, each time she comes, whoever she visits, they have to ask her to leave early. But she's our mum. We love her. It's awful.'

'I'm very sorry to hear that,' Stephen had said.

'The thing is, she has changed again these last days. I rang her today, because I hadn't heard from her for a few days, and that's not normal. Instead of her telling me I was going to Hell, she started crying and saying *she* was going to Hell. Something about hurting St Joseph. I tried to tell her that wasn't true, but of course, I don't go to Mass any more, so I haven't any authority. So I was wondering if you could talk to her? It's terrible – I'd almost rather she was back lecturing me – she is so upset. She isn't well. I think when Dad died, she sort of went back to the orphanage with the nuns, if you know what I mean.'

'I will go and call on her right now,' promised Stephen. 'Could you give me her address again? Father Hugh and I were a bit concerned as she wasn't at morning Mass today.'

'That's bad,' said her son, worriedly.

'Now, don't worry. May I have your permission to share her story with Father Hugh?'

'Definitely.'

'Give me your phone number and I will tell you how I get on. It sounds like your mother needs help, and I will do my best to give it.'

So now Stephen was praying for Maura in the church. On impulse, he went and lit a candle in front of St Joseph before leaving, the saint's kind face as calm and patient as ever, even with the faint crack around his neck.

Dear Saint Joseph, Our Lady's husband, and also dear cheerful, normal, kind unofficial saint who was Maura's husband. Please, both of you, pray for poor Maura, and pray for me, that I can bring her some peace.

Stephen was surprised to find that Maura's flat was in the same block as Bridie's. He rang the bell and she opened the door, her face immediately white when she saw him.

'Did Sister Margaret send you?' she said, fearfully. 'I would never tell on Sister Bridget.'

'No, not at all,' said Father Stephen, perplexed. 'Sisters Margaret and Bridget are in fact in Ireland for a funeral. I've just come to check on you, as your son rang and said he was worried you weren't well, and we didn't see you at Mass today.'

'I'm very sorry,' said Maura, starting to cry.

'Please don't be upset, Maura,' said Father Stephen, his heart wrung to see such vulnerability in his most difficult parishioner. 'You don't have to go to daily Mass. I just wanted to check on you. May I come in?'

Maura opened the door and brought him in, and for a moment the similarity between her and Bridie's flats struck him. Both had walls covered with holy pictures, both had happy family photos on the walls, both had small statues of saints, but the atmosphere was completely different. Instead of a mug and a plate of biscuits on the coffee table, Maura had pious leaflets with titles like 'Ireland's damnation', or 'Mary is holding back the hand of her son from smiting the world'. The flat was totally silent, and cold.

'Your flat is very cold, Maura,' Stephen said gently.

'I'm very sorry, Father,' she said meekly, and put on the electric fire immediately.

'Why didn't you have it on for yourself?' he said.

'For penance. For the wicked thing I did to St Joseph, and for not owning up.'

'What was that, Maura?' he said.

And Maura told him about breaking the statue . . . and also about how she would never tell anyone that Sister Bridget had cheated at bingo . . .

'Where is Pangur?' said Sister Cecilia, at the B&B reception, glancing down around her feet.

'Presumably up in the library, where he is allowed,' said

318

Em, but when Cecilia went up the stairs again, there was no Pangur waiting outside the closed library door, and a sudden feeling of dread gripped her.

She went downstairs quickly. She could see through the windows that snow was falling heavily again.

'Has the garden door been open?' she asked Em.

'Well, yes. Chris came in just now for a hot cup of tea and then went out to finish the fence, though he'll probably be back in soon if it keeps snowing.' said Em. *If she is going to moan about heating or something I really am going to complain to Sister Bridget when she comes back,* Em thought. *This is unbearable.*

Sister Cecilia opened the door and rushed out into the falling snow without stopping to put on wellies or a coat.

'Pangur!' she cried. She could see lots of pawprints leading down to the bottom of the garden, and squinting against the bright falling flakes, she made her way down, where, to her horror, she saw a gap in the fence leading out to the street behind, and Chris holding a fence panel.

Oh God, help! Cecilia prayed.

'Did you leave the fence panel out when you went to make your tea?' she demanded, urgently.

'Yes, yes I did,' he said. 'It was only for five minutes.'

'Pangur has got out and is lost in the snow!' said Sister Cecilia, and stepping through the gap in the fence out onto the street, she rushed off, in a steadily faster and thicker snowfall, to find him.

No little white cat was to be seen. The roads and pavements were getting covered with deeper and deeper snow, and cars had their headlights on.

Please Lord, protect my little Pangur, pleaded Cecilia. *He is such an innocent little cat. He knows nothing about the world. Don't let him get hurt!*

'Pangur! Pangur!' she cried, but there was no answering miaow.

Pet Paradise was lit up and still open and Sister Cecilia ran to it, like a lighthouse in a storm.

The door burst open and Jackie, with a sinking heart, saw the grumpy old nun she had served a fortnight ago.

'Has anyone seen a little white cat?' the nun cried as she entered. 'He is out in the snow and I am worried something terrible has happened to him. Please, please, you have got to help me!'

Jackie looked at the shop clock. Not long until closing time. There were no customers, and the thought of that nun's kitten lost in the snowstorm was very upsetting. She made a decision, taking pity on the wild-eyed Cecilia, locked the till and grabbed the shop keys.

'I'll help you look!' she said.

'Thank you! Thank you!' said Cecilia, nearly in tears.

Aaah, she's not so bad after all, thought Jackie. *And she really loves her cat.*

But they had no luck. They went up and down the road calling Pangur's name, stopping to look up into the bare branches of trees, and calling again, but he was nowhere to be found. The snow kept falling heavier and heavier, and the evening light was getting dimmer, until streetlamps were coming on in the dusk, shining out through whirling swathes of snow, and it was impossible to see. Jackie had a winter coat and gloves and hat on, but she was increasingly concerned for the old nun who had no such protection.

'I'm sorry, Sister,' she said, linking Cecilia's arm, noticing how she was shaking. 'I think we'd better go back to the convent. He's probably been a sensible little cat and gone home already.'

*

'And I absolve you from your sins in the name of the Father, the Son, and the Holy Spirit,' said Father Stephen, blessing Maura. 'Now Maura, you can be at peace. Everything is all right. You have accepted my penance, haven't you? You understand it?'

She nodded. 'Thank you, Father,' she said. 'I'm sorry for all the trouble I have caused.'

'It's nothing, Maura. When I spoke to your son Ben, it was obvious how much he loves you. His sisters do too. Your penance is that you must stop telling them they are wicked, because that's obviously not true, and you must stop listening to the voice in you that seems to be telling you that *you* are wicked too, as that is not true either. That voice doesn't come from God – the voice of God is gentle, and brings peace. I want to take these leaflets away with me, Maura, and dispose of them, and the rest of your penance is that I want you to stop going to the prayer groups where they give you these leaflets. I don't think they are doing you any good. If anyone from them tries to contact you, tell them that I said they are to leave you alone, and to contact me if they have any problem with that. I think you are missing your husband very much and I think you need some bereavement counselling, and maybe a check-up at the doctor, and a good rest. Do you agree?'

Maura nodded. 'I didn't use to be like this, Father.'

'I know, Maura. Ben told me all about it. He said you were a lovely mother. He wants you to come back and stay with him, and his sisters want to come and see you. They all love you.'

'After everything I said?'

'Yes. They forgive you. They just want you well again. Maura – maybe the shock of breaking the statue was a blessing really. Maybe St Joseph brought you to your senses. He was a good husband, like your husband was to you. They are both up in Heaven, looking down, wanting you to get well. And you DID fix St Joseph's head back on!' he smiled, trying to coax an answering one from Maura.

'But Sister Margaret is so cross with me,' said Maura, fearfully, and Stephen had an insight into the anxious little girl who had been brought up by the nuns with such lack of love.

'Maura – please don't worry. Sister Margaret is NOTHING like the Sisters who brought you up. But she was very wrong to threaten you the way she did. She was just cross with you because she was worried about Sister Bridget, that's all, and about what Mrs Sanders was saying about her fixing the bingo, but she had absolutely no right to tell you what you can or can't say.'

'Yes. But it wasn't even true, Father. Mrs Sanders rang me and told me that it was a big lie she made up that Sister Bridget cheated and I wasn't to repeat it. Can you tell Sister Margaret that?'

'Of course I will talk to Sister Margaret,' said Stephen, reassuringly, but his mind was whirring. *Sister Bridget COULD tell the numbers of the bingo balls without looking – he had seen her do it himself. What was Mrs Sanders doing? What had actually happened? It was very wrong of them to treat poor Maura like this. She had enough troubles.* 'But first of all, Maura, I will ring your son. He is going to come and collect you and bring you to his house so you can have a good rest for as long as you want, and get all the help you need to get better.'

Thirty-Four

After a beautiful sunset over the island, Margaret drew the curtains and they all sat around the table together. For the evening meal George and Matthew had made a warm and filling vegetable soup served with soda bread they had bought in Knock earlier.

'What was the cottage like when you were growing up, Sister Bridget?' asked George, serving up the soup.

'Well, much smaller than this,' said Bridget. 'Hmm, that soup smells out of this world, George, thank you. Declan did a great job extending it on either side and building upwards. The sitting room was the main room, with this lovely big dresser on one wall and a big turf fire and the pots hanging over it. There was no electricity or running water – we had gas lamps and we went across the fields to the well and brought water back in buckets – we cooked and drank and washed in it. Lovely clear, pure, soft water. We were lucky really. No pollution or contamination. The vegetables we ate were all organic, because we had no money for anything to help them grow. There was no bathroom, let alone en suites, but we didn't know the lack of them then. Declan built on the kitchen to the side but we lived and cooked in the same room and only two bedrooms – one for the parents, one for the children. There was just Mary and me, but in bigger families the children would sleep top to toe at times.'

'I'm glad Mary has kept the picture of The Sacred Heart up,' said JJ. 'And the one with the Immaculate Heart of Mary. Sure, every home had them. Could we say the rosary in thanksgiving before we go to bed, Sisters, do you think?'

'I do,' said Bridget, smiling at him. His happiness went a long way to soothing the pain in her heart after the funeral.

Peter and Margaret cleared the table and washed up together in the little kitchen Declan had put in, as the others relaxed and chatted in the sitting room. Declan's extension was very tasteful, bright and modern, but country-style and respectful of the original house.

'He did a good job here, I'll say that for him,' said Peter. 'He was a good builder.'

'Are you going to tell Bridget who you are, Peter?' said Margaret, quietly. 'I thought she might guess when you said it was hard to leave the island.'

'I think if she hasn't guessed, I might let sleeping dogs lie,' said Peter. 'But I'm going to be nice to her, Margaret, don't worry. It did help talking to you. I want to move on and not dwell in the past – forgive and forget – I've carried the bitterness too long, and it's only been hurting me. I'm going to concentrate on making this a good week for JJ, and I'm truly grateful to Bridget for making it possible. I can see you are right, and I was wrong.'

'That's big of you, Peter,' said Margaret. 'Do you have any family here?'

'My parents died years ago, God rest them. I never saw

them again after I left the priesthood and was on the streets – I'm sorry for that now,' he said, sadly. 'They'd be buried over in Gurteen graveyard. I had two sisters, but they sold the family home and went off and married – I don't even know where they are living – they could be anywhere – the USA, Canada, anywhere. I didn't want to contact family as I just felt it would cause grief and upset to everyone, especially that their son and brother the priest they were so proud of had brought shame on them. I thought everyone would be better off if they thought I was dead. The years have gone by and it has just seemed easier to forget all about it. I do sometimes wonder.'

'I'll pray about that, Peter,' said Margaret. 'I'll pray you find your family again.'

'Thank you, Margaret. I don't know what I think about God, or about prayer any more, but I'm beginning to suspect you might have more chance of getting through than me. Hugh offered to help me trace them, but I don't want to cause trouble. I don't even know if they are alive. JJ had one sister, and he lost touch with her years ago – once he was on the streets he was too ashamed to go home. We're all each other has got, but I'm glad for it. If there IS a God, I thank God for JJ, at any rate.'

Em was waiting at reception when Cecilia came back, with Jackie at her side.

'Has he returned?' asked Cecilia, desperately. She was shaking with cold and fear.

'What's happened?' said Katy, walking into reception. 'Oh Sister! You look frozen!'

'She's been looking for her cat Pangur,' explained Jackie. 'She came into my shop to ask for help. We've been up and down the road, calling, but had no luck. I said he might have come home.'

'I've checked downstairs and he isn't anywhere, and all the doors are shut upstairs and he's not on the landing,' said Em. 'I'm afraid Sister Cecilia is right – he must have got out into the garden. He was so excited by the snow, poor Pangur. Chris is so sorry, Sister.'

'I'm going to pray in the chapel,' said Sister Cecilia, desperately.

'You must change out of those wet clothes first, Sister, or you will get your death of cold,' said Katy, firmly. Although she was nearly seventy years older than Katy, Sister Cecilia listened and granted her words authority, and allowed her to help her upstairs to her bedroom.

'Thanks for helping,' said Em to Jackie.

'I'm so sorry the cat is lost. I thought she was just a grumpy old nun, but she loves that cat like a child, doesn't she?' Jackie replied. 'I couldn't help but be sorry for her.'

'No, you're right,' said Em. 'Poor Sister Cecilia. Poor Pangur too. I would be so sad if I lost my Kylie. She has been curled up down here in her basket whilst all this has been going on.'

'Can I leave you my number so you can give me a ring later, if the little cat is found?' Jackie said. 'I don't think I'll be able to sleep until I hear.'

'Thanks again,' said Em, smiling at her, as Jackie scribbled down her number on some paper. 'That was really kind of you.'

'Oh no problem. She was so upset – I couldn't not help,' Jackie replied.

'I'll wait outside and we will go down to the chapel and pray together,' said Katy.

Sister Cecilia looked at her bed and longed to see little

Pangur curled up there. Outside in the dark night the snow was still falling, and her heart was breaking to think of him lost and cold and afraid. She took off her wet cold things and changed into a fresh habit and warm tights and slippers. She left her wet things, uncharacteristically, in a pile on the floor. There was no time for anything but prayer.

Margaret and Peter made hot drinks for everyone, and they all sat up and chatted for a while. Then George and Matthew made their apologies and went up to bed, and JJ asked if they could say the rosary. Margaret was surprised to see Peter hesitate, but then stay. Peter had no rosary, but she noticed an olive wood one on the mantelpiece, which she guessed must have belonged to Mary.

'I know it's Friday, but can we pray the Joyful Mysteries instead of the Sorrowful? As that's how I feel,' said JJ.

'I feel so lucky to be with you, my love,' said George, upstairs in the silence of their room. They could hear the comforting rhythmic call and response of the rosary from downstairs as they lay in bed. The curtains were open, the rain had cleared the sky of clouds, and through the window, they could see the stars.

As soon as Cecilia and Katy passed on their way to the chapel, Kylie woke up, and went to follow them down the corridor.

'Oh no you don't,' said Em, grabbing her. 'Sister Cecilia won't want you bothering her whilst Pangur is lost.'

Cecilia and Katy knelt down in the little dark chapel, lit only by the flickering tea light in its red case in front of the tabernacle.

'Why don't we remember that God is the Good Shepherd?'

said Katy, gently to Sister Cecilia. 'He cares for little sparrows – he loves little Pangur. If he can find the lost sheep, he can find a lost kitten.'

Cecilia nodded, but a tear coursed down her face, and the hand Katy reached out to hold felt very light and fragile, the elderly skin delicate and easily bruised.

Suddenly there was a loud miaow, and both looked down in sudden hope, only to have it dashed when they saw Kylie, pawing at Cecilia's skirt.

'I am so sorry!' said Em, breathlessly entering. 'I tried to stop her following you but she just wriggled out of my arms and ran.'

'Let her,' said Cecilia. 'If I had been more welcoming to her when we went to the library, and not brought her back down, maybe Pangur wouldn't have wandered off and gone out in the garden.'

'So the last time you saw Pangur was in the library?' said Katy.

'Not in it. We were about to go in,' said Cecilia. 'Then I saw Kylie and picked her up and returned her to reception.'

Kylie miaowed loudly again, ran to the chapel door, and miaowed once more.

'I think she wants us to follow her,' said Katy. 'Come on.'

The little cat ran ahead, looking back to check they were following her, and ran up the stairs to the library, sitting outside it.

'But the library door is closed. It has been closed all the time you were out searching,' said Em. 'I checked all the doors upstairs.'

Kylie sat outside and scratched the door.

'Wait a minute,' said Cecilia, a wild hope rising. 'I opened the library door, and then Kylie started pawing at my skirt, so I picked her up and brought her down to reception.'

'And now I remember, I passed the library door this afternoon when I went to get something from my room and it was slightly ajar, and I could see nobody was there, so I closed it. You were saying how we needed to stop drafts, Sister,' said Katy. 'I didn't think to check if Pangur was there, because you are always together.'

But Cecilia hadn't waited to hear. She had already opened the door and was inside, and within a minute a small white kitten, who had been peacefully sleeping in an armchair as the snow was falling outside, was purring in her arms, as she kissed and cried over him in joy, and a black and white kitten was weaving around her feet, purring too.

Thirty-Five

Saturday morning on the island dawned bright and dry. They had a quiet, restful morning. Matthew read his book about Paul Henry, and George looked up places to visit in Connemara and worked out on the map how long it would take. Peter strummed his guitar quietly, JJ alternately napped in his chair and silently said his rosary.

'Could I have a word, Peter?' said Margaret. Peter put down his guitar and went outside with her.

Five minutes later, they returned, Peter to play guitar again, and Margaret to find Bridget in their bedroom, and invite her for a walk along the road.

'Would you like to know what the problem has been with Peter?' asked Margaret, as they set off up the path. I asked him this morning for permission to tell you.'

As soon as they got back a somewhat shell-shocked Bridget asked to see Peter alone.

'You aren't Peter Sims – you are Patrick Connolly, aren't you? I am so, so sorry, Patrick,' she said. 'I didn't recognise you – I knew there was something familiar about you, but I didn't put two and two together. I don't know what to say. I am so sorry. I really had no idea, back then, that you were in love with Mary. I am so sorry. No wonder you hated me.'

'No, I held on to the grudge for decades longer than I should have, Bridget. Hugh and Margaret both pointed that out. They both love you very much. I am sorry about the way I have treated you,' said Patrick. 'I just want to thank you for all your kindness to JJ and myself, and let everything in the past go. I changed my name to do that, years ago, but I realise now I hadn't really changed my mind or heart.'

'Well, I'm so sorry,' said Bridget. 'I really am. Sorry for all you've been through.'

Patrick put out his hand. 'Let me take responsibility for my own wrong choices, Bridget. And as Margaret pointed out, I haven't had a bad life. I'm even quite proud of what I've done with it,' he said, smiling, 'now that I have let go of the anger. I've met some remarkable people over the years – and I can see now that you are one of them.'

'Oh, I wish you were right,' said Bridget, sadly. 'I seem to be making so many mistakes. Mary is so angry with me about Declan telling me about his illness and keeping it from her, and the idea I gave Declan about giving the cottage to JJ. I have said sorry, but she won't forgive me. I don't know how to put it right.'

'You are not responsible for other people's anger,' said Patrick. 'That might seem like a trite saying, but it's true, and I should know. You have said sorry – she is the one who has to decide what to do with it. She has to forgive you, Bridget, or she'll find no peace.'

'Well, I'm just so sorry again, Patrick,' said Bridget. 'I'll be praying to God to put all my mistakes right.'

'Well, as far as I'm concerned, that's all in the past now, and I am sorry for my rudeness to you,' said Patrick, smiling.

At lunch Patrick broke the news of his real name to the others, and how he was really from the island.

'I've just told Sister Bridget – JJ knew already, and Father Hugh, of course – that my name was not always Peter Sims, but Patrick Connolly. We both grew up on this island together, but as I'm a bit younger, I went to school with Mary, Bridget's sister. I know you will be wondering why I changed my name . . . I was Father Patrick Connolly before I took to the drink and ended up on the streets. I felt I brought shame on my family, and it was easier to go by a different name.'

'So – what do we call you now?' asked George. 'This is deliciously dramatic!' Everyone laughed, and Patrick visibly relaxed.

'I hardly know myself,' said Patrick. 'There's no one around here who knows me now. Let's try Patrick. I can't be back on the island and not go by my true name.'

'To Patrick!' said George, lifting his glass of water. 'A noble name! Welcome back!'

It was decided after lunch that George and Matthew, Bridget and Margaret and JJ would drive off the island and go to Roundstone. The Sisters and JJ would pray in the church and George and Matthew would go and get food, then they would all go to Gurteen to pray at JJ's parents' grave. JJ had brought a plastic dome enclosing artificial flowers and a statue of Our Lady at Knock, which the shopkeeper had assured him would be perfect to put on a grave, and would withstand the rain and the wind and the sand blowing in from the shore on the exposed graveyard site.

'Will you be all right on your own, Patrick?' said Bridget.

'I'll be fine, Bridget, thank you,' said Patrick, smiling. 'I need some time to get used to my old identity. I have my guitar. I think I'll sit outside and sing to the mountains. It will be nice to have some time alone here – this is my church.'

The others had gone. He washed up the lunch things, made himself a cup of tea and, wearing a coat and woollen hat, went and stood outside. Without thinking, looking up at the mountains, he found himself, to his surprise, praying the beginning of Psalm 121:

I lift up mine eyes to the mountains, from whence shall come my help?
My help is in the name of the Lord, who made Heaven and Earth.

Patrick tentatively started saying snippets of prayers from memory, tasting the words on his lips as he spoke them out into the quietness, his heart moved with peace and joy as he heard his voice saying the familiar words. 'O Lord, open my lips, and my tongue shall announce thy praise. Incline unto my aid O Lord, O Lord, make haste to help me.'

He found the tears rolling down his cheeks. It seemed only yesterday he had left the island. So many years had passed. So much had happened. He had suffered so much. He had felt so much pain, and when others had helped him – Hugh and the AA – he had recognised that pain and hopefully relieved it in others. He had lost faith in an institution – but he had found it again in people. He had re-discovered goodness – in Hugh and JJ and the AA and its members – and now, he finally admitted, in Bridget too, and Father Stephen and Em and Chris and George and Matthew, Margaret and Katy and even grumpy old Cecilia and her love for Pangur. He smiled at the memory of catching her in his arms. And he finally let go of all the anger he had felt for so long.

And then he heard it. Not so much in his head but in his heart, and somehow part of the beauty that was everywhere around him.

'All shall be well,' it said.

And in spite of the unholy mess, the waste, the pain, the lies, the shame, the deliberate cruelty and the genuine mistakes, in spite of everything, he suddenly believed again, that it could be true.

'This must be the most beautiful graveyard on earth!' said George. 'Look at the view – mountains, sea, golden beach stretching for miles. It's just spectacular!' They had arrived at Gurteen beach, and together had walked with JJ up the long sandy path from the beach to the graveyard. He had only been in Ireland a couple of days, but already seemed stronger. Matthew carried the rather gaudy plastic dome, which he found intensely moving in the context of JJ and his visit to his parents' grave after so many years.

'I myself might have chosen traditional slate stone, or pottery, as a memorial,' he said quietly to George, 'but there is something about this which reminds me of Mexican folk art, especially decorations for The Day of the Dead, or even the popular art seen and sold at Indian shrines. It is obvious it means a great deal to JJ, so I find it an honour to carry it, in what is really a religious ceremony, visiting a grave.'

George beamed at Matthew, full of love for this serious, kind, gentle and humble academic, and still overwhelmed, every day, at the luck that had brought him into his life. *Though Miguel, I know that you and your angels up in Heaven would say it was not luck, but blessings, even for an agnostic like me. So thank you!*

added George, sending up a thought to Miguel who, George was becoming more and more convinced, was still looking after him even after death. A robin appeared, singing, and flew past Margaret and Bridget and JJ, down past Matthew and George.

'Our loved ones up in Heaven are thinking of us,' Bridget called down, as she and Margaret and JJ reached the top.

I know you are, dear Miguel, thought George. *Love never ends.*

JJ was very pleased to find his parents' grave not too overgrown. 'The people here are very good,' he said, as Matthew passed him the dome and he left it on the grave. 'Now, thanks be to God I am here after all these years. I can die in peace now. We'll say an Our Father and a Hail Mary now we are here.' JJ slightly swayed with tiredness, his hands grasping his rosary beads.

'Then we'll go back,' said Bridget. 'You don't want to get worn out. We can always come again tomorrow. We have a week after all.'

They were back at the cottage having tea, when a car appeared on the hill and drove right down to the cottage. The gate opened and there was a knock at the door. Bridget could hardly believe who she was seeing when she opened it.

'Mary!' said Bridget, shocked.

'I need to see JJ,' said Mary, coming in.

'Hello Mary!' said JJ, very calmly. 'How are you?'

'JJ – I have found your sister!' she blurted out. JJ grasped the sides of the chair in shock. 'I volunteer in a charity shop in Galway, and a lovely woman has been coming in to buy jigsaws for her grandmother. I sold her a few with Connemara scenes, and I said I was from the island, and she said her grandmother was from the island too and wanted to meet me.

I went to see her today. We talked about the island, and it turned out she had a brother years ago, JJ, who had gone to work in England. She had never stopped praying she would see him again!'

'Oh, thanks be to God!' said Bridget. 'That's wonderful!'

'And I want you to have the house to keep, JJ. I want you to be able to look your sister Bernie in the eyes and tell her you are a homeowner, and bring her back here and show her what you have at the end of your life. Because I am so sorry, and I know Declan was very sorry, at the way you were treated in England. That's why he wanted to give you the cottage. I didn't want to do it – I wanted to keep it for myself – but I can see this was selfish now,' said Mary.

'She's alive,' said JJ, wonderingly. 'Little Bernie is alive. And she wants to see me.'

'She does. She is a widow, but she has a lovely son and daughter-in-law, and a granddaughter, and even a gorgeous little great grandson called Rory. And they ALL want to meet you! I left a very excited house, I can tell you! You have a grand big family now. You're an uncle, and a great uncle, and a great-great uncle!'

'Thanks be to God!' said JJ, making the sign of the cross with his rosary beads, his hands shaking. 'Well, you must stay and have a cup of tea. We bought some barm brack when we were out. I cannot thank you enough.'

'Well, I don't know . . .' said Mary, suddenly awkward.

'May I ask you a question, Mary?' said JJ.

'Anything,' said Mary, taking the seat George pulled up for her.

'What were you going to do with the cottage?' said JJ.

'Oh, that's not important,' said Mary, hastily.

'Just humour me,' said JJ. 'Because I am very intrigued by

the guest book. It is a very welcoming book, but it says we must not go into the studio. That it is private.'

'I'll move my paintings out, don't worry,' said Mary. 'This is where I have come to paint over the years. It's been my refuge. But I can paint anywhere.'

'So now, would you let us go and see the paintings?' said JJ.

'No, you don't want to be bothering with them,' said Mary.

'Would you do a sick man a favour?' said JJ, surprisingly firmly.

'Well, all right,' said Mary, reluctantly.

'And Dr Matthew, will you come with us?' said JJ, linking Mary's arm. 'My friend is very keen on art,' he explained to Mary, as they crossed the yard to the studio.

'Really,' said Mary, blushing. 'They are nothing . . . just my paintings . . .' but she found herself opening the studio all the same.

'These are BEAUTIFUL!' said Matthew, as he stepped inside and saw all the canvases. 'And you say you painted them?'

Mary blushed. 'I did.'

'You are extremely talented. These are very, very impressive,' said Matthew, going from one to another. 'You can see the influence of Paul Henry, but there is something new too, something modern, a sense of feeling and . . . there is something sad and longing about these – something unrequited. But also full of love for the small details. The way you have painted the fuchsia bush outside the cottage in this one, for example. It is so tender. You obviously love this cottage, this landscape, very much. Have you been showing them in galleries?'

'No – the only other person I've shown them to is my friend Lizzie. My family may have seen them but they just see them as clutter. My daughter wanted to clear them out anyway to extend the self-catering capacity.'

'She absolutely mustn't!' said Matthew, firmly.

As if on cue, there was the sound of a car, as a Ford Fiesta drove down and parked behind Mary's Mini. The door slammed and Deirdre burst out.

Thirty-Six

'Mum! I got your note about giving the cottage to JJ! I absolutely forbid you to give this cottage away. Our family needs it!' shouted the furious young woman.

'Your mother won't be giving it away to anyone,' said JJ firmly.

'Oh . . . good,' said Deirdre, the wind taken out of her sails. 'I'm sorry – but it's just we use it for self-catering and I've just split up from my husband and I need it . . .'

'Your mother needs it,' continued JJ. 'She needs it for her painting, which my friend here, Doctor Matthew Woodburn, who is a lecturer at the University of Fairbridge, says is TREMENDOUS.'

'It really is,' agreed Matthew. 'Your mother is exceptionally talented, and is obviously inspired by this cottage and the landscape around it.'

'But what about showing Bernie that you made something of yourself and have a home?' said Mary, anxiously to JJ.

'Why would I need to do that?' said JJ to Mary. 'Wouldn't that be a lie? The truth is I have no home, that I spent years on the streets, but that the good Lord had mercy on me, and sent Patrick Connolly to look for me and rescue me and look after me at the end of my days.'

'Patrick Connolly?' said Mary, shocked. 'Is that man with the beard – the man with you – is that Patrick Connolly?'

'Yes, Mary, it is,' said Patrick, who had come outside to find out who was shouting.

They looked at each other, each registering the difference the years had made, but also recognising the one they had loved.

'Oh God. Why are you here? I loved you, you know,' Mary blurted out, as if she could not help herself.

'Mum! What are you saying?' said Deirdre in distress. 'She's not herself – we only buried Dad yesterday,' she said to everyone.

'Come inside, Deirdre dear,' said Bridget. 'You look worn out. Come and have some tea and leave your mother and Patrick to talk.' Deirdre looked with bewilderment at her mother and the tall, distinguished, grey-bearded man, standing facing each other.

'Mum?' she said.

'Go inside with your aunt,' Mary said firmly.

Suddenly everyone was inside, and only Patrick and Mary were left standing outside in the yard.

'Why did you leave me?' she said.

'What do you mean?' said Patrick, confused.

'As soon as Declan showed interest in me, you disappeared.'

'But you were in love with Declan!' said Patrick.

'No. I had had a bit of a crush on him as my big sister's boyfriend, but I never imagined marrying him. But then Bridget decided to be a nun, and pass Declan on to me, though I had never asked her to, and he decided I would do, and everyone was so sure – our parents were so happy – and you were nowhere to be seen. I was only sixteen, Patrick. I didn't have the confidence to say what I really wanted, especially when the person I did want didn't seem to want me.'

'Are you telling me,' stuttered Patrick, 'that if I had told you when you got engaged that I loved you, you would have thrown Declan over for me?'

'Of course I would!' said Mary. 'I loved you. I always wanted to marry you. And I thought you wanted to marry me. Don't you remember you gave me a grass ring and asked me to marry you when we were ten? I said "yes" then and I meant it! I just always took it for granted that one day we would be married. I never talked about it – I thought it was just between me and you. But suddenly, when I was sent over to England to work, everything changed. I didn't have a chance. Everyone was so sure Declan was the one for me. You ignored me, and then suddenly went back to Ireland, saying you were going off to be a priest, even before Declan and I were married. I couldn't ask for you back from God. I just thought I must have made a mistake – that you didn't love me at all, and that I should marry Declan and make everyone happy.'

'But Mary – I did love you,' said Patrick, his voice shocked. 'I loved you so much. I have never loved another woman like you. But I had nothing to offer you. I stepped aside so he could give you everything you wanted, you deserved.'

'But I wanted YOU!' shouted Mary suddenly, so that even in the cottage they could hear.

'More tea?' said Bridget, a little desperately, but JJ was already at the door, opening it, shamelessly eavesdropping on the couple, who were oblivious to everyone but each other.

'What right had you to "step aside"?' shouted quiet Mary. 'I never wanted to have big money. I hated the lifestyle, all the swanky dinner parties. All I wanted all those years ago was this – this cottage I was born in – on this island I love – and to be here with you. I was a good wife to Declan, and I was never unfaithful, but I never forgot you. Even when I heard that you had left the priesthood, I never stopped praying for you. I thought you'd be married yourself by now, with a family of your own.'

'Oh Mary,' said Patrick, heartbroken. 'I'm so sorry. Fifty years apart. What a waste.'

He took a step towards her, and before they knew what they were doing, they were in each other's arms.

'Mum!' said Deirdre, shocked, from the doorway.

'So now, don't waste any more time,' came JJ's voice. Patrick and Mary broke apart, but kept holding each other's hands.

'Mum – how could you?' Deirdre said, crying, and ran to her car.

'Deirdre!' said Mary, going to run after her, but Patrick refused to let go of her hand.

'Leave her, Mary. She'll need some time,' said Patrick.

Bridget and Margaret had got to Deirdre, and stopped her getting into the car. She burst into tears and Margaret led her back into the house. Bridget came towards them, hesitantly.

'Mary – I just wanted to say I am so, so sorry for everything. I had no idea all those years ago you were in love with Patrick, and he with you, and I should never have bundled you into that engagement. I am so sorry to both of you for all the time you have had apart – and I just want to give you my blessing. Keep this cottage – keep it and be together the way you should have all those years ago.'

'Hey Bridget, hold on there! Declan's funeral was only yesterday – don't be at your organising again!' said Patrick, but he smiled as he said it.

'Oh, I'm so sorry,' said Bridget, crestfallen. 'I'm doing it again!'

Mary went forward and hugged her. 'It's all right, Bridget, and I'm so sorry I've been so angry with you. Thank you for helping Declan at the end of his life. It wasn't your fault he didn't confide in me. And he died at peace, which is all any of us could hope for. And if it wasn't for you helping JJ, and bringing him to the cottage, I would never have met Patrick again. But Patrick is right. It's too soon for either of us. There is a lot to sort out. Deirdre and Tom need helping. We haven't even scattered poor Declan's ashes.' Her voice wobbled then, and she wiped her eyes. Yet she still didn't let go of Patrick's hand.

'I lift up mine eyes to the mountains,' quoted Patrick, 'from whence shall come my help.' He smiled down at Mary. 'I have a feeling that all shall be well at last.'

Epilogue

Mary and Patrick went for a walk, and when they got back, Deirdre had left. Margaret assured her that she was much calmer. She had even broken down and told them about her marriage problems with Tom, and his gambling, and JJ had given her great advice about support groups, and explained to her that using the money from renting out the cottage was not helping, but only feeding his addiction.

Mary reluctantly said a temporary 'goodbye' to Patrick and the others, and went back to her home in Galway, bringing Bridget with her, who was a great help to her sister and family in the following week. Margaret and the others had a wonderful week in Connemara, visiting Roundstone, Clifden, Kylemore Abbey, and back to Gurteen again, this time for Patrick to find and pray at his parents' grave, finding only peace when he got there.

When JJ and Patrick, George and Matthew drove to pick Bridget up at the end of the holiday, Bridget looked as rested and peaceful as they felt. Bridget had been forgiven by her sister and, as importantly, had forgiven herself. And then, at the very end of the holiday, Mary joined Bridget and the others and took JJ to see his little sister Bernie, and his new, extended family. Many tears were shed, and the sister and brother, who had spent so many decades apart, felt the last pieces had been found in the jigsaw puzzle of their lives.

They returned to Fairbridge and to the B&B to find things little, and yet much, changed. Sister Cecilia was now often accompanied on her trips to the laundry and library by not just one, but two kittens, both of whom she admitted to being very fond of. Although she would never be a touchy feely sort of woman, she was much more demonstrative to each of them than anyone had ever seen, and the kittens obviously adored her. Furthermore, Cecilia and Em, who had just discovered she and Chris were expecting a baby, were much better friends, and could always be relied on to have conversations about their two cats. Em had a new friend in Jackie, from Pets Paradise, and she and Cecilia were often treated to samples from the shop, so Kylie and Pangur accumulated an inordinate number of cat toys. Although jumping in and out of laundry baskets and chasing each other around the garden, whether snowy or not, still remained their favourite thing to do.

Katy reported that bingo had gone well the week they were all away. George's mother had been a great help. She had brought some visiting friends along and they all raved about the cupcakes as well as the larger cake prizes. One of George's mother's friends actually won a big cake, and had been very impressed to learn that Father Hugh had done all the baking.

Maura had gone to live with her son Ben, who wrote to Father Stephen saying his mother was getting help, and was feeling better by the day, and had completely stopped telling anyone, including herself, that they were going to Hell.

In the days after they returned Father Stephen, Margaret and

Bridget had all been separately praying about Maura, and Margaret spoke to Bridget about her feelings of uneasiness, which Sister Bridget said she shared. Father Stephen was just at the point of asking Margaret to come and speak to him when, to his relief, Margaret rang to organise a meeting with Father Hugh and Father Stephen, where the two Sisters sat in the presbytery kitchen and confessed about the cake and the silencing.

'I wanted to protect Bridget, but I was wrong,' said Margaret. 'I wanted you both to know, as I am parish Sister to Father Hugh, but also I know Father Stephen has been very kind to Maura and is in contact with her son.'

'And I was wrong to ever rig the bingo,' said Bridget, blushing.

'And you also threatened Mrs Sanders?' said Father Stephen to Margaret.

'Yes. But she apologised first and offered to tell Maura it had never happened,' said Margaret, also blushing. Just speaking it out loud made her realise how bad the situation was. 'It's pretty bad, isn't it? I had this mad fear the local papers would get hold of it and Bridget and the parish wouldn't cope, and I was glad she offered to deny that it had ever happened, but I shouldn't have given in to it. I'm so sorry.'

'And I am so sorry too,' said Bridget.

'Well', said Father Hugh slowly. 'I think you will both have to throw yourselves on their mercy. You know where Mrs Sanders lives, and then Father Stephen can check with Maura's son if she is well enough to see you.'

'But I said sorry to YOU. I don't blame you for trying to silence us. You're worrying about nothing,' said George's mum, when Margaret and Bridget, sitting opposite her, had finished apologising.

346

'Not really,' said Bridget. 'I cheated at bingo so someone would like me.'

'Not really,' said Margaret. 'I had no right to threaten you.'

George's mother looked at them both. 'You really are making things difficult, you know that? You know if I accept your apology, I am going to then have to go along with you and apologise to Maura too?'

Margaret laughed ruefully. 'Yes, that's how it works, I'm afraid.'

'"The quality of Mercy is not strained." I know my Shakespeare,' she said resignedly. 'I accept your apology. So come on – let's go to Maura. You do know she still can decide to tell the other people at bingo?'

'Yes,' said Margaret and Bridget, 'but we are hoping she will have mercy on us.'

'Honestly – you are both potty,' grumbled George's mum, but she still got her coat.

'You want to apologise to me?' said Maura, slightly bewildered, after Margaret had explained why they had come to find her at her son's house.

'Yes. Sorry for threatening you. I wanted to protect Sister Bridget, but I was wrong,' said Margaret.

'And sorry for lying to you and telling you it hadn't happened, when it had,' said George's mum, who was finding this novel experience of apologising embarrassing but also strangely moving. They were just talking in the sitting room of a small terraced house, but it felt more momentous, somehow, deeply ordinary but also lifted above the ordinary in some way.

'And sorry for fixing who won the cake in the first place,' said Bridget.

'So you DID do it?' said Maura.

'Yes,' said Bridget. 'I am sorry. I wasn't myself. Or not my best self, anyway. I am ashamed. I will never do that again.'

'Well,' said Maura, taking a deep breath, 'I have to tell you. I think, from what you said in the Hall, Sister Margaret, that you might have guessed. I went to confession and told Father Stephen that I broke the statue of St Joseph and then glued his head back on. He was very kind to me, and told me God forgave me,' said Maura. 'I wasn't MY best self either, when I did that, or when I said horrible things to my children, or to other people, so I accept your apology. I forgive you all. I won't tell anyone about the cake, Sister Bridget, and I hope you won't tell anyone I broke the statue. And,' she finished bravely, 'when I come back to Fairbridge, Mrs Sanders, I want to go and apologise to your son and his partner for what I said to them in the theatre lobby, after the pantomime. I really am so sorry. It was a terrible thing to say, I know that now. I didn't even remember to tell Father Stephen about it in confession.'

'God will have heard,' said Bridget. 'You are forgiven already.'

'But I still have to make it right,' said Maura. 'I want to go to confession about it and say sorry to Mrs Sanders' son and the other man. He looked very upset.'

'Call me Annabel, Maura,' said George's mother, the redoubtable Mrs Annabel Sanders, who found she had tears in her eyes. 'You can ALL call me Annabel. And thank you, Maura. That will mean a great deal.'

Maura's son entered the sitting room to offer tea just as the women spontaneously decided to hug each other.

'Would you like some tea and biscuits?' he said, smiling at

them, greatly surprised and relieved to walk into the room and discover his mother surrounded by such an atmosphere of love.

'I've got a cake in the car,' said Bridget, and then blushed, and Ben was astonished to see his mum and all the other women burst into peals of laughter.

JJ, instead of fading away, got stronger and fitter by the day. Thomas Amis recovered from his hip operation, took back his gardening duties, and Patrick, as he now preferred to be called, wondered to his friend Father Hugh what he should do next.

'We'll pray about it,' said Hugh, delighted that his friend was so happy. Patrick had come back to Mass, and was writing regular letters to Mary. In August, she wrote a very special letter to him and JJ:

Dear Patrick and JJ,

I have been thinking about our future. Thank you both for all you have done to help Deirdre and Tom. I have signed over the house in Galway to them. Tom has done so well with the groups and support you put him in touch with, but he insisted the property should be in Deirdre's name. My friend Lizzie's fiancée, an experienced accountant, will be running the business for me, but Tom is still a senior manager, and I have every hope that things will be fine for him and Deirdre and that in time I can pass the business on to safe hands.

So I have been thinking. I want to go and live permanently in the cottage – but now it is too big for just me. I remember hearing that JJ once said it would be a lovely respite house for people, and

I wondered if you would both be interested in helping me make this happen? I would want to keep painting in my studio, and I have already had interest from a few galleries Dr Woodburn put me in touch with, but I would hope that you both could run the respite house itself. There is room to build new accommodation, and no shortage of funds to do this. Please let me know.

Love from Mary x

It was a few days later that Mary was in the cottage, and saw a car descend the hill. It drew up outside the gate, and she went out to see who it was.

'I've got a letter for you,' said Patrick, getting out. He passed an envelope to Mary.

She smiled and read it.

Dear Mary,

Patrick and I would be delighted to help you run the Island Respite Centre.

   When can we come?
   Yours faithfully,
   JJ

'But before you answer,' said Patrick, picking a piece of grass growing between the yard stones, and twisting it into a knotted ring, then getting down on one knee.

'Mary O'Sullivan – then Mary Lynch – will you do me the honour of being my wife? I don't mind whether you take my name or not – but you've got me, body and soul!'

She laughed and put out her hand for him to place the grass ring on her finger.

'Patrick Connolly – I would be only too happy to accept!'

'I'll get you a proper ring in Galway,' he promised, kissing her.

'On the one condition that it is in the shape of a grass ring!' said Mary, as she flung her arms around him, and, in front of a background fit for any of Paul Henry's paintings – or hers – kissed him back.

Author's Note

I had such fun taking Sisters Bridget, Margaret and Cecilia, and their friends George and Matthew, to beautiful Italy in my first book *Small Miracles*, and was delighted when Harvill Secker suggested they might go on another trip in a second book. 'Can you think of another lovely setting?' I was asked, and I immediately thought of Connemara, in the West of Ireland, where my mother was from. It is one of the most beautiful places in the world, and I love it so much. Perhaps this second book could be about Irish Sister Bridget, and the family she loved so well? My parents separately emigrated from Ireland in the 1950s, and met each other in England, so I had plenty of their stories to draw on, and many happy memories of childhood holidays in Galway.

I also had a sadder story, one I had heard on a radio programme sometime in the 1990s. I can't remember what the programme was called, but I remember I was washing up at the sink when I heard a report on the problems of elderly Irish men who had, like my parents, come over to England in the 1950s, but unlike them had ended up homeless on the streets of London. These were men who had worked as labourers on building sites, like my dad, and had been paid in cash, or had their paycheques cashed in pubs. My dad never drank alcohol, but I knew that many of his peers – who were lonely, away from home and often experiencing prejudice – had looked for comfort in drink. Their employers took their labour but did not look after their welfare, not paying their National Insurance. The radio programme explained that many of these men, now elderly, had problems with alcoholism and had become utterly destitute. Not eligible for state benefits, they were reliant on charities. They longed to go back to Ireland but were unable to return because of the shame they felt they would bring on their families. I remember crying when I listened to the report about the men, who were the same age as my dad, imagining them coming over young and hopeful but ending up exploited and lonely and in such messes.

I was also very moved when I read, in 2019, of the tragic story of Joseph Tuohy who, as a little five-year-old boy in Tipperary, Ireland, was cruelly separated from his mother when she was sent to one of the now notorious Magdalene Laundries. Joseph was heartbroken and spent his childhood in institutions in Ireland, later experiencing mental health problems. He emigrated to London, where he experienced many difficulties, including homelessness, but was a kind and sensitive man. When Joseph died, aged 83, only an undertaker and his friend Brian Boylan were at his cremation, but Brian contacted Margaret Brown at the charity the Forgotten Irish and they ensured that this gentle, kind, humble man was at least honoured in his death, organising a beautiful public funeral Mass back in Dublin, attended by hundreds, and burying him back in Tipperary. I wondered if this might inspire my plot, but when, with my own parents both dead, I started writing the character of the old Irish man who needed help, I loved him so much, and felt so protective of him, I couldn't bear to give him such a sad ending. I think that the Forgotten Irish and charities like the Irish Chaplaincy and the Irish Centre are so inspiring and I am very grateful for the encouragement of

Eddie Gilmore of the Irish Chaplaincy when I told him my plan to write about an elderly Irish man, longing to go home.

I knew that many readers of *Small Miracles* had found the book comforting, and I wanted *Sweet Mercies* to comfort people too. I wanted to continue to write optimistic books, as I knew that when I was a carer for my parents, such feel-good books had kept me going. How could I write a book that might link those sad Irish histories with Sister Bridget, and how could I truthfully do justice to what had really happened to others, whilst keeping my fictional story uplifting and hopeful?

So then I thought about focusing on Sister Bridget, always so optimistic and positive. Her family was so important to her. How about if I made her family partly responsible for the suffering of an elderly Irish man she meets? What if Sister Bridget had to cope with the shock of discovering that things with her Irish family – even the Catholic Church itself in Ireland – were not as good as she believed them to be? And how would this affect her faith and her sense of self, and her place in the community of St Philomena? I wondered whether the story could be about how she reacts to this news and whether somehow, after I put poor Sister Bridget through the mill, things could be put right and there still be a happy ending for her and her family and the man her family had hurt. I thought that Sister Margaret might be just the person to support Sister Bridget through this crisis, and kind Father Hugh too.

I also wanted to carry on the stories about the other characters from *Small Miracles*. What was next for George and Matthew, and George's difficult mother? How would Cecilia be, coming back down to earth after her experience in Italy? (No spoilers!) I had introduced a little kitten at the end of *Small Miracles* – maybe I could have fun with Cecilia and this new addition to the community? I loved continuing the stories of other characters from *Small Miracles*, and bringing new ones in, and had great fun writing the Bingo scenes. I have deliberately written *Sweet Mercies* so that if you haven't yet read *Small Miracles* you can still fully enjoy it, and I hope very much that it captures your heart and makes you smile, and maybe even makes you book a holiday in Connemara!

I was very worried that anyone might mistakenly think that I was basing the fictional unscrupulous builder Declan works for in England on a real, identifiable person, so I deliberately never gave him a surname – he is just Declan's uncle, and his mother's brother, and the plot is purely based on stories heard on the radio show and things online I have read since. The island and the families on it, and Mary's cottage, are also fictional, although based on my memories of visiting the real island my mother and her family grew up on. For similar reasons I do not mention the name of the island and am deliberately vague about where it is, but Knock and Kylemore and Clifden and Roundstone and Gurteen are real places I mention, and I can only recommend visiting them! I went to Roundstone for two research visits whilst writing this book, and can't wait to return!

Neither Sister Bridget in fiction, nor I in reality, has met her hero Daniel O'Donnell, and unlike Sister Bridget, I don't have a Daniel O'Donnell tea towel. I did, however, buy his records for my parents, and although I am not really a country music fan myself, whilst researching this book and getting into Sister Bridget's mindset I did go to one of his post-pandemic concerts and saw what a lovely experience he creates and how happy he makes so many people. I now have a mug with Daniel O'Donnell on, and I did write lots of this book drinking tea from it, with his music playing in the background!

I can now really understand why people like Sister Bridget and my parents, who left so much behind when they left Ireland, find him comforting and fun to listen to. I am sure it would be fun to dance to his songs at a Bingo session at St Philomena's Church Hall!

Acknowledgements

As always, I need to thank people.

I must thank my agent Jo Unwin for her belief in me as a writer and her enthusiasm for the nuns, and her assistants, first Nisha Bailey and now Daisy Arendell, for all their ongoing support and help.

I would also like to thank my agent for my children's books, Anne Clark, for her generosity in letting me have time to explore writing for adults and her support for the nuns – I still have lots of books for children I want to write for you, Anne!

I want to thank Liz Foley, publishing director of Harvill Secker, and my wonderful editor Mikaela Pedlow, for all their enthusiasm and kindness and creative and personal support when I was writing *Sweet Mercies*. During the past year I caught Covid twice, with all the accompanying brain fog, and I would particularly like to thank Mikaela and my copy-editor Fiona Brown for their patience in dealing with my slowness and in sorting out the timeline muddles I got into.

Thank you to managing editor Rhiannon Roy, production manager Konrad Kirkham and proofreader Carolyn McAndrew for all your work getting *Sweet Mercies* into print!

Thank you to illustrator Harriet Seed and designer Dan Mogford for another gorgeous cover!

Thank you to Maya Koffi and Helia Daryani, my publicity and marketing team, for your work in bringing the book to readers and booksellers.

Ongoing thanks are due again to Katie Fforde, AJ Pearce and Julie Cohen, who helped me bring my nuns to life in the first place. It's a privilege to be able to have written a second book about the nuns and I would never have been able to do that without their original help.

I have lots more people to thank, and I don't want to forget anyone, so I would like to say a big thank you to everyone who told me that they loved *Small Miracles* and that they were looking forward to the sequel! This kept me going as I wrote it.

Thank you to my friends Katherine Mezzacappa (also known as the writer Katie Hutton) and to Dr Monica Tobon, who helped me so much in writing the kitten characters. I have never had a kitten myself, and photographs and stories and advice from these two wonderful women, along with watching kitten videos on the internet, were essential and fun research! I now really want one, but I am not sure if my dog would agree!

Thank you to my friend Katy (the artist Kate Wilson) for laughing in the right places when I told her the plot of *Sweet Mercies*, and, along with Elizabeth Foley, for insisting that Maura got an apology! Thanks to Fiona MacCarthy, who read the very first pages of *Sweet Mercies* and gave me the thumbs up to carry on, Virginia Moffatt and Ruth Washington, who are always such kind friends to talk with about writing, to Janie and Mickey Wilson at Chez Castillon, in whose house it is a wonderful place to write, to Jo Thomas, whose encouragement on retreat at Chez Castillon was much appreciated, and to Clare and Edmund Weiner, who have heard so much on Zoom about my writing deadlines and have given me so much support!

I am not a nun, or a religious sister myself, so I really need again to give so much thanks to the wonderful #nunsoftwitter for their wise support and advice and enthusiasm. Thanks especially to those who read early versions of *Sweet Mercies*: Sister Miriam McNulty @BirgitteUna for her confidence-boosting encouragement, @SisterWalburga who was so kind and made such insightful comments about Confession, which prompted me to make important changes, Sister Cathy Edge @knittingnun and Sister Silvana Dallanegra RSCJ @Silvanarscj, who talked to me about Katy's interest in finding out about community life, and helped me devise a timetable for her, and patiently explained to me that she was not yet a Novice! Silvana was also kind enough to book a Zoom call with me, also pointing out that convents wouldn't normally have Christmas trees in early December, and, thank goodness, noticing a real timeline and liturgical muddle I got into about when Christmas actually ended!

Last but not least, I want to thank my family. Thank you to Graeme, my gorgeous and kind husband, for all your love and encouragement and endless supply of hugs, cups of tea and delicious meals, and to Joanna, Michael, Laura and Christina, my lovely children, for all your support and confidence-boosting. Finally, though he won't read it, thank you (even though I don't always feel that grateful!) to Barney our cockapoo, for being my little personal trainer and manager, stealing my pens, interrupting my writing when he is bored, having cuddles with me, making me laugh and for enthusiastically making me get up and move away from my computer!

About the author

Anne Booth has had all sorts of jobs, including washing-up in a restaurant, working as a tour guide in a haunted almshouse, bookselling, lecturing at a university and being a long-term carer for her elderly parents. She has published 25 children's books and *Small Miracles* was her first novel for adults. Throughout her youth she wanted to be a nun, and although she has ended up happily married with four children, she still feels inspired by the many nuns and religious Sisters she has met.